BRANDON SANDERSON

This special signed edition
is limited to
2,500 numbered copies.

This is copy __49__ .

LEGION Skin Deep

LEGION Skin Deep

BRANDON SANDERSON

SUBTERRANEAN PRESS 2014

ISBN
978-1-59606-690-8

First Edition

Subterranean Press
PO Box 190106
Burton, MI 48519

subterraneanpress.com

For Greg Creer,
Who was the first person other than myself
to ever read one of my books. Thank you
for the encouragement, my friend!

Part One

1

"**What's her** angle?" Ivy asked, walking around the table with her arms folded. Today, she wore her blonde hair in a severe bun, which was stuck through with several dangerous-looking pins.

I tried, unsuccessfully, to ignore her.

"Gold digger, perhaps?" Tobias asked. Dark-skinned and stately, he had pulled a chair over to the table so he could sit beside me. He wore his usual relaxed suit with no tie, and fit in well with this room of crystalline lighting and piano music. "Many a woman has seen only Stephen's wealth, and not his acumen."

"She's the daughter of a real estate magnate," Ivy said with a dismissive wave. "She has wealth coming out of her nose." Ivy leaned down beside the table, inspecting my dinner companion. "A nose, by the way, which seems to have had as much work done on it as her chest."

I forced out a smile, trying to keep my attention on my dinner companion. I was used to Ivy and Tobias by now. I relied upon them.

But it can be damn hard to enjoy a date when your hallucinations are along.

"So . . ." said Sylvia, my date. "Malcom tells me you're some kind of detective?" She gave me a timid smile. Resplendent in diamonds and a tight black dress, Sylvia was an acquaintance of a mutual friend who worried about me far too much. I wondered how much research Sylvia had done on me before agreeing to the blind date.

"A detective?" I said. "Yes, I suppose you could say that."

"I just did!" Sylvia replied with a chittering laugh.

Ivy rolled her eyes, refusing the seat Tobias pulled over for her.

"Though honestly," I said to Sylvia, "the word 'detective' probably gives you the wrong idea. I just help people with very specialized problems."

"Like Batman!" Sylvia said.

Tobias spat out his lemonade in a spray before him. It spotted the tablecloth, though Sylvia—of course—couldn't see it.

"Not . . . really like that," I said.

"I was just being silly," Sylvia said, taking another drink of her wine. She'd had a lot of that for a meal that she'd only just begun. "What kind of problems do you solve? Like, computer problems? Security problems? Logic problems?"

"Yes. All three of those, and then some."

"That . . . doesn't sound very specialized to me," Sylvia said.

She had a point. "It's difficult to explain. I'm a specialist, just in lots of areas."

"Like what?"

"Anything. Depends on the problem."

"She's hiding things," Ivy said, arms still folded. "I'm telling you, Steve. She's got an angle."

"Everyone does," I replied.

"What?" Sylvia asked, frowning as a server with a cloth over her arm made our salad plates vanish.

"Nothing," I said.

Sylvia shifted in her chair, then took another drink. "You were talking to *them*, weren't you?"

"So you *have* read up on me."

"A girl has to be careful, you know. There are some real psychos in the world."

"I assure you," I said. "It's all under control. I see things, but I'm completely aware of what is real and what is not."

"Be careful, Stephen," Tobias said from my side. "This is dangerous territory for a first date. Perhaps a discussion of the architecture instead?"

I realized I'd been tapping my fork against my bread plate, and stopped.

"This building is a Renton McKay design," Tobias continued in his calm, reassuring way. "Note the open nature of the room, with the movable fixtures, and geo-metric designs in ascending patterns. They can rebuild the interior every year or so, creating a restaurant that is half eatery, half art installation."

"My psychology really isn't that interesting," I said. "Not like this building. Did you know that it was built by Renton McKay? He—"

"So you see things," Sylvia interrupted. "Like visions?"

I sighed. "Nothing so grand. I see people who aren't there."

"Like that guy," she said. "In that movie."

"Sure. Like that. Only he was crazy, and I'm not."

"Oh, yeah," Ivy said. "What a great way to put her at ease. Explain in depth how *not* crazy you are."

"Aren't you supposed to be a therapist?" I snapped back at her. "Less sarcasm would be delightful."

That was a tall order for Ivy. Sarcasm was kind of her native tongue, though she was fluent in "stern disap-pointment" and "light condescension" as well. She was also a good friend. Well, imaginary friend.

She just had a thing about me and women. Ever since Sandra abandoned us, at least.

Sylvia regarded me with a stiff posture, and only then did I realize I'd spoken out loud to Ivy. As Sylvia noticed me looking at her, she plastered on a smile as fake as red dye #6. Inside, I winced. She was quite attractive, despite what Ivy claimed—and no matter how crowded my life had become, it also got terribly lonely.

"So . . ." Sylvia said, then trailed off. Entrées arrived. She had chic lettuce wraps. I'd chosen a safe-sounding chicken dish. "So, uh . . . You were speaking to one of them, just now? An imaginary person?" She obviously considered it polite to ask. Perhaps the proper lady's book of etiquette had a chapter on how to make small talk about a man's psychological disabilities.

"Yes," I said. "That was one of them. Ivy."

"A . . . lady?"

"A woman," I said. "She's only occasionally a lady."

Ivy snorted. "Your maturity is stunning, Steve."

"How many of your personalities are female?" Sylvia asked. She hadn't touched her food yet.

"They aren't personalities," I said. "They're separate from me. I don't have dissociative identity disorder. If anything, I'm schizophrenic."

That is a subject of some debate among psychologists. Despite my hallucinations, I don't fit the profile for schizophrenia. I don't fit *any* of the profiles. But why should that matter? I get along just fine. Mostly.

I smiled at Sylvia, who still hadn't started her food. "It's not a big deal. My aspects are probably just an effect of a lonely childhood, spent mostly by myself."

"Good," Tobias said. "Now transition the conversation away from your eccentricities and start talking about her."

"Yes," Ivy said. "Find out what she's hiding."

"Do you have siblings?" I asked.

Sylvia hesitated, then finally picked up her silverware. Never had I been so happy to see a fork move. "Two sisters," she said, "both older. Maria is a consultant for a marketing firm. Georgia lives in the Cayman Islands. She's an attorney . . ."

I relaxed as she continued. Tobias raised his glass of lemonade to me in congratulations. Disaster avoided.

"You're going to have to talk about it with her eventually," Ivy said. "We aren't exactly something she can ignore."

"Yes," I said softly. "But for now, I'll settle for surviving the first date."

"What was that?" Sylvia looked at us, hesitating in her narrative.

"Nothing," I said.

"She was speaking about her father," Tobias said. "A banker. Retired."

"How long was he in banking?" I asked, glad that one of us had been paying attention.

"Forty-eight years! We kept saying he didn't need to continue on . . ."

I smiled and began cutting my chicken as she talked.

"Perimeter clear," a voice said from behind me.

I started, looking over my shoulder. J.C. stood there, wearing a busboy's uniform and carrying a tray of dirty dishes. Lean, tough, and square-jawed, J.C. is a cold-blooded killer. Or so he claims. I think it means he likes to murder amphibians.

He was a hallucination, of course. J.C., the plates he was carrying, the handgun he had holstered inconspicuously under his white server's jacket . . . all hallucinations. Despite that, he'd saved my life several times.

That didn't mean I was pleased to see him.

"What are you doing here?" I hissed.

"Watching out for assassins," J.C. said.

"I'm on a date!"

"Which means you'll be distracted," J.C. said. "Perfect time for an assassination."

"I told you to stay home!"

"Yeah, I know. The assassins would have heard that too. That's why I had to come." He nudged me with an elbow. I felt it. He might be imaginary, but he felt perfectly real to me. "She's a looker, Skinny. Nice work!"

"Half of her is plastic," Ivy said dryly.

"Same goes for my car," J.C. said. "It still looks nice." He grinned at Ivy, then leaned down to me. "I don't suppose you could . . ." He nodded toward Ivy, then raised his hands to his chest, making a cupping motion.

"J.C.," Ivy said flatly. "Did you just try to get Steve to imagine me with a larger chest?"

J.C. shrugged.

"You," she said, "are the most loathsome non-being on the planet. Really. You should feel proud. Nobody has imagined anything more slimy, *ever*."

The two of them had an off-again on-again relationship. Apparently, "off-again" had started when I wasn't looking. I really had no idea what to make of it—this was the first time two of my aspects had become romantically entangled.

Curiously, J.C. had been completely unable to say the words about me imagining Ivy with a different body shape. He didn't like to confront the fact that he was a hallucination. It made him uncomfortable.

J.C. continued looking the room over. Despite his obvious hangups, he was keen-eyed and very good with security. He'd notice things I would not, so perhaps it was good he'd decided to join us.

"What?" I asked him. "Is there something wrong?"

"He's just paranoid," Ivy said. "Remember when he thought the postman was a terrorist?"

J.C. stopped scanning, his attention focusing sharply on a woman sitting three tables over. Dark-skinned and wearing a nice pantsuit, she turned toward her window as soon as I noticed her. That window reflected back our way, and it was dark outside. She could still be watching.

"I'll check it out," J.C. said, moving away from our table.

"Stephen . . ." Tobias said.

I glanced back at our table and found Sylvia staring at me again, her fork held loosely as if forgotten, her eyes wide.

I forced myself to chuckle. "Sorry! Got distracted by something."

"By what?"

"Nothing. You were saying something about your mother—"

"What distracted you?"

"An aspect," I said, reluctant.

"A hallucination, you mean."

"Yes. I left him home. He came on his own."

Sylvia stared intently at her food. "That's interesting. Tell me more."

Being polite again. I leaned forward. "It's not what you think, Sylvia. My aspects are just pieces of me, receptacles for my knowledge. Like . . . memories that get up and walk around."

"She's not buying it," Ivy noted. "Breathing quickly. Fingers tense . . . Steve, she knows more about you than you think. She's not acting shocked, but instead like she's been set up on a date with Jack the Ripper and is trying to keep her cool."

I nodded at the information. "It's nothing to worry about." Had I said that already? "Each of my aspects help me in some way. Ivy is a psychologist. Tobias is a historian. They—"

"What about the one that just arrived?" Sylvia asked, looking up and meeting my eyes. "The one who came when you weren't expecting?"

"Lie," Tobias said.

"Lie," Ivy said. "Tell her he's a ballet dancer or something."

"J.C.," I said instead, "is ex-Navy SEAL. He helps me with that sort of thing."

"*That* sort of thing?"

"Security situations. Covert operations. Any time I might be in danger."

"Does he tell you to kill people?"

"It's not like that. Okay, well, it is *kind* of like that. But he's usually joking."

Ivy groaned.

Sylvia stood up. "Excuse me. I need the restroom."

"Of course."

Sylvia took her purse and shawl and left.

"Not coming back?" I asked Ivy.

"Are you kidding? You just told her that an invisible man who tells you to kill people just showed up when you didn't want him to."

"Not one of our smoothest interactions," Tobias agreed.

Ivy sighed and sat down in Sylvia's seat. "Better than last time, at least. She lasted . . . what? Half an hour?"

"Twenty minutes," Tobias said, glancing at the restaurant's grandfather clock.

"We're going to need to get over this," I whispered. "We can't keep going to pieces every time romance is potentially involved."

"You didn't need to say what you did about J.C.," Ivy said. "You could have made something up. Instead, you told her the truth. The frightening, embarrassing, J.C.-filled truth."

I picked up my drink. Lemonade in a fancy wine glass. I turned it about. "My life is fake, Ivy. Fake friends. Fake conversations. Often, on Wilson's day off, I don't speak to a single real person. I guess I don't want to start a relationship with lies."

The three of us sat in silence until J.C. came jogging back, dancing to the side of a real server as they passed one another.

"What?" he asked, glancing at Ivy. "You chased the chick off already?"

I raised my glass to him.

"Don't be too hard on yourself, Stephen," Tobias said, resting his hand on my shoulder. "Sandra is a difficult woman to forget, but the scars will eventually heal."

"Scars don't heal, Tobias," I said. "That's kind of the definition of the word *scar*." I turned my glass around, looking at the light on the ice.

"Yeah, great, whatever," J.C. said. "Emotions and metaphors and stuff. Look, we've got a problem."

I looked at him.

"The woman we saw earlier?" J.C. said, pointing. "She—" He cut off. The woman's seat was empty, her meal left half-eaten.

"Time to go?" I asked.

"Yeah," J.C. said. "*Now.*"

2

"**Zen Rigby,**" J.C. said as we rushed from the restaurant. "Private security—and, in this case, those are fancy words for 'killer on retainer.' She has a list of suspected hits as long as your psychological profile, Skinny. No proof. She's good."

"Wait," Ivy said from my other side. "You're saying that an assassin really *did* show up at dinner?"

"Apparently," I replied. J.C. could only know what I did, so if he was saying these things, they were dredged from deep in my memory. I periodically looked over lists of operatives, spies, and professional assassins for missions I did.

"Great," Ivy said, not looking at J.C. "He's going to be insufferable to live with now."

On the way out of the restaurant, at J.C.'s prompting, I looked at the reservation list. That simple glance dumped the information there into my mind, and gave the aspects access to it.

"Carol Westminster," J.C. said, picking a name off the list. "She's used that alias before. It was Zen for sure."

We stopped at the valet stand outside, the rainy evening making cars swish as they drove past on the wet road. The weather dampened the city's normal pungency—so instead of unwashed hobo, it smelled like recently washed hobo. A man asked for our valet ticket, but I ignored him, texting Wilson to bring our car.

"You said she's on retainer, J.C.," I said as I texted. "Whom does she work for?"

"Not sure," J.C. said. "Last I heard, she was looking for a new home. Zen isn't one of those 'hire for a random hit' assassins. Companies bring her on and keep her long-term, use her to clean up messes, fix problems in legally ambiguous ways."

I knew all of this, deep down, but J.C. had to tell it to me. I'm not crazy, I'm compartmentalized. Unfortunately, my aspects . . . well, *they* tend to be a little unhinged. Tobias stood to the side, muttering that Stan—the voice he hears sometimes—hadn't warned him of the rain. Ivy pointedly did not look at the series of small wormholes in the post nearby. Had it always been this bad?

"It could just be a coincidence," Tobias said to me, shaking his head and turning away from his inspection of the sky. "Assassins go out for dinner like everyone else."

"I suppose," J.C. said. "If it is a coincidence, though, I'm gonna be annoyed."

"Looking forward to shooting someone tonight?" Ivy asked.

"Well, yeah, obviously. But that's not it. I hate coincidences. Life is much simpler when you can just assume that everyone is trying to kill you."

Wilson texted back. *Old friend called. Wanted to speak with you. He is in car. Okay?*

I texted back. *Who?*

Yol Chay.

I frowned. Yol? Was the assassin his? *Fine,* I texted.

A few minutes out, Wilson texted to me.

"Yo," J.C. said, pointing. "Scope it."

Nearby, Sylvia was getting into a car with a man in a suit. Glen, reporter for the *Mag.* He shut the door for Sylvia, glanced at me and shrugged, tipping his antiquated fedora before climbing in the other side of the car.

"I *knew* she had an angle!" Ivy aid. "It was a setup! I'll bet she was recording the entire date."

I groaned. The *Mag* was a tabloid of the worst kind—meaning that it published enough truths mixed with its fabrications that people kind of trusted it. For most of my life I'd avoided mainstream media attention, but recently the papers and news websites had latched on to me.

J.C. shook his head in annoyance, then jogged off to scout the perimeter as we waited for the car.

"I *did* warn you something was up," Ivy said, arms folded as we stood beneath the canopy with the valets, rain pattering above.

"I know."

"You're normally more suspicious than this. I'm worried that you are developing a blind spot for women."

"Noted."

"And J.C. is disobeying you again. Coming on his own when you pointedly left him at home? We haven't ever discussed what happened in Israel."

"We solved the case. That's all that happened."

"J.C. shot your gun, Steve. He—an aspect—shot *real people*."

"He moved my arm," I said. "I did the shooting."

"That's a blurring between us that has never happened before." She met my eyes. "You're trying to find Sandra again; I think you purposely sabotaged this date to have an excuse to avoid future ones."

"You're jumping to conclusions."

"I'd better be," Ivy said. "We had an equilibrium, Steve. Things were working. I don't want to start worrying about aspects vanishing again."

My limo finally pulled up, Wilson—my butler—driving. It was late evening, and the regular driver only worked a normal eight-hour shift.

"Who's that in the back?" J.C. said, jogging up and trying to get a clear view through the tinted windows.

"Yol Chay," I said.

"Huh," J.C. said, rubbing his chin.

"Think he's involved?" I asked.

"I'd bet your life on it."

Delightful. Well, a meeting with Yol was always interesting, if nothing else. The restaurant valet pulled open the door for me. I moved to step in, but J.C. put his hand on my chest and stopped me, unholstering his side-arm and peering in.

I glanced at Ivy and rolled my eyes, but she wasn't looking at me. Instead, she watched J.C., smiling fondly. What was *up* with those two?

J.C. stood back and nodded, removing his hand from my chest. Yol Chay lounged inside my limo. He wore a pure white suit, a silver bow tie, and a polished set of black-and-white oxford shoes. He topped it all with sunglasses that had diamonds studding the rims—an extremely odd outfit for a fifty-year-old Korean business-man. For Yol, though, this was actually reserved.

"Steve!" he said, holding out a fist to be bumped and speaking with a moderately thick Korean accent. He said the name *Stee-vuh*. "How are you, you crazy dog?"

"Dumped," I said, letting my aspects climb in first, so the valet didn't close the door on them. "The date didn't even last an hour."

"What? What is wrong with the women these days?"

"I don't know," I said, climbing in and sitting down as my aspects arranged themselves. "I guess they want a guy who doesn't remind them of a serial killer."

"Boring," Yol said. "Who wouldn't want to date you? You're a steal! One body, forty people. Infinite variety."

He didn't quite understand how my aspects worked, but I forgave him that. *I* wasn't always sure how they worked.

I let Yol serve me a cup of lemonade. Helping him with his problem a few years back had been some of the most fun, and least stress, I'd ever encountered on a project. Even if it *had* forced me to learn to play the saxophone.

"How many today?" Yol asked, nodding to the rest of the limo.

"Only three."

"Is the spook here?"

"I'm *not* CIA," J.C. said. "I'm Special Forces, you twit."

"Is he annoyed to see me?" Yol asked, grinning behind his garish sunglasses.

"You could say that," I replied.

Yol's grin deepened, then he took out his phone and tapped a few buttons. "J.C., I just donated ten grand in your name to the Brady Campaign to Prevent Gun Violence. I just thought you'd like to know."

J.C. growled. Like, *literally* growled.

I leaned back, inspecting Yol as the limo drove us. Another followed behind, filled with Yol's people. Yol had given Wilson instructions, apparently, as this wasn't the way home. "You play along with my aspects, Yol," I said. "Most others don't. Why is that?"

"It's not play to you, is it?" he asked, lounging.

"No."

"Then it isn't to me either." His phone chirped the sound of some bird.

"That's actually the call of an eagle," Tobias said. "Most people are surprised to hear how they really sound, as the American media uses the call of the red-tailed hawk when showing an eagle. They don't think the eagle sounds regal enough. And so we lie to ourselves about the very identity of our national icon . . ."

And Yol used this as his ringtone. Interesting. The man answered the phone and began speaking in Korean.

"Do we *have* to deal with this joker?" J.C. said.

"I like him," Ivy said, sitting beside Yol. "Besides, you yourself said he was probably involved with that assassin."

"Yeah, well," J.C. said. "We could get the truth out of him. Use the old five-point persuasion method." He made a fist and pounded it into his other hand.

"You're terrible," Ivy said.

"What? He's so weird, he'd probably get off on it."

Yol hung up his phone.

"Any problems?" I asked.

"News of my latest album."

"Good news?"

Yol shrugged. He had released five music albums. All had flopped spectacularly. When you were worth 1.2 billion from a life of koon commodities investing, a little thing like poor sales on your rap albums was not going to stop you from making more.

"So . . ." Yol said. "I have an issue I might need help with."

"Finally!" J.C. said. "This had better not involve trying to make people listen to that awful music of his." He paused. "Actually, if we need a new form of torture . . ."

"Does this job involve a woman named Zen?" I asked.

"Who?" Yol frowned.

"Professional assassin," I replied. "She was watching me at dinner."

"Could be wanting a date," Yol said cheerfully.

I raised an eyebrow.

"Our problem," Yol said, "might involve some danger, and our rivals are not above hiring such . . . individuals. She's not working for me though, I promise you that."

"This job," I said. "Is it interesting?"

Yol grinned. "I need you to recover a corpse."

"Oooo . . ." J.C. said.

"Hardly worth our time," Tobias said.

"There's more," Ivy said, studying Yol's expression.

"What's the hitch?" I asked Yol.

"It's not the corpse that is important," Yol said, leaning in. "It's what the corpse knows."

3

"**Innovation Information** Incorporated," J.C. said, reading the sign outside the business campus as we pulled through the guarded gate. "Even *I* can tell that's a stupid name." He hesitated a moment. "It is a stupid name, right?"

"The name is a little obvious," I replied.

"Founded by engineers," Yol said, "run by engineers, and—unfortunately—named by engineers. They're waiting for us inside. Note, Steve, that what I'm asking you to do goes beyond friendship. Deal with this for me, and our debt will be settled, and then some."

"If a hit woman is really involved, Yol," I said reluctantly, "that's not going to be enough. I'm not going to risk my life for a favor."

"What about wealth?"

"I'm already rich," I said.

"Not riches, *wealth*. Complete financial independence."

That gave me pause. It was true; I had money. But my delusions required a lot of space and investment. Many rooms in my mansion, multiple seats on the plane each time I fly, fleets of cars and drivers whenever I wanted to go somewhere for an extended time. Perhaps I could have bought a smaller house and forced my aspects to live in the basement or shacks on the lawn. The problem was that when they were unhappy—when the illusion of it started to break down—things got . . . bad for me.

I was finally dealing with this thing. Whatever twisted psychology made me tick, I was far more stable now than I had been at the start. I wanted to keep it that way.

"Are you in personal danger?" I asked him.

"I don't know," Yol said. "I might be." He handed me an envelope.

"Money?" I asked.

"Shares in I3," Yol said. "I purchased the company six months ago. The things this company is working on are revolutionary. That envelope gives you a ten percent stake. I've already filed the paperwork. It's yours, whether you take the job or not. A consultation fee."

I fingered the envelope. "If I don't solve your problem, this will be worthless, eh?"

Yol grinned. "You got it. But if you do solve it, that envelope could be worth tens of millions. Maybe hundreds of millions."

"Damn," J.C. said.

"Language," Ivy said, punching him in the shoulder. At this rate, those two were either heading for a full-blown screaming match or a makeout session. I could never tell.

I looked at Tobias, who sat across from me in the limo. He leaned forward, clasping his hands before him, looking me in the eye. "We could do a lot with that money," he said. "We might have the resources, finally, to track *her* down."

Sandra knew things about me, things about how I thought. She understood aspects. Hell, she'd taught me how they work. She'd captivated me.

And then she'd gone. In an instant.

"The camera," I said.

"The camera doesn't work," Tobias said. "Arnaud said he could be *years* away from figuring it out."

I fingered the envelope.

"She's actively blocking your efforts to find her, Stephen," Tobias said. "You can't deny that. Sandra doesn't want to be found. To get to her, we'll need resources. Freedom to ignore cases for a while, money to overcome roadblocks."

I glanced at Ivy, who shook her head. She and Tobias disagreed on what we should be doing in regard to Sandra—but she'd had her say earlier.

I looked back at Yol. "I assume that I have to agree before I can know about the technology you people are involved in?"

Yol spread his hands. "I trust you, Steve. That money is yours. Go in. Hear them out. That's all I'm asking. You can say yes or no afterward."

"All right," I said, pocketing the envelope. "Let me hear what your people have to say."

☰☰

4

I₃ **wa**ₛ one of those "new" technology companies, the kind decorated like a daycare, with bright walls painted in primary colors and beanbag chairs set at every intersection. Yol popped some ice cream bars out of a chest freezer and tossed one to each of his bodyguards. I declined, hands behind my back, but he then wagged one at the empty air between us.

"Sure," Ivy said, holding out her hands.

I pointed, and Yol tossed one in her direction. Which was a problem. Those who work closely with me know to just pantomime, letting my mind fill in the details. Since Yol *actually* threw the thing, my ability to imagine broke down for a moment.

The bar split into two. Ivy caught one, sidestepping the other—the real one—which hit the wall and bounced to the floor.

"I didn't need two," Ivy said, rolling her eyes. She stepped over the fallen ice cream bar and unwrapped hers, but she looked uncomfortable. Any time a flaw appeared in my ability to mediate between my imaginary world and the real one, we were in dangerous territory.

We went on, passing glass-walled meeting rooms. Most of these were empty, as one would expect at this hour, but every table was covered in small plastic bricks in various states of construction. Apparently at I3, business meetings were supplied with plenty of Legos to accompany the conversation.

"The receptionist at the front desk is new," Ivy noted. "She had trouble finding the visitor name badges."

"Either that," Tobias said, "or visitors are rare here."

"Security is *awful*," J.C. growled.

I looked at him, frowning. "The doors are key carded. That's good security."

J.C. snorted. "Key cards? Please. Look at all of these windows. The bright colors, the inviting carpets . . . and is that a *tire swing*? This place just screams 'hold the door for the guy behind you.' Key cards are useless. At least most of the computers are facing away from windows."

I could imagine how this place might feel during the day, with its playful atmosphere, treat bins in the halls and catchy slogans on the walls. It was the type of environment carefully calculated to make creative types feel comfortable. Like a gorilla enclosure for nerds. The lingering scents in the air spoke of an in-house cafeteria, probably free, to keep the engineers plump and fed—and to keep them on campus. Why go home when you can have a meal here at six? And since you're hanging around, you might as well get some work done . . .

That sense of playful creativity seemed thin, now. We passed engineers working into the night, but they hunched over their computers. They'd glance at us, then shrink down farther and not look up again. The foosball table and arcade machines stood unused in the lounge. It felt like even in the evening this place should have born a pleasant buzz of chatter. Instead, the only sounds were hushed whispers and the occasional beep from an idle game machine.

Ivy looked to me, and seemed encouraged that I'd noticed all of this. She gestured, indicating that I should go farther. *What does it mean?*

"The engineers know," I said to Yol. "There has been a security breach, and they're aware of it. They're worried that the company is in danger."

"Yeah," Yol said. "Word should never have gotten to them."

"How did it?"

"You know these IT types," Yol said from behind his sparkling sunglasses. "Freedom of information, employee involvement, all of that nonsense. The higher-ups held a meeting to explain what had happened, and they invited everyone but the damn cleaning lady."

"Language," Ivy said.

"Ivy would like you not to swear," I said.

"Did I swear?" Yol asked, genuinely confused.

"Ivy has a bit of puritan in her," I said. "Yol, what *is* this technology? What do they develop here?"

Yol stopped beside a meeting room—a more secure one, its only glass a small, square window on its door. A handful of men and women waited inside. "I'll let them tell you," Yol said as one of his security guards held open the door.

5

"**E**very cell in your body contains seven hundred and fifty megs of data," the engineer said. "For comparison, one of your fingers holds as much information as the *entire internet*. Of course, your information is repeated and redundant, but the fact remains that cells are capable of great storage."

Garvas, the engineer, was an affable man in a button-down shirt with a pair of aviator sunglasses hanging from the pocket. He wasn't particularly overweight, but had some of the round edges that came from a life working a desk job. He was building a dinosaur out of Legos on the table as he spoke, while Yol paced outside, taking a call.

"Do you have any idea of the potential there?" Garvas continued, snapping on the head. "As the years pass, technology shrinks, and people grow tired of carrying around bulky laptops, phones, tablets. Our goal is to find a way to do away with that by using the body itself."

I glanced at my aspects. Ivy and Tobias sat at the table with us. J.C. stood by the door, yawning.

"The human body is an incredibly efficient machine," said another engineer. A thin man with an eager attitude, Laramie had built his Legos into an ever-growing tower. "It has great storage, self-replicating cells, and comes with its own power generator. The body is also very long-lived, by current manufacturing standards."

"So you were turning human bodies," I said, "into computers."

"They're *already* computers," Garvas said. "We were simply adding a few new features."

"Imagine," said the third engineer—a thin, arrow-faced woman named Loralee. "Instead of carrying a laptop, what if you made use of the organic computer already built into you? Your thumb becomes storage. Your eyes are the screen. Instead of a bulky battery, you eat an extra sandwich in the morning."

"That," J.C. said, "sounds *freakish.*"

"I'm inclined to agree," I said.

"What?" Garvas asked.

"Figure of speech," I said. "So, your thumb becomes storage. It looks like, what. A . . . um . . . USB drive?"

"He was going to say 'thumb drive,' " Laramie said. "We really need to stop using thumbs as an example."

"But it's so *neat*!" Loralee said.

"Regardless," Garvas said, "what we were doing didn't change the look of the organ." He held up his thumb.

"You've had the procedure *done*?" I asked. "You're testing on yourselves?"

"Freaks," J.C. said, shifting uncomfortably. "This is going to be about zombies. I'm calling it now."

"We've done some very initial tests," Garvas said. "Most of what we just told you is just a dream, a goal. Here, we've been working on the storage aspect exclusively, and have made good progress. We can embed information into cells, and it will stay there, reproduced by the body into new cells. My thumb doubles as backup for my laptop. As you can see, there are no adverse effects."

"We keep it in the DNA of the muscles," Laramie said, excited. "Your genetic material has tons of extraneous data anyway. We mimic that—all we have to do is add in a little extra string of information, with marks to tell the body to ignore it. Like commented-out sections of code."

"I'm sorry," J.C. said. "I don't speak super-geek. What did he just say?"

"When you 'comment out' something in computer code," Ivy explained, "you write lines, but tell the program to ignore them. That way, you can leave messages to other programmers about the code."

"Yup," J.C. said. "Gibberish. Ask him about the zombies."

"Steve," Ivy said to me, pointedly ignoring J.C., "these people are serious and excited. Their eyes light up when they talk, but there are reservations. They are being honest with you, but they *are* afraid."

"You say this is perfectly safe?" I asked the three.

"Sure," Garvas said. "People have been doing this with bacteria for years."

"The trouble is not the storage," Loralee said. "It's access. Sure, we can store all of this in our cells—but writing and reading it is very difficult. We have to inject data to get it in, and have to remove cells to retrieve it."

"One of our teammates, Panos Maheras, was working on a prototype delivery mechanism involving a virus," Garvas said. "The virus infiltrates the cells carrying a payload of genetic data, which it then splices into the DNA."

"Oh, *lovely*," Ivy said.

I grimaced.

"It's *perfectly safe*," Garvas said, a little nervous. "Panos's virus had fail-safes to prevent it from over-reproducing. We have done only limited trials, and have been very careful. And note, the virus route was only *one* method we were researching."

"The world will soon change," Laramie said, excited. "Eventually, we will be able to write to the genetic hard disk of every human body, using its own hormones to—"

I held up a hand. "What can the virus you made do *right now*?"

"Worst case?" Loralee asked.

"I'm not here to talk about ponies and flowers."

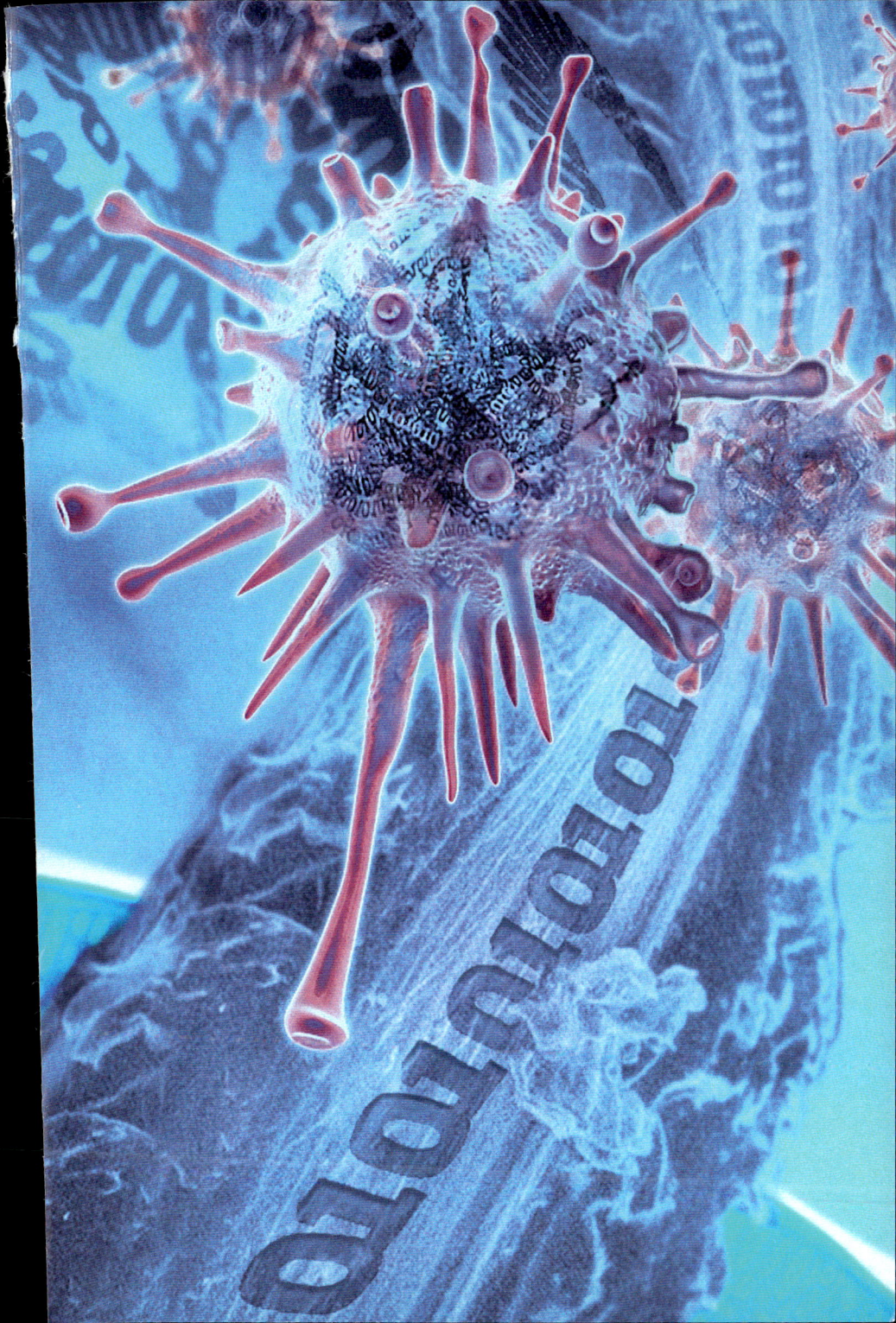

"Worst case," Loralee said, looking to the others, "the virus that Panos developed could be used to deliver huge chunks of useless data to people's DNA—or it could cut out chunks of their DNA."

"So . . . zombies?" J.C. said.

Ivy grimaced. "Normally, I'd call him an idiot. But . . . yeah, this kind of sounds like zombies."

Not again, I thought. "I hate zombies."

The engineers all gave me baffled looks.

". . .Zombies?" Loralee asked.

"That's where this is going, isn't it?" I asked. "You turning people into zombies by accident?"

"Wow," Garvas said. "That's *way* more awesome than what we actually did."

The other two looked at him, and he shrugged.

"Mister Leeds," Laramie said, looking back to me. "This is not science fiction. Removing chunks of someone's DNA doesn't immediately produce some kind of zombie. It just creates an abnormal cell. One that, in our experiments, has a habit of proliferating uncontrollably."

"Not zombies," I said, feeling cold. "Cancer. You created a virus that gives people cancer."

Garvas winced. "Kind of?"

"It was an unintended result that is perfectly manageable," Laramie said, "and only dangerous if used malignly. And why would anyone want to do that?"

We all stared at him for a moment.

"Let's shoot him," J.C. said.

"Thank heavens," Tobias replied. "You hadn't suggested we shoot someone in over an hour, J.C. I was beginning to think something was wrong."

"No, listen," J.C. said. "We can shoot Pinhead McWedgy over there, and it will teach everyone in this room an important life lesson. One about not being a stupid mad scientist."

I sighed, ignoring the aspects. "You said the virus was developed by a man named Panos? I'll want to talk to him."

"You can't," Garvas said. "He's . . . kind of dead."

"How surprising," Tobias said as Ivy sighed and massaged her forehead.

"What?" I asked, turning to Ivy.

"Yol said a body was involved," Ivy said. "And their company is about storing data in human cells, so . . ."

I looked to Garvas. "He had it in him, didn't he? The way to create this virus? He stored the data for your product inside his own cells."

"Yes," Garvas said. "And somebody stole the corpse."

6

"Security Nightmare," J.C. said as we made our way to the office of Panos, the deceased gene splicer.

"So far as we can tell," Loralee said, "Panos's death was perfectly natural. We were all devastated when he had his fall, as he was a friend. But nobody thought it was anything more than a random accident on the ski slopes."

"Yeah," J.C. said, walking with my other two aspects just behind him, "because scientists working on doomsday viruses dying in freak accidents isn't *at all* suspicious."

"Occasionally, J.C.," Tobias said, "accidents *do* happen. If someone wanted his secrets, I suspect killing him and stealing his body would be low on the list of methods."

"Are you sure he's dead?" I asked Garvas, who walked on my other side. "It could be some kind of hoax, part of an espionage ploy of some sort."

"We're very sure," Garvas replied. "I saw the corpse. The neck doesn't . . . uh . . . turn that way on someone alive."

"We'll want to corroborate that," J.C. said. "Get coroner reports, photos if possible."

I nodded absently.

"If we follow the simplest line of events," Ivy said, "this is quite logical. He dies. Someone discovers that his cells hide information. They snatch the body. I'm not saying it couldn't be something else, but I find what they're saying to be plausible."

"When did the body disappear?" I asked.

"Yesterday," Loralee said. "Which was two days after the accident. The funeral was to be today."

We stopped in the hallway beside a wall painted with cheerful groups of bubbles, and Garvas used his key card to open the next door.

"Do you have any leads?" I asked him.

"Nothing," he replied. "Or, well, too many. Our area of research is a hot one, and lots of biotech companies are involved in the race. Any one of our less scrupulous rivals could be behind the theft." He pulled open the door for me.

I took the door from Garvas and held it, much to the man's confusion. If I didn't, though, he was likely to walk through while my aspects were trying to enter. The engineers entered. Once they'd gone in, my aspects went through, and I followed. Where had Yol run off to?

"Finding out who did this should be easy," J.C. said to me. "We just have to figure out who hired that assassin to watch us. What I don't get is why everyone is so worried. So the nerds accidentally invented a cancer machine. Big deal. I've got one of those already." J.C. held up a cellphone and wiggled it.

"You have a mobile phone?" Ivy asked, exasperated.

"Sure," J.C. said. "Everyone does."

"And who are you going to call? Santa?"

J.C. stuffed the phone away, drawing his lips to a line. Ivy danced around the fact that none of them were real, but she always seemed—deep down—to be okay with it, unlike J.C. As we walked along this new hallway, Ivy fell in beside him and began saying some calming things, as if embarrassed for calling out his hallucinatory nature.

This newer area of the building was less like a kindergarten, more like a dentist's office, with individual rooms along a hallway decorated in tans with fake plants beside doorways. Garvas fished out another key card as we reached Panos's office.

"Garvas," I asked, "why didn't you go to the government with your virus?"

"They'd have just wanted to use it as a weapon."

"No," I said, putting my hand on his arm. "I doubt it. A weapon like this wouldn't serve a tactical purpose in war. Give the enemy troops cancer? It would take months or years to take effect, and even then would be of marginal value. A weapon like this would only be useful as a threat against a civilian population."

"It's not supposed to be a weapon at all."

"And gunpowder was first just used to make fireworks," I said.

"I mentioned that we were looking for other methods to read and write into our cells, right?" Garvas said. "Ones that didn't use the virus?"

I nodded.

"Let's just say that we started those projects because some of us were concerned about the virus approach. Research on Panos's project was halted as we tried to find a way to do all of this with amino acids."

"You still should have gone to the government."

"And what do you think they'd have done?" Garvas asked, looking me right in the eye. "Pat us on the heads? Thank us? Do you know what happens to laboratories that invent things like this? They vanish. Either they get consumed by the government or they get dismantled. Our research here is important . . . and, well, lucrative. We don't want to get shut down; we don't want to be the subject of a huge investigation. We just want this whole problem to go away."

He pulled open the door and revealed a small, neat office. The walls were decorated with an array of uniformly framed, autographed pictures of science fiction actors.

"Go," I said to my aspects, holding Garvas back.

The three entered the office, poking and prodding at objects on the desk and walls.

"He was of Greek descent," Ivy said, inspecting some books on the wall and a set of photos. "Second-generation, I'd say, but still spoke the language."

"What?" J.C. said. "Panos isn't a w—"

"Watch it," Ivy said.

"—Mexican name?"

"No," Tobias said. He leaned down beside the desk. "Stephen, some aid, please?"

I walked over and moved the papers on the desk so Tobias could get a good look at each of them. "Dues to a local fablab . . ." Tobias said. "Brochure for a Linux convention . . . D.I.Y. magazine . . . Our friend here was a maker."

"Speak dumb person, please," J.C. said.

"It's a subculture of technophiles and creative types, J.C.," Tobias said. "A parallel, or perhaps an outgrowth, of the open source software movement. They value hands-on craftsmanship and collaboration, particularly in the creative application of technology."

"He kept each name badge from conventions he attended," Ivy said, pointing toward a stack of them. "And each is signed not by celebrities, but by—I'd guess—people whose talks he attended. I recognize a few of the names."

"See that rubber wedge on the floor?" J.C. said with a grunt. "There's a scuff on the carpet. He often stuffed the wedge under his door to prop it open, circumventing the auto-lock. He liked to leave his office open for people to stop by and chat."

I poked at a few stickers stuck to the top of his desk. *Support Open Source*, *Information for Every Body*, *Words Should Be Free*.

Tobias had me sit at the computer. It wasn't password protected. J.C. raised an eyebrow.

Panos's latest website visits were forums, where he posted energetically, but politely, about information and technology issues. "He was enthusiastic," I said, scanning some of his emails, "and talkative. People genuinely liked him. He often attended nerdy conventions, and though he would be reticent to talk about them at first, if you could pry a little bit out of him, the rest would come out like a flood. He was always tinkering with things. The Legos were his idea, weren't they?"

Garvas stepped up beside me. "How . . ."

"He believed in your work," I continued, narrowing my eyes at one of Panos's posts on a Linux forum. "But he didn't like your corporate structure, did he?"

"Like a lot of us, he felt that investors were an annoying but necessary part of doing what we loved." Garvas hesitated. "He didn't sell us out, Leeds, if that's what you're wondering. He *wouldn't* have sold us out."

"I agree," I said, turning around in the chair. "If this man were going to betray his company, he'd just have posted everything on the internet. I find it highly unlikely that he'd sell your files to some other evil corporation rather than just giving them away."

Garvas relaxed.

"I'll need that list of your rival companies," I said. "And coroner's reports, with photos of the body. Specifics on how the corpse vanished. I'll also want details about where Panos lived, his family, and any non-work friends you know about."

"So . . . you're agreeing to help us?"

"I'll find the body, Garvas," I said, standing. "But first I'm going to go strangle your employer."

7

I **found Yol** sitting alone in a cafeteria, surrounded by clean white tables, chairs of green, red, yellow. Each table sported a jar filled with lemons.

Empty, yet decorated with perky colors, the room felt . . . as if it were holding its breath. Waiting for something. I waved for my aspects to wait outside, then walked in to confront Yol alone. He'd removed his garish sunglasses; without them, he looked almost like an ordinary businessman. Did he wear the glasses to pretend he was a star, or did he wear them to keep people from seeing those keen eyes of his, so certain and so wily?

"You set me up," I said, taking a seat beside him. "Ruthlessly, like a pro."

Yol said nothing.

"If this story breaks," I said, "and everything about 13 goes to hell, I'll be implicated as part-owner in the company."

I waited for Ivy to chastise me for the curse, bland though it was. But she was outside.

"You could tell the truth," Yol said. "Shouldn't be too hard to prove that you only got your shares today."

"No good. I'm a story, Yol. An eccentric. I don't get the benefit of the doubt with the press. If I'm connected in any way, no protests will keep me out of the tabloids, and you know it. You gave me shares *specifically* so I'd be in the pot with you, you bastard."

Yol sighed. He looked far older when you could see his eyes. "Maybe," he said, "I just wanted you to feel like I do. I knew *nothing* of the whole cancer fiasco when I bought this place. They dropped the worst of it on me two weeks ago."

"Yol," I said, "you need to talk to the authorities. This is bigger than me or you."

"I know. And I am. The feds are sending CDC officials tonight. The engineers are going to be quarantined; I probably will be too. I haven't told anyone else yet. But Stephen, the government is wrong; they're looking at this *wrong*. This isn't about a disease, but about information."

"The corpse," I said, nodding. "How could I3 let this happen? Didn't they consider that he was *literally* a walking hard drive?"

"The body was to be cremated," Yol said. "Part of an in-house agreement. It wasn't supposed to be an issue. And even still, the information might not be easy to get.

Everyone here is supposed to encrypt the data they store inside their cells. You've heard of a one-time pad?"

"Sure," I said. "Random encryption that requires a unique key to decode. Supposed to be unbreakable."

"Mathematically, it's the *only* unbreakable form of encryption," Yol said. "The process isn't very practical for everyday use, but what people were doing here wasn't about practicality, not yet. Company policy insisted on such encryption—before they put data in their bodies, they encrypt it with a unique key. To read that data, then, you'd need that exact key. We don't have the one Panos used, unfortunately."

"Assuming he actually followed policy and encrypted his data."

Yol grimaced. "You noticed?"

"Not the most interested in security, our deceased friend."

"Well, we have to hope he used a key—because if he did, the people who have his body won't be able to read what he stored. And we might be safe."

"Unless they find the key."

Yol pushed a thick folder toward me. "Exactly. Before we arrived, I had them print this out for you."

"And it is?"

"Panos's net interactions. Everything he's done over the last few months—every email sent, every forum post. We haven't been able to find anything in it, but I thought you should have it just in case."

"You're assuming I'm going to help you."

"You told Garvas—"

"I told him I'd find the corpse. I'm not sure I'll return it to you when I do."

"That's fine," Yol said, standing up, taking his sunglasses out of his pocket. "We have our data, Stephen. We just don't want it falling into the wrong hands. Tell me you disagree."

"I'm pretty sure that your hands *are* the wrong hands." I paused. "Did you kill him, Yol?"

"Panos? No. As far as I can tell, it really *was* an accident."

I studied him, and he met my eyes before slipping on the ridiculous sunglasses. Trustworthy? I'd always thought so in the past. He tapped the packet of information. "I'll see that Garvas and his team get you everything else you asked for."

"If it were only your company," I said, "I'd probably just let you burn."

"I know that. But people are in danger."

Damn him. He was right. I stood up.

"You have my number," Yol said. "I'll likely be on lockdown here, but I should still be able to talk. You, however, need to make a quick exit before the feds arrive."

"Fine." I brushed past him, heading toward the door.

"Finding the decryption key isn't enough," Yol said after me. "We don't know how many copies of it there are—and that's assuming Panos even followed encryption protocol in the first place. Find that body, Stephen, and *burn it*. That's what I wish I'd done to this whole building weeks ago."

I opened the door, stepping out and waving to Ivy, Tobias, and J.C. They fell in with me as we walked.

"J.C.," I said, "use that phone of yours. Call the other aspects. Send them to the White Room. We've got work to do."

Part Two

I**'ve got** a lot of aspects. Forty-seven, to be exact, with Arnaud being the latest to join us. I don't usually need all of them—in fact, imagining more than four or five at a time is taxing, something I can't do for long. That limitation is yet another thing that makes my psychologists salivate. A psychotic who finds it more tiring to create his fantasy world than live in the real one?

On occasion, a job comes along that requires extra effort, and I need the attention of a large number of aspects. That's why I made the White Room. Blank walls, floor, and ceiling painted the same uniform matte white; smooth, cool surfaces, unbroken save for lights in the ceiling. Soundproofed and calm, here there were no distractions—nothing to focus on but the dozens of imaginary people who flooded in through the double doors.

I don't consciously choose how my aspects look, but something about me seems to appreciate variety. Lua, a

Samoan, was a beefy fellow with a vast smile. He wore sturdy cargo pants and a jacket covered in pockets—appropriate for a survivalist. Mi Won, Korean, was our surgeon and field medic. Ngozi—forensic investigation—was a six-foot-four black woman, while Flip was squat, fat, and often tired.

It went on, and on, and on. They'd joined me slowly, one case at a time, as I'd needed to learn some new skill—packing my overcrowded brain with an increasingly diverse array of proficiencies. They acted just like real people would, chatting in a variety of languages. Audrey looked disheveled; she'd obviously been napping. Clive and Owen wore golfing outfits, and Clive carried a driver over his shoulder. I hadn't realized that Owen had finally gotten him to pick up the sport. Kalyani, decked out in a bright red and gold silk sari, rolled her eyes as J.C. called her "Achmed" again, but I could tell he was growing fond of her. It was tough *not* to be fond of Kalyani.

"Mister Steve!" Kalyani said. "How was your date? Fun, I hope?"

"It was a step forward," I said, looking around the room. "Have you seen Armando?"

"Oh! Mister Steve." The diminutive Indian woman took me by the arm. "Some of us tried to get him to come down. He refused. He says he is on a hunger strike until his throne is returned to him."

I winced. Armando was getting worse. Nearby, Ivy gave me a pointed look.

"Mister Steve," Kalyani said, "you should have my husband Rahul join us."

"I've explained this before, Kalyani. Your husband is not one of my aspects."

"But Rahul is *very* helpful," Kalyani said. "He's a photographer, and since Armando is so unhelpful lately . . ."

"I'll consider it," I said, which seemed to placate her. Kalyani was new, and didn't yet know how all this worked. I couldn't create new aspects at will, and though many of my aspects spoke of their lives—their families, friends, and hobbies—I never actually *saw* any of this. Good thing too. Keeping track of forty-seven hallucinations is tough enough. If I had to imagine their in-laws too, I just might end up going crazy.

Tobias cleared his throat, trying to draw everyone's attention. That proved to be futile before the jabbering hoard of aspects; getting together at once was too novel, and they were enjoying it. So J.C. pulled out his sidearm and shot once into the air.

The room immediately silenced, then was filled with the sounds of aspects grousing and complaining as they rubbed their ears. Tobias stepped out of the way of a small trail of dust that floated down from above.

I glared at J.C. "You realize, genius, that now I'm going to have to imagine a *hole* in the ceiling every time we come in here?"

J.C. gave a little shrug, holstering his weapon. He at least had the decency to look embarrassed.

Tobias patted me on the arm. "I'll patch the hole," he told me, then turned to the now-silenced crowd. "A corpse has been stolen. We have been employed to recover it."

Ivy walked among the aspects, delivering sheets of paper.

"You'll find the details explained here," Tobias continued. Though they all knew what I did, sometimes going through the motions of delivering information was better for us all. "It is important you understand that lives are at stake. Perhaps many lives. We need a plan, and quickly. Get to work."

Ivy finished distributing the sheets, ending next to me. She handed me the last group of papers.

"I already know the details," I said.

"Your sheet is different," Ivy said. "It's everything you know about I3's rival companies."

I glanced it over, and was surprised at how much information it contained. I'd spent the ride here pondering the things Yol had told me, and hadn't read his briefings beyond glancing at the names of the three companies he thought most likely to have stolen the corpse. Well, information about each company was apparently tucked in the back of my brain. I flipped through the pages, thoughtful. I hadn't done any research on biotech companies since Ignacio had . . . left us. I'd assumed that knowledge like this would have gone with him.

"Thanks," I said to Ivy.

"No problem."

My aspects spread through the White Room, each starting to work in his or her own way. Kalyani sat on the floor beside a wall and took out a bright red marker. Dylan paced. Lua sidled up to whomever was closest and started a conversation. Most wrote their ideas, using the walls like whiteboards. Some sketched as they wrote, others had a linear progression of ideas, others kept writing things and crossing them out.

I read through Ivy's pages to refresh my memory, then dug into the material Yol had given me. This included the coroner's report, with pictures of the dead man who did indeed look very dead. Liza herself had filled out the report. Might need to visit her, unfortunately.

Once done reading, I strolled through the room looking over each aspect's work, Tobias at my side. Some aspects focused on whether or not Yol was playing us. Others—like Ivy—extrapolated from what we knew about Panos, trying to decide where they thought he'd be most likely to hide the data key. Still others worked on the problem of the virus.

After one circuit through the room, I leaned back against the wall and picked up the larger stack of papers Yol had given me—the one that contained the record of Panos's web and email interactions over the last few months. It was thick, but this time I didn't worry about paying conscious attention to what I was reading. I just wanted to do a quick speed read to dump it into my brain so the aspects could play with it.

That still took over an hour. By the time I stood up, stretching, much of the white space in the room was filled with theories, ideas, and—in Marinda's case—large floral patterns and an impressively detailed sketch of a dragon. I clasped my hands behind my back and did another circuit of the room, encouraging those who had gotten bored, asking questions about what they'd written, breaking up a few arguments.

In the midst of it I passed Audrey, who was writing her comments in the middle of the air before her, using her finger instead of a pen.

I stopped and raised an eyebrow at her. "Taking liberties, I see."

Audrey shrugged. Self-described as "curvaceous," she had long dark hair and a pretty face. For an expert in handwriting analysis, her penmanship was awful.

"There wasn't space left on the wall," Audrey said.

"I'm sure," I said, looking at her hovering text. A second later a pane of glass appeared in the room where she had been writing, making it seem like she'd been writing on glass all along. I felt a headache coming on.

"Oh, that's no fun," she said, folding her arms.

"It is what must be, Audrey," I said. "There are rules."

"Rules you made up."

"Rules we all live by," I said, "for our own good." I frowned, reading what she'd written. "Biochemistry equations? Since when have you been interested in that?"

She shrugged. "I figured that somebody ought to do a little studying on the topic, and I had the time, since you pointedly refuse to imagine me a pet."

I rested my fingers on the pane of glass, looking over her cramped notes. She was trying to figure out the method Panos had used to create the virus. There were large gaps in her diagrams, however—breaks that looked as if they'd been ripped free of the writing. What was left went barely beyond basic chemistry.

"It's not going to work, Audrey," I said. "This just isn't something we can do anymore."

"Shouldn't it still be in there, somewhere?"

"No. It's gone."

"But—"

"Gone," I said firmly.

"You are one messed-up person."

"I'm the sanest one in this room."

"Technically," she said, "you're also the most insane."

I ignored the comment, squatting down beside the pane of glass, inspecting some other notations she'd made on other topics. "Searching for patterns in the things Panos wrote online?"

"I thought there might be hidden messages in his forum posts," Audrey explained.

I nodded. When I'd studied handwriting analysis—and, in doing so, created Audrey—I'd done a little tangential research into cryptography. The two disciplines moved in the same circles, and some of the books

I'd read had described decoding messages by noticing intentional changes in handwriting, such as a writer crossing some of their *T*s at a different slant to convey hidden information.

That meant Audrey had some small cryptography expertise. More than any of the rest of us did. "This could be useful," I said, tapping the pane of glass.

"Might be more useful," she noted, "if I—you—had any *real* understanding of cryptography. Do you have time to download some more books, perhaps?"

"You just want to go on more missions," I said, standing.

"Are you kidding? You get *shot at* on those missions."

"Only once in a while."

"Often enough. I'm not so comfortable with being imaginary that I want to see you dead on the ground. You're literally my whole world, Steve-O." She paused. "Though, to be honest, I've always been curious what would happen if you took LSD . . ."

"I'll see what I can do about the cryptography," I said. "Continue with the analysis of his forum posts. Stop with the chemistry sham."

She sighed, but reached out and started to erase the equations with her sleeve. I walked away, pulling out my phone and bringing up some books on cryptography. If I studied further, would I create another aspect? Or would Audrey really acquire the ability, as she implied? I wanted to say the first was more likely, but Audrey—as the most self-aware of all my aspects—got away with things I wouldn't have expected.

Tobias joined me as I sorted through the volumes available electronically.

"Report?" I asked him.

"General consensus is that this technology is viable," Tobias said, "and the threat is real, though Mi Won wants to think more about the effects of dumping rampant DNA strains into the body's muscles. J.C. says we'll want to confirm independently that I3 is in lockdown and that the feds are really involved. That will tell us a great deal about how honest Mister Chay is being with us."

"Good idea. What's that contact we have at Homeland Security?"

"Elsie," Tobias said. "You found her cat."

Yes, her cat. Not all of my missions involve terrorists or the fate of the world. Some are far more simple and mundane. Like locating a teleporting cat.

"Give her a call," I said absently. "See if she'll confirm for us what Yol said about contacting the authorities."

Tobias stopped beside me. "Call her?"

I looked up from my screen, then blushed. "Right. Sorry. I've been talking to Audrey." She tended to throw me off-balance.

"Ah, dearest Audrey," Tobias said. "I sincerely think she must be some kind of compensating factor in your psychology, a way to blow off a little steam, so to speak. Genius is often accompanied by quirks of the mind. Why,

Nikola Tesla had an arbitrary, and baffling, aversion to *pearls* of all things. He'd send people away who came to him wearing them, and it is said . . ."

He continued on. I relaxed to the sound of his voice, choosing a book on advanced cryptography. Tobias eventually wound back around to his report on what the aspects had determined. "This brings us to our next course of action," he said. "Owen's suggestion is perhaps the most relevant, and Ivy won't be able to complete her psychological analysis unless we know more about the subject. Beginning by visiting Panos's family is advised. From there, Ngozi needs more information from the coroner. We may want to go there next."

"Reverse those," I said. "It's . . . what, three in the morning?"

"Six."

"Already?" I said, surprised. I didn't feel that tired. The engagement of a new mission, a puzzle to solve, kept me alert. "Well, still. I feel more comfortable about visiting a coroner's office this early than I do about waking Panos's family. Liza gets to work at . . . what, seven?"

"Eight."

So I had time to kill. "What leads do we have on the corporations who might be behind this?"

"J.C. has some thoughts. He wants to talk to you."

I found him leaning against the wall near where Ivy was working; he was chattering away and generally distracting her. I grabbed him by the shoulder and pulled him away. "Tobias said you have something for me."

"Our assassin," he said. "Zen Rigby."

"Yes, and?" J.C. couldn't have any new information on her—he only knew what I knew, and we'd dredged that well already.

"I've been thinking, Skinny," J.C. said. "Why did she show up when you were on your date?"

"Because her employers knew Yol was likely to go to me."

"Yeah, but why start surveillance on you that early? Look, they have the body, right?"

"So we assume."

"Therefore, the reason to watch you is to tail you and see if you find the data key. There was no reason to watch you *before* Yol arrived. It tipped their hand, you see? They should have waited until you were called in to I3."

I chewed on that for a minute. We liked to make fun of J.C., but the truth was, he was one of my most practical aspects. A lot of them spent their days dreaming and thinking. J.C. kept me alive.

"It does seem odd," I agreed. "But what does it mean?"

"It means we don't have all the facts," J.C. said. "Zen might have been trying to bug us, for instance, hoping we'd go to I3 and reveal information."

I looked at him sharply. "Wardrobe change?"

"Good place to start," he said. "But there are a host of other reasons she could have been there so early. Perhaps she's employed by a *third* company that knows something is up with I3, but doesn't quite know what. Or maybe she's not involved in this case at all."

"You don't believe that."

"I don't," he agreed. "But let's tread lightly, eh? Zen is dangerous. I ran across her a couple of times in black ops missions. She left corpses, sometimes operatives— sometimes just innocent bystanders."

I nodded.

"You'll want to carry a sidearm," J.C. said. "You realize that if it comes to a confrontation, I won't be able to shoot her."

"Because of past familiarity?" I said, giving him an out. I didn't like to push him to confront what he was—instead offering reasons why, despite being my bodyguard, he could never actually interact with any-one we met.

Except that one time when he had done just that.

"Nah," J.C. said. "I can't shoot her because I'm not really here."

I started. Had he just . . .? "J.C.," I said. "This is a big step for you."

"Nah, I've got this figured out. That Arnaud guy, he's pretty smart."

"Arnaud?" I looked across the room toward the slen-der, balding Frenchman who was our newest addition.

"Yeah," J.C. said, hand on my shoulder. "He has this theory, see. That we're not figments, or whosits, or whatever crazy term you feel like using at the moment. He said . . . well, it's a lot of nerd talk, but it means I'm a real boy for sure. I'm just not here."

"Is that so?" I wasn't certain what to think of this.

"Yup," J.C. said. "You should hear what he has to say. Hey, chrome-dome!"

Arnaud pointed at himself, then hustled over as J.C. waved. J.C. put his hand around the diminutive Frenchman, as if they were best friends—the gesture seemed to make Arnaud distinctly uncomfortable. It was a little like the cat buddying up to the mouse.

"Let him have it," J.C. said.

"It? What it are you speaking of?" Arnaud spoke with a smooth French accent, like butter melting over a browned game hen.

"You know," J.C said. "The things you said about us?"

Arnaud adjusted his spectacles. "Well, um, you see, in quantum physics we talk about possibilities. One interpretation says that dimensions are infinite, and everything that can happen, has happened. It seems to follow if this is true, then each of us aspects somewhere has existed in some dimension or realm of possibility as a real person. A curious thought, would you not agree, Étienne?"

"Curious indeed," I said. "It—"

"So I'm real," J.C. interjected. "The smart guy just said it."

"No, no," Arnaud said. "I merely indicated that it is likely that somewhere, in another place and time, there really is a person who matches—"

J.C. shoved him aside and wrapped his arm around my shoulders, turning me away from Arnaud. "I've got it figured out, Skinny. We're all from this other place, see. And when you need some help, you reach out and *snatch* us. You're some kind of physics wizard."

"A . . . physics wizard?"

"Yup. And I'm no Navy SEAL. I've just got to accept that." He paused. "I'm an Interdimensional Time Ranger."

I looked at him, grinning.

But he was dead serious.

"J.C.," I said. "That's as ridiculous as Owen's ghost theory."

"No it's not," J.C. said, stubborn. "Look, back in that Jerusalem mission. What happened there at the end?"

I hesitated. I had been surrounded, hands shaking, holding a gun I barely knew how to use. In that moment, J.C. had *taken hold* of my arm and directed it, causing me to fire my gun in the precise pattern needed to bring down every enemy.

"I learn quickly," I said. "Physics, math, languages . . . I just need to spend a short time studying, and I can become an expert—via an aspect. Maybe gunplay isn't different. I studied it, fired a few times at the range, and became an expert. But this skill is different—you can't help me by talking—so I couldn't use you properly until I imagined you guiding me. It's not so different from what Kalyani does in guiding me through a conversation in another language."

"You're stretching," J.C. said. "Why hasn't this worked for any other skill you've tried?"

I didn't know.

"I'm a Time Ranger," J.C. said stubbornly.

"If that were true—which it's *not*—wouldn't you be angry at me for grabbing you from your other life and trapping your quantum ghost here?"

"Nah," J.C. said. "It's what I signed up for. The creed of the Time Ranger. We have to protect the universe, and for now that means protecting you as best I can."

"Oh, for the love of—"

"Hey," J.C. interrupted. "Aren't we tight for time? You should be moving."

"We can't do much until morning arrives," I said, but allowed myself to be moved on from the topic. I waved Tobias over. "Keep everyone working. I'm going to go take a shower and do some reading. After that, we're hitting the field."

"Will do," Tobias said. "And the field team is?"

"Standard," I said. "You, Ivy, J.C., and . . ." I looked through the room. "And we'll see who else."

Tobias gave me a curious look.

"Have the team meet me in the garage, ready to go, at seven thirty."

☷

9

I‌turned the cryptography book to text-to-voice, cranked the volume, and set it to 5x speed. The following shower was long and refreshing. I didn't think about the problem—I just learned.

When I stepped into my bedroom in my bathrobe, I found that Wilson had set out breakfast for me, along with a tall glass of lemonade. I sent him a text, asking him to have the driver prep the SUV—much less conspicuous than taking the limo—for a seven thirty departure.

I finished the book while eating, then made a call to Elsie, my contact in Homeland Security. I woke her up, unfortunately, but she was still willing to check on the matter for me. I put in a call to the coroner's office—got the voicemail, but left a message for Liza—and as I was finishing, got a text back from Elsie. 13 was indeed under lockdown, with the CDC investigating and the FBI involved.

I strode into the garage a short time later, dressed and somewhat refreshed, right on time for our departure. There I found Wilson himself—square-faced, bifocaled, and graying on top—flicking a speck of something off a chauffeur's cap, which he proceeded to put on his head.

"Wait," I said. "Isn't Thomas supposed to be in this morning?"

"Unfortunately," Wilson said, "he is not coming to work today. Or ever, apparently, as per his message this morning."

"Oh, no," I said. "What happened?"

"You do not recall explaining to him that you were a Satanist, Master Leeds?"

"Two percent Satanist," I said. "And Xavier is very progressive for a devil-worshiper. He's never made me sacrifice anything other than imaginary chickens."

"Yes, well . . ."

I sighed. Another servant lost. "We can call in a driver for the day. We had a long night last night. You don't need to do work this early."

"I don't mind," Wilson said. "Somebody needs to look out for you, Master Leeds. Did you sleep at all?"

"Uh . . ."

"I see. And did you happen to eat anything at dinner last night before you ended up in the tabloids?"

"The story is out already, is it?"

"Written up in the *Mag* and posted on *Squawker* this morning—along with an exposé by Miss Bianca herself.

You skipped dinner, and you skipped lunch yesterday as well, insisting that you didn't want to spoil your appetite for the date."

More like didn't want to throw up from nervousness. "No wonder that breakfast tasted so good." I reached for the door handle to the SUV.

Wilson rested his hand on my arm. "Do not become so preoccupied with saving the world, Master Leeds, that you forget to take care of yourself." He patted my arm, then climbed into the driver's seat.

My team waited inside, all but Audrey, who burst into the garage wearing a sweater and a scarf. No other aspect had appeared upon my reading the book; Audrey had gained the knowledge, as she'd expected. I was glad—each new aspect put a strain on me, and I'd rather have old ones learn new things. Though, having Audrey along on the mission could be its own special brand of difficult.

"Audrey," I said as I opened the door for her, "it's almost June. A scarf?"

"Well," she said with a grin, "what good is being imaginary if you can't ignore the weather?" She threw her scarf dramatically over one shoulder, then piled into the car, elbowing J.C. on her way past.

"If I shoot you, woman," he growled at her, "it will hurt. My bullets can affect interdimensional matter."

"Mine can go around corners," she said. "And make flowers grow." She settled in between Ivy and Tobias, and didn't put on her seat belt.

This was going to be an interesting mission.

We pulled out onto the roadway. Morning was upon us, the day bright, and rush hour well under way. I watched out the window, lost in thought for a time, until I noticed J.C. fishing in Ivy's purse.

"Uh . . ." I said.

"Don't turn," J.C. said, batting away Ivy's hand as she tried to snatch the purse back. He came out with her compact makeup mirror and held it up to glance over his shoulder out the back window, not wanting to present his profile.

"Yeah," he said, "someone's probably following us."

"Probably?" Ivy asked.

"Hard to say for certain," J.C. said, shifting the mirror. "The car doesn't have a front license plate."

"You think it's her?" I asked. "The assassin?"

"Again," J.C. said, "no way to tell for certain."

"Maybe there is a way," Audrey said, tapping her head and the new knowledge inside of it. "Wanna try some hacking, Steve-O?"

"Hacking?" Ivy said. "As in computer hacking?"

"No, as in coughing," Audrey said, rolling her eyes. "Here, I'm going to write some instructions for you."

I watched with curiosity as she scribbled down a list of instructions, then handed them to me. It was imaginary paper—not that I could tell. I took it and read the instructions, then glanced at Audrey.

"Trust me," Audrey said.

"I only read you one book."

"It was enough."

I studied her, then shrugged and got out my phone. Worth a try. Following her instructions, I called up F.I.G, the restaurant where I'd eaten—or, well, ordered food— last night. It rang, and fortunately the breakfast staff was already in. An unfamiliar voice answered, asking, "Hello?"

I followed Audrey's instructions. "Yeah, hey," I said. "My wife ate there last night—but we had a family emergency, and she had to run before finishing her food. In fact, she was in such a hurry, she used the business credit card to pay instead of our home one. I was wondering if I could swap the cards."

"Okay," the woman on the phone said. "What's the name?"

"Carol Westminster," I said, using the alias Zen had used for her reservation.

A few minutes passed. Hopefully the receipts from last night were still handy. Indeed, after shuffling about a moment, the woman came back on the phone. "Okay, what's the new card name?"

"Which one did she use?"

"It's a KeyTrust card," the woman said, starting to sound suspicious. "Ends in 3409."

"Oh!" I replied. "Well, that's the right one after all. Thanks anyway."

"Great, thanks." The woman sounded annoyed as she hung up the phone. I wrote the number down in my pocket notebook.

"You call that hacking?" J.C. said. "What was the point?"

"Wait and see," Audrey said.

I was already dialing the bank's credit card fraud prevention number. We continued in the car, taking an exit onto the southbound highway as I listened to holding music. Beside me, J.C. kept an eye on our supposed tail with Ivy's mirror. He nodded at me. They'd followed us onto the highway.

When I finally got through the menus, holding patterns, and warnings my call might be recorded, I ended up with a nice-sounding man with a Southern accent on the other side of the line. "How can I help you?" he asked.

"I need to report a stolen credit card," I said. "My wife's purse got taken from our house last night."

"All right. Name on the card?"

"Carol Westminster."

"And the card number?"

"I don't have it," I said, trying to sound exasperated. "Did you miss the part about the card being lost?"

"Sir, you just need to look online—"

"I tried! All I can see are the last four digits."

"You need to—"

"Someone could be spending my money *right now*," I cut in. "Do we have time for this?"

"Sir, you have fraud protection."

"I'm sorry, I'm sorry. I'm just worried. It's not your fault. I just don't know what to do. Please, you can help, right?"

The man on the other line breathed out, as if my tone change indicated he'd just dodged a potentially frustrating incident. "Just tell me the last four digits, then," he said, sounding more relaxed.

"The computer says 3409."

"Okay, let's see . . . Do you know your PIN number, Mister Westminster?"

"Uh . . ."

"Social security number attached to the card?"

"805-31-3719," I said with confidence.

There was a pause. "That doesn't match our records, sir."

"But it *is* my social security number."

"The number I have is probably your wife's, sir."

"Why does that matter?"

"I can't let you make changes until I authenticate, sir," the man said in the neutral, patient voice of one accustomed to talking on the phone all day to people who deserved to be strangled.

"Are you *sure*?" I asked.

"Yes, sir. I'm sorry."

"Well, I suppose you could call her," I said. "She's off to work, and I don't have her social handy."

"I can do that," the man said. "Is the number we have on file all right?"

"Which one is that?" I asked. "Her cell was in her purse."

"555-626-9013."

"Drat," I said, writing down quickly. "That's the stolen phone's number. I'll just have to call her when she gets to work and have her call you."

"Very well. Is there anything else, sir?"

"No. Thank you."

I hung up, then rotated the pad to display the number to the others. "The assassin's phone number."

"Great," J.C. said. "Now you can ask her out."

I turned the pad around and looked at the number. "You know, it was shocking how easy that was, all things considered."

"Rule number one of decryption," Audrey said. "If you don't have to break the code, don't. People are usually far less secure than the encryption strategies they employ."

"So what do we do with this?" I asked.

"Well, first there's a little app I need you to download onto your phone," Audrey said. "J.C., which of the three competitors do you think is most likely to have hired the woman?"

"Exeltec," J.C. said without missing a heartbeat. "Of the three, they're the most desperate. Years of funding with no discernible progress, investors breathing down their necks, and a history of moral ambiguity and espionage. Subject of three investigations, but no conclusive findings."

"That packet has their CEO's phone numbers," Audrey said.

I smiled and started working on the phone. In short time, I had my mobile set up to send fake information to Zen's caller ID, indicating I was Nathan Haight, owner of Exeltec.

"Have Wilson ready to honk," Audrey said.

I told him to be ready, then dialed.

It rang once. Twice.

Then picked up.

"Here," a curt, female voice said. "What is it? I'm busy."

I gestured to Wilson. He honked loudly.

I heard it over the phone as well. Zen was most certainly tailing us. I hit the button on my phone's app that imitated static on the line, then said something, which I knew would be distorted beyond recognition.

Zen cursed, then she said, "I don't care how nervous the other partners are. Bothering me repeatedly isn't going to make this go faster. I'll call in with a report when I know something. Until then, leave me alone."

She hung up.

"That," J.C. said, "was the strangest hacking I've ever seen."

"That's because you don't know what hacking really is," Audrey said, sounding smug. "You Imagine geeks in front of a computer. But in reality, most people 'hacking' today—at least as far as the media calls it—just spend their time on the phone trying to pry out information."

"So we know she's following us," Ivy said, "*and* we know the name of our rival company. Which tells us who has the corpse."

"Not for certain," I said. "But it looks good." I tapped my phone, thoughtful, as Wilson pulled off the highway and started driving through downtown. "Advice?"

"We need to avoid getting in over our heads," Ivy said. "If that's humanly possible for us."

"I agree," Tobias said. "Stephen, if we can find proof that Exeltec stole the body, the CDC might be willing to raid their offices."

"We could just raid their offices ourselves," J.C. said. "Cut out the middleman."

"I'd rather not do anything specifically illegal," Tobias replied.

"Don't worry," J.C. said. "As an Interdimensional Time Ranger, I have code 876 special authorization to ignore local legal statutes in times of emergency. Look, Skinny, we're going to end up compromising Exeltec eventually. I can feel it. Even if they aren't storing the body in their local offices, there will be a trail to it in there somewhere."

"For what it's worth," Audrey added. "I'm with J.C. Breaking in sounds like fun."

I sat back, thinking. "We'll go to the coroner," I finally said, getting a nod from Tobias and Ivy. "I'd rather find proof incriminating Exeltec, and then set up an official raid." A plan was beginning to form in my head. "Besides," I added, "breaking in isn't the *only* way to find out what Exeltec knows . . ."

10

The car rolled down a waking urban street, lamps flickering off now that the sun was fully up, like servants lowering their heads before their king. The city morgue was near the hospital, situated in a spread-out office complex that could have easily held three or four exciting internet start-ups. We passed carefully-trimmed hedges and trees with last year's Christmas lights still wrapped around them, dormant until the season started up again.

"All right," J.C. said to me. "You ready for this?"

"Ready?" I said.

"We're being tailed by an assassin, Skinny," he said. "That feeling between your shoulder blades, that's the knowledge that someone has you in their sights. She could squeeze the trigger at any moment."

"Don't be silly," Ivy said. "She's not going to hurt us as long as she thinks we're leading her to important information."

"Are you sure?" J.C. said. "Because I'm not. At any moment, her higher-ups could decide that you working for Yol is a very, very bad thing. They could decide to remove the competition and take their chances at finding the key on their own."

The way he said it, cold and straightforward, made me squirm.

"You just don't like being followed," Ivy said.

"Damn right."

"Language."

"Look," J.C. said, "Zen has information we'd really like to know. If we capture her, that alone might give us the proof we need. We know where she is, and we have a momentary advantage. How well do you think you could pull off a quiet evacuation?"

"Not well," I said.

"Let's try it anyway," J.C. said, pointing. "See that turn right ahead, as we move into the parking lot? The hedge there will hide us from the view of the car following us. You need to bail from the vehicle there—don't worry, I'll help you—and have Jeeves park in front of the building right beside the hedges. We can get the drop on Zen and turn this chase on its head."

"Reckless," Ivy said.

It was, but as the turn approached, I made a decision. "Let's do it," I said. "Wilson, I'm slipping out of the car at the next turn. Drive as if nothing has happened;

don't slow more than normal. Park right in front of the morgue, then wait."

He adjusted the rearview mirror so he could meet my eyes. He didn't say anything, but I could see that he was concerned.

The turning of the mirror gave me a good glimpse of the dark sedan behind us. I felt under my jacket for the sidearm J.C. had insisted I bring. This was *not* how I liked missions to go. I'd rather spend ten hours in a room trying to figure out a puzzle or a safe with no lock. Why, lately, did guns always seem to get involved?

I moved to the side door, then crouched down, grabbing the handle. J.C. moved over behind me, hand on my shoulder.

"Five, four, three . . ." he counted.

I took a deep breath.

"Two . . . *One!*"

I cracked the door right as Wilson turned the car around the hedge. J.C. *heaved* against my back, somehow pushing me in just the right way so that when I left the car, I hit in a curling roll. It still hurt. The momentum of the car's turn clicked the door shut and I rolled up into a crouch beside the hedge, where I waited until I heard the car behind us start to turn.

I slipped through the hedge to the other side right as the car turned around it, following Wilson. This meant that I was separated from Zen by the squat wall of densely packed foliage. It ran all the way along the parking lot here.

I scurried along the hedge, head down, keeping pace with Zen's car. It passed Wilson as he parked, then continued on in a presumably nonsuspicious way toward another section of the parking lot. I caught brief glimpses of black car through holes in the hedge—a shadowed driver, but nobody else visible. The car pulled into a parking stall a short distance from where the hedge ended.

Ahead, the leaves rustled, and J.C. slipped through, handgun out, joining me. "Nice work," he whispered. "We'll make a Ranger out of you yet."

"It was your push," I said. "Sent me tumbling exactly the right way."

"I said I'd help."

I said nothing, too nervous to continue the conversation. I was manifesting something new, an extension of my previous . . . framework. What else could I learn to do by having one of my aspects guide my fingers or steps?

I peeked through the hedge, then took out my handgun. J.C. motioned furiously for me to hide it in front of myself, so cars passing along the street to my right wouldn't see. Then J.C. nodded toward an opening in the hedge.

I took a deep breath before scrambling through and crossing the short distance to Zen's car. J.C. tailed me. I came up beside the car in a crouch.

"Ready?" J.C. asked.

I nodded.

"Finger on the trigger, Skinny. This is for real."

I nodded again. The passenger's side window, just above me, was open. Palms sweating, I threw myself to my feet and leveled my gun through the open window at the driver.

It wasn't the assassin.

The **driver** was a dark-haired kid, maybe eighteen, wearing a hoodie. He cried out, dropping the pair of binoculars he'd been using to look toward my SUV, his face going white as snow as he stared down my handgun.

That was most certainly *not* Zen Rigby.

"In the car, Skinny," J.C. said, looking around the parking lot. "Back seat, so he can't grapple you. Tell him to keep quiet. Don't look suspicious."

"Hands where I can see them," I told the kid, hoping he didn't see that my gun was shaking. "Don't say a word." I pulled open the back door, slipped in, but kept the gun on him.

The kid remained quiet save for a whine in the back of his throat. He was either terrified, or was a very good actor.

"Where's Zen?" I said to him, lifting the gun up beside the youth's head.

"Who?" he said.

"No games. *Where is she?*"

"I don't . . . I don't know anything . . ." The kid actually started weeping.

"Damn it," J.C. said, standing by the front window. "You think he's acting?"

"No idea," I said back.

"I should fetch Ivy."

"No," I said, not wanting to be left alone. I inspected the kid's weeping face reflected in the rearview mirror. Mediterranean skin tone . . . Same nose . . .

"Don't kill me," the kid whispered. "I just wanted to know what you did with him."

"You're Panos's brother," I guessed.

The kid nodded, still sobbing.

"Oh hell," J.C. said. "No wonder it was so easy to spot the tail. *Two* people were following us: an amateur and a professional. I'm an idiot."

I felt cold. I'd heard Wilson's honk through the line when on the phone with Zen, so she had been nearby, yet we hadn't spotted her. Zen had been invisible to us all along.

Bad.

"What's your name?" I asked the youth.

"Dion."

"Well, Dion, I'm putting the gun away. If you are who you say, then you don't need to be afraid. I'm going to need you to come with me, and if you start to run, or cry out, or anything like that . . . well, I'll have to make sure you stop."

The youth nodded.

I climbed from the car, gun holstered, and pulled the kid out by his shoulder. A quick frisk determined he wasn't armed, though he considered himself quite the spy. Flashlight, ski mask, binoculars, a mobile phone which I took and turned off. I marched him across the parking lot, fully aware that this whole exchange would have looked *very* suspicious to anyone watching. With J.C.'s coaching, though, I maintained the air of someone who knew what he was doing—arm on the youth's shoulder, walking confidently. We were in the government complex; hopefully, anyone who spotted us would think I was a cop.

If they didn't, well, it wouldn't be the first time the police had been called to deal with me. I think they kept a department pool going on the frequency of it.

I shoved Dion into my SUV, then climbed inside, feeling a little more secure with the tinted windows and more of my aspects in attendance. Dion moved to the back seat and slumped there, forcing Audrey to climb onto Tobias's lap—an event so unexpected, the aging aspect almost seemed to choke.

"Wilson, please give me warning if anyone approaches," I said. "All right, Dion. Spill it. Why are you following me?"

"They stole Panos's body," Dion said.

"And by 'they' you mean . . ."

"I3."

"And why on earth would they do such a thing?"

"The information," Dion said. "He had it stored in his cells, you know? All of their secrets. All the terrible things they were going to do."

I shared a look with J.C., who then facepalmed. Panos had been talking to his family about his research. Wonderful. J.C. removed his hand and mouthed to me, *security nightmare.*

"And what kind of terrible things," I said, "do you assume I3 was going to do?"

"I . . ." Dion looked to the side. "You know. *Corporate* things."

"Like take away casual Fridays," Audrey guessed.

So Panos hadn't completely confided in his brother. I tapped my fingers on the armrest. The family assumed that Yol and his people had taken the body to keep their information hidden—and, to be honest, that wasn't far from the truth. They'd been planning to see it burned, after all. Someone had merely gotten to Panos first.

"And you're following me," I said to the kid. "Why?"

"You were all over the internet this morning," Dion said. "Getting into a car with that weird Asian guy who owns I3. I figured out that you were supposed to crack the code on Panos's body. Seems obvious. I mean, you're some kind of superspy hacker or something, right?"

"That's *exactly* what we are," Audrey said. "Steve-O, tell him that's what we are." When I said nothing, she elbowed Tobias, in whose lap she was still sitting. "Tell him, grandpa."

"Stephen," Tobias said, somewhat uncomfortable, "this youth sounds earnest."

"He's being honest," Ivy said, inspecting him, "so far as I can tell."

"You should reassure him," Tobias said. "Look at the poor lad. He looks like he still thinks you're going to shoot him."

Indeed, Panos had his hands clasped, eyes down, but he was trembling.

I softened my tone. "I wasn't hired to crack the body's code," I told him. "I3 has plenty of backups on all their information. I'm here to find the corpse."

Dion looked up.

"No," I said, "I3 didn't take it. They would have been perfectly content to let it be cremated."

"I don't think he believes you, Steve," Ivy said.

"Look," I said to Dion, "I don't care what happens with I3. I just want to make sure the information in that corpse is accounted for, all right? And for now, I need you to wait here."

"Why—"

"Because I don't know what to do with you." I glanced at Wilson, who nodded. He'd keep an eye on the kid. "Go climb in the front seat," I told Dion. "When I get back, we can have a long conversation about all of this. For now, I have to go deal with a very surly coroner."

12

The city coroner was housed in a sterile-smelling little office beside the city morgue, which was only one set of rooms in a larger medical complex. Technically, Liza liked to be called a "medical examiner," and she was always surprisingly busy for a person who seemed to spend all of her time playing internet games.

At the stroke of eight, I strode through the medical complex lobby—suffering the glare of a security guard who was far too large for the little cubby they'd given him—and knocked politely on the coroner's office door. Liza's secretary—I forget his name—opened the door with an obviously reluctant expression.

"She's waiting for you," the young man said. "I wouldn't call her excited, though."

"Great. Thanks . . ."

"John," Tobias filled in.

". . . John."

The secretary nodded, walking back to his desk and shuffling papers. I strolled down a short hallway to a nice office, hung with official-looking diplomas and the like. I managed to get a glimpse of Facebook reflected in one of them as Liza turned off her tablet and looked up at me.

"I'm busy, Leeds," she said.

Dressed in a white labcoat over jeans and a pink buttoned blouse, Liza was in her late fifties, and was tall enough that she was very tired of answering whether or not she'd played basketball in school. It was fortunate her clients were, for the most part, dead—as that was the only type of person who didn't seem to bother her.

"Well, this shouldn't take long," I said, leaning against the doorframe and folding my arms, partially to block Tobias's adoring stare. What he saw in the woman, I'd never know.

"I don't have to do anything for you," Liza said, making a good show of turning toward her computer screen, as if she had tons and tons of work to do. "You're not involved in any kind of official case. Last I heard, the department had decided not to involve you anymore."

She said that last part a touch too triumphantly. Ivy and J.C. shared a look. The authorities weren't . . . particularly fond of us these days.

"One of your bodies went missing," I said to her. "Isn't anyone worried about that?"

"Not my problem," Liza said. "My part was done. Death pronounced, identity confirmed, no autopsy required. The morgue had a lapse. Well, you can talk to them about it."

Not a chance. They wouldn't let me in—they didn't have the authority. But Liza could; this *was* her department, no matter what she said.

"And the police aren't concerned about the breach?" I asked. "Sergeant Graves hasn't been poking around, wondering how such a terrible security snafu happened?"

Liza hesitated.

"Ah," Ivy said. "Good guess, Steve. Push more there."

"This is your division," I said to Liza. "Don't you even want to know how it happened? I can help."

"Every time you 'help,' Leeds, some kind of catastrophe follows."

"Seems like a catastrophe already happened."

"Hit her where it hurts," Ivy said. "Mention the hassle."

"Think of the paperwork, Liza," I said. "A body missing. Investigations, questions, people poking around, *meetings you'll have to attend*."

Liza couldn't completely cover her sour grimace. Beside me, Ivy grinned in satisfaction.

"All this," Liza said, leaning back, "for a body that should never have been here."

"What do you mean?" I asked.

" There was no *reason* for us to keep the corpse. Kin had identified him; no foul play was suspected. I should have released the body to the family's chosen mortician for embalming. But no. Not allowed. This corpse had to stay here, and nobody would tell me why. The commissioner himself insisted." She narrowed her eyes at me. "Now you. What was special about that guy, Leeds?"

The commissioner? Yol had done some work to keep this body in custody. Made sense. If he'd had the corpse released, then given it some kind of crazy security, that would have advertised to the world that there was something special about it. A quick call to ensure Panos stayed in the city morgue, locked up tight, was far less suspicious.

It just hadn't worked.

"We're going to have to give something up, Steve," Ivy told me. "She's digging her heels in. Time for the big guns."

I sighed. "You sure?" I asked under my breath.

"Yes, unfortunately."

"One interview," I said, meeting Liza's eyes. "One hour."

She leaned forward in her chair. "Buying me off?"

"Yes, and?"

She tapped the top of her table with an idle finger. "I'm a medical examiner. I'm not interested in publishing."

"I didn't say the interview had to be with you," I said. "Anyone you like—anyone in the medical community you need something from. *You* get *me* as barter."

Liza smiled. "Anyone?"

"Yes. One hour."

"No. As long as they want."

"That's too open-ended, Liza."

"So is the list of ways you're annoying. Take it or leave it, Leeds. I don't owe you anything."

"We're going to regret this, aren't we?" Tobias asked.

I nodded, thinking of the hours spent being prodded by some psychologist who was looking to make a name for themselves. Another paper in another journal, treating me like a strange species of sea cucumber to be dissected and displayed.

Time was ticking though, and it was either this or tell Liza why the body was so important.

"Deal," I said.

She didn't smile. Smiling was far too human an expression for Liza. She did seem satisfied, though, as she grabbed her keys off the table and led me down the hallway, my aspects trailing.

The air grew appreciably colder as we approached the morgue. A key card unlocked the door, which was of heavy, thick metal. Inside the room, one could see why Liza had chosen to work here—not only was it frigid, all this chrome probably reminded her of the spaceship that had dropped her off on our planet.

The door swung closed behind us, thumping into place. Liza settled in beside the wall, arms folded, watching to prevent any shenanigans. "Fifteen minutes, Leeds. Get to it."

I surveyed the room, which had three metal tables on wheels, a counter with various medical paraphernalia, and a wall full of large corpse drawers.

"All right," I said to the four aspects, "I want to know how they got the body out."

"We need proof too," J.C. said, poking through the room. "Something to tie Exeltec to the crime."

"That would be wonderful," I said to him, "but honestly, we don't want to be too leading. Maybe they don't have it. Focus on what we know. Find me clues on how the thieves stored or moved the body, and that might lead us right to it."

The others nodded. I turned around slowly, taking the whole room in, absorbing it into my subconscious. Then I closed my eyes.

My delusions started talking.

"No windows," J.C. said. "Only one exit."

"Unless those ceiling tiles are removable," Ivy noted.

"Nah," J.C. replied. "I've seen the security specs for this building. Remember the Coppervein case? No crawl space. No air ducts. Nothing funny about the architecture."

"This equipment *has* been used lately," Tobias said. "I know little of its purpose, though. Stephen, you really *should* recruit a coroner of our own eventually."

"We *do* have Ngozi," Audrey said. "Forensic investigation. Why didn't we bring her?"

Because of you, Audrey, I thought. *My subconscious gave you an important skill and inserted you into my team*. Why? I missed the days when I'd had someone to ask about things like this. When Sandra had been with me, everything had made sense for the first time in my life.

"This place is secure," Ivy said, sounding dissatisfied. "Inside job, perhaps? One of the morgue workers?"

"Could one of the workers here have been bribed?" I asked, opening my eyes and looking toward Liza.

"I thought of that," she said, arms still folded. "But I was the last one in the office that night. I came in, checked everything and turned off the lights. Security says nobody came in overnight."

"I'll want to talk to security, then," I said. "Who else was here that day?"

Liza shrugged. "Family. A priest. Always accompanied. This room doesn't open for anyone other than me and two of our technicians. Even the security guard can't get in without calling one of us. But that's all irrelevant— the body was still here when I left for the night."

"You're sure?"

"Yeah, I had to write down some numbers for paperwork. I checked on it specifically."

"We'll want to fingerprint the place," J.C. said. "Like it or not, we might have to go through the precinct."

I nodded. "I assume the police have already done forensics."

"Why would you assume that?" Liza asked.

We all looked at her. "Uh . . . you know. Because there was a *crime*?"

"A corpse was stolen," Liza said dryly. "Nobody was hurt, we have no actual signs of a break-in, and there is no money involved. The official word is that they are 'working' on the case, but let me tell you—finding this body is low on their list of priorities. They're more worried about the break-in itself; they'll want someone's hide for that . . ."

She refolded her arms, then repositioned and folded them again. She was trying to play it cool, but she *was* obviously worried. Ivy nodded at me, obviously pleased that I could read Liza so well. Well, it wasn't hard. I picked up things from my aspects now and then.

"Security cameras?" J.C. asked as he inspected the corners of the room. I repeated the question so Liza could hear it.

"Just out in the hallways," she said.

"Isn't that a little sparse?" I asked.

"The whole place is wired with alarms. If someone tries to break in, the security guard's desk will light up like Christmas." She grimaced. "We used to turn it on only at night, but they've had it on for two days straight now. Have to get permission to open a damn window these days . . ."

I looked at the team.

"Stephen," Tobias said, "we're going to need Ngozi."

I sighed. Well, it wasn't *too* long a drive to go back and pick her up.

"Here," J.C. said, pulling out his phone. "Let me give her a call."

"I don't think . . ." I said, but he was already dialing.

"Yeah, Achmed, we need your help," he said. "What? Of course I have your number. No, I have *not* been stalking you. Look, can you find Ngozi? How should I know where she is? Probably washing her hands a hundred times or something. No, I have *not* been stalking her either." He lowered the phone, giving the rest of us a suffering look. He raised it back up, and a short time later, continued. "Great. Let's video conference."

Tobias and I looked over J.C.'s shoulders as Kalyani's face appeared on the screen, perky and excited. She waved, then turned the phone toward Ngozi, who sat reading on her bed.

What to say about Ngozi? She was from Nigeria, with deep brown skin, and had been educated at Oxford. She was also deathly afraid of germs—so much so that when Kalyani held the phone toward her, Ngozi shied away visibly. She shook her head, and Kalyani was obliged to stand there, holding the phone.

"What's up?" Ngozi asked with a clipped, Nigerian accent.

"Crime scene investigation," I said.

"You're going to come get me?"

"Well, I guess we kind of thought . . ." I hesitated, then looked to J.C. "I don't know if this is going to work, J.C. We've never done anything like this before."

"Worth a try, though, right?"

I looked toward Ivy, who seemed skeptical, but Tobias shrugged. "What harm can it do, Stephen? Getting Ngozi out of the house is difficult sometimes."

"I heard that," Ngozi said. "It's not *difficult*. I just require proper preparation."

"Yeah," J.C. said, "like a hazmat suit."

"Please," Ngozi said, rolling her eyes. "Just because I like things clean."

"Clean?" I asked her.

"Very clean. Do you know the kinds of poisons that are pumped into the air every day by all those cars and factories? Where do you think that all goes? Do you ever wonder what that crusty blackness is on your skin after you hold a handrail on your way down the steps into the subway? And think of the *people*. Coughing into their hands, wiping their snotty nostrils, touching everything and everyone, and—"

"We get it, Ngozi," I said. I looked at Tobias, who nodded encouragingly. J.C. was right; phones among my aspects could be a valuable resource. I took the phone from J.C. Nearby, Liza watched me with what seemed like the first genuine emotion she'd displayed all morning: Fascination. She might not be a psychologist, but physicians of all varieties tend to find my . . . quirks captivating.

Good for her. As long as it kept her from thinking about how much—or little—time I had remaining of her original "fifteen minute" restriction.

"We're going to try this over the phone," I said to Ngozi. "We're at the icebox. By all accounts, the body was here at night, but gone the next morning. Nothing suspicious on the hallway security cameras." Liza nodded when I checked with her on this one. "There isn't a camera in this room specifically, but the building does have an intense security system. So how did they get the body out?"

Ngozi leaned forward, still not taking the camera from Kalyani, but inspecting me with curiosity. "Show me the room."

I walked around it, scanning the place, fully aware that to Liza's perspective, I was holding nothing. Ngozi hummed to herself as I walked. Some show tune; I wasn't certain which one.

"So," she said after I'd spent a few minutes scanning the place, "you're sure the body is gone?"

"Of course it's gone," I said, pointing the camera toward the still-open corpse drawer.

"Well," Ngozi said, "it's going to be hard to do any traditional forensics here. But the question we should ask first is, 'Do we need to?' You'd be surprised at how often something is reported stolen, only to be found lost—or stashed—someplace very close to where the theft happened. If getting the body out of the room would be so hard, maybe it never did leave the room."

I looked at the other drawers. Then, with a sigh, I put the phone aside and began pulling them open one at a time.

After a few minutes, Liza walked over and helped me. "We did this," she mentioned, but didn't stop me from double-checking. Only three of the other drawers had corpses, and we checked each one carefully. None were Panos.

From there, I looked in the room's cabinets, closets, and even drawers that were too small for a corpse. It was a long process, and one that I was actually pleased to find unfruitful. Discovering several bags full of elbows or whatnot wouldn't have been particularly appealing.

I dusted off my hands and looked toward the phone and Ngozi's image. Kalyani had joined her on the bed, and the two had been chatting about how I really *did* need to stop working so much and settle down with someone nice. And, preferably, someone sane.

"What next?" I said to the phone.

"Locard's principle," Ngozi said.

"Which is?"

"Basically," she said, "the principle states that whenever there is contact, or an exchange, evidence is left behind. We have very little to go on, as the victim was already dead when abducted, and presumably still zipped up tight. But the perpetrator will have left behind signs they were here. I don't suppose we can get a DNA sweep of the room . . ."

I looked hopefully at Liza and asked, to which I got a sniff of amusement. The case wasn't nearly important enough for that. "We can try for fingerprints on our own," I said to Ngozi. "But the police aren't going to help."

"Let's do obvious contact points first," Ngozi said. "Close up on the drawer handle please."

I brought the phone over and put it very close to the handle of the corpse drawer. "Great," Ngozi said after a minute. "Now the door into the room."

I did so, passing Liza, who was checking her watch.

"Time might be running out, Ngozi," I said softly.

"My art isn't exactly something that can be rushed," she noted back at me. "Particularly long-distance."

I showed her the door handle, not really certain what she was looking for. Ngozi had me pull the door open to look at the other side. The door *was* heavy, made to swing shut after anyone who left. Once I was outside, I couldn't open it again. Liza had to unlock it with a key card.

"All right, Leeds," Liza said as I turned the camera to show the strike plate on the inside of the door frame. "You—"

"Bingo," Ngozi said.

I froze in place, then looked back at the door frame. Ignoring the rest of what Liza said, I knelt down, trying to see what Ngozi had.

"See those dust marks?" Ngozi asked.

"Um . . . no?"

"Look closely. Someone put tape here, then pulled it off, leaving behind enough gum to attract dust."

Liza stooped down beside me. "Did you hear me?"

"Tape," I asked. "Do you have some tape?"

"Why—"

"Yo," J.C. said from inside the room, holding up a roll of the translucent industrial tape that lay on the counter.

I brushed past Liza and fetched the tape—J.C. had to set down his imaginary copy before I could see the real one—then rushed back. I placed a strip of it over the strike plate, stepped out of the room, and let the door slide closed.

It thumped into place. That thump covered the lack of a click. When I pushed on the door, it opened without needing help from the inside.

"We know how they got into the room," I said.

"So?" Liza asked. "We knew they'd gotten in some-how. How does this help?"

"It tells us it was likely someone who visited the day before the body went missing," I said. "The last visitor, perhaps? They would be in a position to tape the door with the least chance of discovery during the day."

"I'm pretty sure I'd have noticed if the door were taped," Liza said.

"Would you have? With the key card unlocking, you never have to turn or twist anything. It's natural for you to push the door and have it just swing open."

She thought about it for a moment. "Plausible," she admitted. "But who did it?"

"Who was last into this room that day?"

"The priest. I had to let him in. The others had gone home for the evening, but I stayed late."

"Had a FreeCell game that you just *had* to finish?" I asked.

"Shut up."

I smiled. "Did you recognize the priest?"

She shook her head. "But he was on the list and his ID was valid."

"Creating a fake ID wouldn't be much," Ivy said to me, "considering what was at stake."

"That's probably our man," I said to Liza. "Come on, I want to talk to your security officer."

As Liza pulled the tape off the door, I thanked Ngozi for her help, turned off the camera, and tossed the phone back to J.C.

"Nice work," Ivy noted to him, smiling.

"Thanks," he said, slipping the phone into a pocket of his cargo pants. "Of course, it's not *actually* a phone. It's a hyper-dimensional time—"

"J.C.," Ivy interrupted.

"Yeah?"

"Don't ruin this moment."

"Oh. Yeah, okay."

13

I hit the restroom in the hallway before going to the security station. I didn't really need to go to the bathroom, but Tobias did.

The room was clean, which I appreciated. The soap dispensers were full, the mirror spotless, and it even had a little chart on the door listing the last cleaning, where the staff had to sign to prove they'd done their job. I washed my hands, looking at myself in the mirror while Tobias finished his pit stop.

My own mundane face looked back at me. I'm never what people expect. Some picture me as some sort of eccentric scientist, others imagine an action star. Instead, they get a rather bland man in his thirties, perfectly normal.

In some ways, I often feel like my White Room. A blank slate. The aspects have all the character. I try very hard to not stand out. Because I am *not crazy*.

I dried my hands and waited for Tobias to wash up, then we rejoined the others outside and walked toward the security station. It consisted of a circular desk with an open center, the type you'd find at a mall beneath a sign proclaiming "Information." I walked up and the security guard looked me over—like I was a piece of pizza and he was trying to decide how long I'd been sitting in the fridge. He didn't ask what I wanted. Liza had called him to tell him to prepare camera footage for me.

The desk really was too small for this hulk of a man. When he leaned forward, the inside front of the desk pressed into his gut; I was left with the impression of a grape being squeezed from the bottom.

"You," the guard said with a deep baritone voice, "are the crazy one, aren't you?"

"Well, that's not actually true," I said. "You see, the standard definition of insanity is—"

He leaned forward farther, and I pitied the poor desk. "You're armed."

"Uh . . ."

"So am I," the guard said softly. "Don't try anything."

"Okaaay," Ivy said from beside me. "Creepy guy manning the security station."

"I like him," J.C. said.

"Of course you do."

The guard slowly lifted a flash drive. "Footage is on here."

I took it. "You're certain the security system was on that night?"

The man nodded. His hand made a fist, as if me even *asking* something so stupid was an offense worthy of a pounding.

"Uh," I said, watching that fist, "Liza says you leave it on during the day now, too?"

"I'm going to catch him," the guard said. "Nobody breaks into *my* building."

"Twice," I said.

The guard eyed me.

"Nobody breaks into your building twice," I said. "Since they did it once already. Actually . . . they might have done it twice already, since the first time they placed the tape on the door—but you might call that more of an infiltration than a break-in."

"Don't give me lip," the man said, pointing at me, "and don't make trouble. Otherwise I'll thump you so hard, it'll knock some of your personalities into the next state."

"Ouch," Audrey said, flipping through a magazine she'd found on his desk. "Ask him why, if he's so amazingly observant, he hasn't noticed that his fly is down."

I smiled, then made a quick exit. Liza watched me go from the doorway of her office.

Outside, I held up the flash drive, then began moving along the side of the building. I waved to Wilson, who was still in the car. Panos's brother sat sullenly in the front passenger seat, drinking a glass of lemonade.

I rounded the building, aspects trailing, so we could get a good look at the exterior. It had small windows, maybe large enough to fit through. No fire escape. I approached a back door; it was locked tight. I gave it a good shake anyway.

"Someone impersonated a priest," I said to the aspects, "and slipped in to inspect the body and place the tape. Then they came back at night to extract the corpse. So why didn't they just take a sample of the body's cells when they were first there, in the room with it?"

I looked toward the others, who all seemed baffled.

"I guess they didn't know where on the body the modified cells were to be found," Tobias finally said. "There are many, many cells in the body. How were they to know which place held the information they wanted?"

"Perhaps." I folded my arms, dissatisfied. *We're missing something,* I thought. *A very important piece of all this. It—*

The back door burst open. The security guard stood there, puffing, hand on his sidearm. He glared at me.

"I just wanted to check," I said, inspecting the now-open doorway. Tape wouldn't work here; the door had a deadbolt. "Nice response time, by the way."

He poked a finger at me. "Don't push me."

He slammed the door. I continued on my way, rounding the corner into a little alleyway between this building and the next, looking for other entrances. I was about halfway down it when I heard the soft click behind me.

I spun, as did my aspects. There stood Zen Rigby beside a large trash bin, holding a paper bag with one hand inside of it, her posture innocent.

"SIG Sauer P239," J.C. said softly, looking at the bag, which undoubtedly held a gun.

"You can tell the type of gun by the way it sounds to *cock*?" Ivy asked.

"Well yeah," J.C. said. "Duh." He looked embarrassed as he said it, though, and gave me a glance. He felt he should have spotted Zen sneaking up on us. But he could only hear or see what I did.

"Mister Leeds," the woman said. Like last night, she wore a pantsuit and white blouse. She was dark and short with straight black hair. No jewelry.

I inclined my head toward her.

"I will need you to divest yourself of your sidearm," Zen said. "With attention and care, please, lest an unfortunate incident result."

I glanced at J.C.

"Do it," he said, though he sounded reluctant. "She probably won't try to kill us here."

"Probably?" Audrey asked, looking pale.

I slowly slid my gun out, then leaned down and set it on the ground before kicking it away. Zen smiled, sack still carried in a way that would make it easy to raise and shoot me.

"You called me earlier," she said. "A ploy which I must commend. I assume the purpose was to determine if I was following you or not?"

I nodded, hands at my sides, breathing quickly. I found myself in situations like this far too often. I wasn't a soldier or a cop; I wasn't cool under fire. I did *not* like having a gun pointed at me.

"Control the situation, Skinny," J.C. said from beside me. "The people who end up dead are the ones who lose control. Don't let your nerves determine how this plays out."

"Now," Zen said, "I'll need that flash drive."

I blinked. The flash drive . . .

She thought the flash drive contained the code to unlock Panos's data. How must it look to her? I got hired by Yol, then spent the night working. I headed to the coroner as soon as possible in the morning, then walked out with a flash drive.

She'd guessed that I'd recovered something important. Ivy laughed, though J.C. looked concerned. I glanced at him.

"If she thinks she has what she needs," he said softly, "we are in serious danger. If you give her the flash drive, don't go anywhere with her."

I backed away from Zen, hands still to the sides, until I was against the wall to the building. She studied me. Her gun was probably suppressed, but it would still make a sound. Relatively exposed as we were, she had to be worried about firing.

My heart beat frantically. Control the situation. Get her talking, perhaps? "Who did you get to impersonate the priest for you?"

She frowned. Then she raised her bag and the gun inside. "I asked you politely for something, Mister Leeds."

"And I'm not going to give it to you," I said. "Until I at least know how you pulled off the heist. It's a quirk of mine. I'm certain you're aware that I'm prone to those."

She hesitated. Then she glanced to the sides.

Looking for my aspects, I thought. People did that, unconsciously, when they were around me.

"Good," Ivy said. "Playing the insanity card does tend to throw people off their game."

Think, think, think. I knocked my head back.

It hit the window behind me. I paused, then began slamming my head back repeatedly, rattling the glass.

Zen was beside me an instant later, grabbing me roughly by the shoulder and towing me away from the building. She glanced in the window—apparently saw nobody there—then threw me to the ground.

"I am not a patient woman, Mister Leeds," she said softly.

I was tempted to give her the drive right then. But I held back, suppressing my worry, and my fear.

Stall. Just a little bit more. "You realize this is all pointless," I lied to her. "Panos already gave the information away. On the internet. Free, for everyone."

She sniffed. "We know that I3 contained his attempts to do that."

He did? And . . . they did?

She pressed the gun down into my gut. Behind her, the window slammed open.

"Leeds!" the security guard shouted. "You crazy man! Do you *want* to die? Because I'm going to strangle you . . . Hey! What's up?"

Zen met my eyes, then threw herself off me and dashed away around the corner. I leaned back as the security guard cursed, stretching out the window. "Was that a gun she was carrying? Damn it, Leeds! What are you doing?"

"Surviving," I said, tired, looking at my aspects. "Move?"

"Now," J.C. said.

We left the shouting guard and made for my car. I scooped up my gun as I passed, and once out in the open, I didn't spot any sign of Zen. I climbed in the back of the vehicle and told Wilson to go.

I didn't feel much safer when we were on the road.

"I can't believe she tried that," Ivy said. "Practically in the open, without much proof that we even had what she wanted."

"She was likely told to bring us in," J.C. said. "She's a professional; she wouldn't have moved this reck-lessly without external pressure. She reported to her superiors we might have something, then was told to recover it."

I nodded, breathing in and out in deep, desperate breaths.

"Tobias," Ivy said, taking over for me. "What do we know about Exeltec?"

"Yol's report included some basic facts," Tobias said. "Biotech company much like I3, but far more . . . energetic, you might say. Founded five years ago, they soon released their key product—a pharmaceutical to help regulate the symptoms of Parkinson's disease.

"Unfortunately for them, a year later a rival company produced a much better alternative. Exeltec's product tanked. The company is owned by ten investors, with the largest stakeholder—the one Stephen imitated on the phone—acting as CEO and president of the board. Together they stand to lose a great deal of money on this company. Their last three products have flopped, and they are under investigation for cutting corners in overseas manufacturing. So, in a word, they're desperate."

I nodded, calmed by Tobias's voice. I plugged the flash drive into my laptop, then started the footage at 10x speed and set the machine on the floor so I could watch it with half an eye. Tobias, often the most observant of my aspects, leaned down to watch in detail.

In the front seat, Wilson and Dion began chatting about the youth's home life. I felt the tremors from being held at gunpoint finally fade, and took stock. Wilson pulled onto the freeway; he wasn't going anywhere specific, but knew me well enough to realize I needed time to put myself together before giving him any specific directions.

Dion glanced in the rearview mirror to get a look at me. He caught me looking back at him and blushed, then slumped down into his seat, answering Wilson's questions about school. Dion had just finished high school, and was prepping for college in the fall. He readily answered Wilson's questions; it was difficult to resist the affable butler. Wilson could handle me, after all. Compared to that, normal people were easy.

"That must have been some event," Wilson said to the young man, in response to an explanation of a recent race. "Now, if you'll forgive the interruption, I should ask Master Leeds where it was he wanted to be going."

"You don't know already?" Dion asked, looking confused. "But where have we been driving?"

"Around," I said. "I needed time to think. Dion, your brother lived with you and your mother, right?"

"Yeah. You know Greek families . . ."

I frowned. "Not sure I do."

"We're a tight lot," Dion said with a shrug. "Moving out on your own . . . well, that's just not done. Hell, I assume Panos would have stayed nearby even after he'd married. There's no resisting the pull of a Greek family."

The key to Panos's corpse might very well be at the family home. At the very least, going there would indicate to Zen that we were still looking for something, which might encourage her to postpone another confrontation.

"Let's head there, Wilson," I said. "I want to talk to the family."

"I *am* the family!" Dion said.

"The rest of the family," I said, getting out my phone and dialing. "Hold on a minute." The phone rang a few times before being picked up.

"Yo, dawg," Yol said.

"I don't think that's a cool phrase any longer, Yol."

"I'm bringing it back, dawg."

"I don't . . . You know what, never mind. I'm pretty sure our bad guys are Exeltec."

"Hmmm. That's unfortunate. I was hoping it was one of the other two. Let me step out so we can talk."

"I wasn't certain they'd even let you answer while on lockdown."

"It's a pain," he said, and I heard the sound of a door closing, "but I've managed a little freedom, since I'm not technically under arrest, I'm just quarantined. The feds let me set up a mobile office here, but nobody can get in or out until we convince them this thing wasn't contagious."

"At least you can talk."

"To an extent. It's a pain, dawg. How am I going to do press interviews for the new album?"

"Seclusion will just add to your celebrity mystique," I said. "Can you tell me anything more about Exeltec."

"It's all in the documents I sent," he explained. "They're . . . well, they're bad news. I had a hunch it would be them. We've caught them trying to slip in spies in the form of engineers seeking employment."

"Yol, they've got a hit man working for them."

"That one you mentioned before?"

"Yeah. Ambushed me in an alley. Held me at gunpoint."

"*Damn.*"

"I'm not going to sit around and let something like that happen again," I said. "I'm going to email you a list of instructions."

"Instructions?" Yol asked. "For what?"

"For keeping me from being killed," I said, taking my laptop from Tobias. "Yol, I have to ask you. What is it you're not telling me about this case?"

The line was silent.

"Yol . . ."

"We didn't kill him," Yol said. "I promise you that."

"But you *were* having him watched," I said. "You had his computer monitored. There's no other way you'd just naturally have a record of all of the things he'd been doing in the last few months, ready to print out when I arrived."

"Yeah," Yol admitted.

"And he was trying to give your information away," I said. "Post everything about the project online."

In the front seat, Dion had turned around and was watching me.

"Some of the engineers didn't like me getting involved," Yol said. "They saw it as selling out. Panos . . . that guy didn't believe in consequences. He'd have posted our research for everyone, so that every terrorist out there knew about it. I don't get such people, with their wikileaks and their open sources."

"You're making it very hard for me to believe," I said, "that you didn't just remove him."

Dion paled.

"I don't do things like that," Yol snapped. "Do you know how much a murder investigation can cost a company?"

I really wished I could trust him. To an extent, I *needed* to. Otherwise, I could very easily end this mission as a corpse myself. "Just follow the instructions in my email," I told him, then hung up.

I ignored Dion and began typing an email while the feed from the security camera continued to play on the other side of my laptop screen. Audrey stood up behind my seat and looked over my shoulder, watching me type.

"You shouldn't be out of your seat belt," Ivy said.

"If we wreck, I'm sure Steve-O will imagine some delightfully gruesome scars for me," Audrey said, then pointed at what I was typing. "Rumors to be spread? About Exeltec? This will make them even *more* desperate."

"I'm counting on it," I said.

"Which will put an even bigger target on our heads!" Audrey said. "What in the world are you planning?"

I didn't answer her, instead finishing up the instructions and shooting off the email to Yol. "Dion," I said, still half-watching the video on the laptop. "Is your family religious?"

"My mom is," he said from the front seat. "I'm an atheist." He said it stubbornly, as if this were something he'd had to defend in the past.

"Panos?"

"Atheist," Dion said. "Mom refused to accept it, of course."

"Who's your family priest?"

"Father Frangos," he said. "Why?"

"Because I think someone impersonated him last night when visiting your brother's remains. Either that, or Father Frangos is involved in the theft of the corpse."

Dion snorted. "He's, like, ninety years old. He's so pious, when my mother told him I was taking after my brother, he fasted for thirty-six hours to pray for me. *Thirty-six* hours. I think the idea of intentionally breaking one of the commandments would kill him on the spot."

The kid seemed to have gotten over his fear of me. Good.

"Ask him what he thought of his brother," Ivy said from the back seat.

"Seems he liked the guy," J.C. said with a grunt.

"Really?" Ivy said to him. "You deduced that all on your own, did you? Steve, I'd like to hear an opinion of Panos that didn't come through Yol's channels. Get the kid talking, if you please."

"Your brother," I said to Dion. "You seem to really dislike the company he was working for."

"It used to be all right," Dion said. "Before it went and got all corporate. That's when the lies started, the extortion. It became about money."

"Unlike other jobs," Audrey said, "which are never, ever about money."

"Your brother continued working there," I said to Dion, ignoring Audrey's commentary. "So he couldn't have been too torn up about the changes at I3. I expect he wanted in on a little of that cash."

Dion twisted around in his seat and fixed me with a glare that could have fried an egg. "Panos cared *nothing* for the money. He only stayed at that place because of their resources."

"So . . . he needed I3's equipment," I said. "And, by extension, their money."

"Yeah, well, it wasn't *about* the money. My brother was going to do great things. Cure diseases. He did things that even the others, traitors though they were, didn't know about. He—" Dion cut off, then turned around immediately in his seat, and refused to respond to further prodding.

I looked at Ivy.

"Serious hero worship going on there," she said, "I suspect that if you prodded, you'd find Dion was planning to study biology and follow in his brother's footsteps. The philosophy, the mannerisms . . . We can learn a lot about Panos by watching his brother."

"So," J.C. said, "you're telling me Panos was an annoying little sh—"

"Anyway," Ivy interrupted, "if it's true that Panos was working on projects even Garvas and the others didn't know about, that could be the true secret Yol is trying to recover."

I nodded.

"Stephen," Tobias said, pointing at the laptop screen. "You'll want to watch this."

I leaned over, then rewound the footage. Tobias, Audrey, and J.C. huddled around, all ignoring Ivy's pointed complaints that none of us were bothering with seat belts. On the small screen, now playing at normal speed, I watched someone leave the bathroom in the medical complex.

The cleaning lady. She pulled a large trash can on wheels, and approached the doorway into the coroner's offices, then opened the door and went in.

"Does *nobody* in this world care about security anymore?" J.C. said, pointing at the screen. "Look at the security guard! He's didn't even *glance* at her."

I froze the frame. The camera was positioned in such a way that we couldn't get a good look at the figure, even when I rewound and froze it again.

"Somewhat small in stature," Tobias said. "Dark-haired, female. I can't pick out anything else. The rest of you?"

J.C. and Audrey shook their heads. I froze the frame on the security guard. It was a different man from the one we'd met, a smaller fellow, who was sitting in the station and reading a paperback novel. I rewound to try to find where the cleaning lady entered the building, but she must have come in the back. I did catch the security guard pushing a button, perhaps to open the back door for someone who had buzzed for the lock to open.

Fast-forwarding, we watched the cleaning lady leave the coroner's offices and go into each room along the hall. Whoever it was, she knew not to break pattern. She cleaned the other offices quickly, then disappeared down the hallway, towing her large trash can.

"That trash can could most certainly hide a body," J.C. said. "I thought the guard said nobody went into those rooms!"

"Cleaning staff is usually considered 'nobody,'" Tobias observed. "And the door into the morgue itself would be locked. Liza said even the security guard wouldn't be able to get in, so presumably the cleaning staff doesn't go into that room, at least not without supervision."

"Does that drive have footage from other nights?" Audrey asked.

"Good idea," I said, searching and finding the two previous nights' footage as well. We watched, and found that at around the same time each night, a cleaning person entered and engaged in a similar activity. But the trash can they brought was smaller, and it was obviously a different person. Female, yes, and with a similar build—but with lighter hair.

"So," Audrey said, "they replaced first the priest and then the cleaning lady."

"This should have been impossible," J.C. said. "Protocol should have made it so."

"And what protocol is that?" Audrey said. "This isn't a high-security facility, J.C. You spend year after year without any kind of incident, and of course you're going to grow lax. Besides, the people who pulled this off were capable. Fake ID, knowledge of the times the cleaning lady entered and left. The uniform is the same, and they even cleaned the entire set of offices so nobody would be suspicious."

I replayed the footage of the thief, wondering if it was Zen herself. The build was right. What was it Audrey had said before? People are usually far less secure than the encryption strategies—or, in this case, security devices—they employ. This could have all been stopped if the guard had glanced at the cleaning lady. But he didn't, and why would he have? What was there *really* in these offices that someone would want to steal?

Just a corpse carrying a doomsday weapon.

I stifled a yawn as we eventually pulled into a residential area. Blast. I'd been hoping to find a chance to squeeze in a nap while we were driving. Even thirty minutes would do me some good. No chance for that now. Instead, I replied to Yol's return email, telling him that yes, I did want to make Exeltec more frantic, and yes, I did know what I was doing. My next set of instructions seemed to placate him.

We pulled up to a quaint white suburban house, rambler style, with a neatly mowed lawn and vines growing up the walls. A careful air of cultivation helped offset the fact that this house—with its siding, its small windows, and its lack of an enclosed garage—was probably a decade or four past its prime.

"You're not going to hurt my family, are you?" Dion asked from the front seat.

"No," I said, "but I might embarrass you a little."

Dion grunted.

"Come introduce me," I said, shoving open the door. "We're on the same side. I promise that when I recover your brother's body, I won't let I3 do anything nefarious with it. In fact, I'll let you watch the cremation—with I3 getting no chance to lay hands on the body—if you want."

Dion sighed, but joined me in climbing from the car and walking toward the house.

14

"**Keep watch,**" I said to J.C. as we approached the house. "I haven't forgotten that Zen is out there."

"We might want to call in some backup," J.C. said.

"More Rescue Rangers?" Ivy asked.

"*Time* Rangers," J.C. snapped. "And no, we don't have temporal substance here. I was talking about real bodyguards. If Skinny hired a few of those, I'd feel a whole lot safer."

I shook my head. "No time, unfortunately."

"Perhaps you should have explained the truth to Zen," Tobias said, jogging up. "Was it wise to let her think we have the information she wants?"

Behind us, Wilson pulled the SUV away—I'd given him instructions to keep driving until I called him for a pickup. I didn't want Zen deciding to apply a little interrogation to my servant. Unfortunately, if she was determined, simply driving away wouldn't be enough to protect him. Perhaps I *should* have told Zen we didn't have her information. Yet my instincts said that the less she knew about what I'd discovered, the better off I'd be. I just needed to have a plan in place to deal with her.

Dion led us up to the house, glanced over his shoulder at me, then sighed and pushed open the door. I grabbed it and held it for my aspects, then slipped in last.

The house smelled old. Of furniture that had been polished over and over, of stale potpourri, and of burned wood from an old hearth. The careful clutter offered a new oddity on each wall and surface—a line of photos in novelty frames down one hallway, a collection of ceramic cats in a shadow box near the door, a sequence of colorful candles on the mantel with a religious tone to them. The house didn't look lived in, it looked decorated. This was a museum for a family's life, and they'd done a lot of living.

Dion hung his coat beside the door. The only coat there; the rest were stored neatly inside an open coat closet. He walked down the hallway, calling for his mother.

I lingered, stepping into the living room, with its rug on top of carpet and its easy chair with worn armrests. My aspects fanned out. I stepped up beside the hearth, inspecting a beautiful wall cross made from glass.

"Catholic?" I asked, noticing Ivy's reverence.

"Close," she said. "Greek Orthodox. That's a depiction of Emperor Constantine."

"Very religious," I said, noting the candles, the paintings, the cross.

"Or just very fond of decoration," she said. "What are we looking for?"

"The decryption code," I said, turning. "Audrey? Any idea what it might look like."

"It's digital," she said. "For a one-time pad, the key is going to be as long as the data being stored. That's why Zen was after the flash drive."

I looked around the room. With all of this stuff, a flash drive could be hidden practically anywhere. Tobias, Audrey, and J.C. started looking. Ivy remained beside me.

"Needle in a haystack?" I asked her softly.

"Possibly," she said, folding her arms, tapping one finger against the opposite forearm. "Let's go look at pictures of the family. Maybe we can determine something from them."

I nodded, walking over to the hallway that led to the kitchen, where I'd spotted pictures of the family. Four in a row were formal photos of each member of the family. The picture of the father was old, from the seventies; he'd died when the boys were children. The mother's picture and Dion's picture had what appeared to be pictures of saints hanging beneath them.

No saint beneath Panos. "A symbol that he'd given up on his faith?" I asked, pointing to the empty spot.

"Nothing so dramatic," Ivy said. "When a member of the Greek Orthodox Church is buried, a picture of

Christ or their patron saint is buried with them. That picture would have been taken down in preparation for his funeral."

I nodded, walking on a little further, searching for pictures of the family interacting. I paused beside one that showed a smiling Panos from not too long ago. He was holding up a fish while his mother—in sunglasses—hugged him from the side.

"Open and friendly, by all accounts," Ivy said. "An idealist who joined with friends from college to start their own company. 'If this works,' he wrote on a forum a few months back, 'then any person in any country could have access to powerful computing. Their own body supplies the energy, the storage, even the processing.' Others on the forum warned about the dangers of wetware. Panos argued with them. He saw all of this as some kind of information revolution, a step forward for humankind."

"Is there anything about those posts of his that doesn't add up?"

"Ask Audrey about that," Ivy said. "I'm focused on Panos the man. Who was he? How would he act?"

"He was working on something," I said. "Curing diseases, is that what Dion said? I'll bet he was really annoyed when the others pulled him off of his virus research because of the cancer scare."

"Yol knows that Panos got further in his research than he let on. It's clear to me. Yol was spying on Panos and is really, really worried about all of this. That implies he's worried about a danger even more cata-strophic than their little cancer scare. That's why Yol brought you in, and why he's so desperate for you to destroy the body."

I nodded slowly. "So what about Panos? What can you guess about him and the key?"

"If he even used one," Ivy said, "I suspect he'd give it to a family member."

"Agreed," I said as Dion finally headed out the back doors, calling for his mother in the backyard.

I felt a moment of concern. Had Zen been here before us? But no. Stepping into the kitchen, I was able to see the mother outside pruning a tree. Dion walked out to her.

I delayed a moment, stepping up to Audrey and J.C.

"So," Audrey was saying, "in the future, do we have flying cars?"

"I'm not from *your* future," J.C. said. "I'm from a parallel dimension, and you're from another one."

"And does yours have flying cars?"

"That's classified," J.C. said. "So far as I can tell you, my dimension is basically like this one—only, I exist there."

"In other words, that one is way, *way* worse."

"I should shoot you, woman."

"Try it."

I stopped between them, but J.C. just grunted. "Don't tempt me," he growled at Audrey.

"No, really," Audrey said. "Shoot me. Go ahead. Then, when it doesn't do anything because we're both *imaginary*, you'll have to admit the truth: That you're crazy, even for a figment of a deranged man's psyche. That he imagined you as a repository for information. That, in truth, you're just a flash drive yourself, J.C."

He glared at her, then stalked away, head down.

"And," Audrey shouted after him, "you—"

I took her by the arm. "Enough."

"It's good for someone to bring him down a notch or two, Steve-O," she said. "Can't have pieces of your brain getting too uppity, can we?"

"What about you?"

"I'm different," she said.

"Oh? And you'd be fine if I just stopped imagining you?"

"You don't know how to do that," she said, uncomfortably.

"I'm pretty sure that if J.C. *did* shoot you, my mind would follow through accordingly. You'd die, Audrey. So be careful what you ask for."

She glanced to the side, then shuffled from one foot to the other. "So . . . uh . . . what did you want?"

"You're the closest thing I've got to a data analyst right now," I said. "The information that Yol gave us. Think about the emails, forum posts, and personal information from Panos's computer. I need to know what he isn't saying."

"What he *isn't* saying?"

"What's hidden, Audrey. Inconsistencies. Clues. I need to know what he was really working on—his secret projects. There's a good chance he hinted at this online somewhere."

"Okay . . . I'll think about it." She'd gone from a niche expertise—handwriting analysis—to something broader. Hopefully this was the start of a trend. I was running out of space for aspects; it was getting harder and harder to contain them, manage them, imagine them all at once. I suspected that was why Audrey had insisted on coming on this mission—deep down, part of me knew that I needed my aspects to begin doubling up on skills.

She looked at me, eyes focusing. "Actually, as I consider it, I might have something for you right now. Viruses."

"What about them?

"Panos spent a *lot* of time on immunology forums, talking about disease, getting into very technical discussions with people who study bacteria and viruses. None of what he said is revelatory, but when you look at the whole . . ."

"His history was in microbial gene splicing," I said. "Makes sense for him to be there."

"But Garvas said they'd abandoned viruses as a method of data delivery," Audrey said. "However, Panos's forum posts on these subjects *increased* once I3 abandoned that part of the project." She looked at me, then grinned. "I figured that out!"

"Nice."

"Well, I mean, I guess *you* figured that out." She folded her arms. "Being an imaginary person makes it difficult to feel any real sense of accomplishment."

"Just imagine your sense of accomplishment," I said. "You're imaginary, so imaginary accomplishment should work for you."

"But if I'm imaginary, and I imagine something, it's *doubly* unreal. Like using a copy machine to copy something that's just been copied."

"Actually," Tobias said, strolling up, "theoretically the imaginary sense of accomplishment would *have* to be imagined by the primary imaginer, so it wouldn't be an iteration as you suggest."

"It doesn't work that way," Audrey said. "Trust me, I'm the expert on being imaginary."

"But . . . If we are all aspects . . ."

"Yeah, but I'm *more* imaginary than you," she said. "Or, well, less. Since I know all about it." She grinned at him, triumphant, as he rubbed his chin, trying to sort through that.

"You're crazy," I said softly, looking at Audrey.

"Huh?"

It had just struck me. Audrey was insane.

Each of my aspects were. I barely noticed Tobias's schizophrenia anymore, let alone Ivy's trypophobia. But the madness was there, lurking. Each aspect had one, whether it be fear of germs, technophobia, or megalomania. I'd never realized what Audrey's was until now.

"You think you're imaginary," I told her.

"Duh."

"But it's not because you're actually imaginary. It's because you have a psychosis that makes you think you're imaginary. You'd think this even if you happened to be real."

It was hard to see. Many of the aspects accepted their lot, but few confronted it. Even Ivy did that with difficulty. But Audrey flaunted it; she reveled in it. That was because, in her brain, she was a real person who was crazy and therefore thought she wasn't real. I'd assumed she was self-aware, but that wasn't it at all. She was as crazy as the others. Her insanity just happened to align with reality.

She glanced at me, then shrugged, and immediately tried to deflect the conversation by asking Tobias about the weather. He, of course, referenced his delusion who lived in the satellite far above. I shook my head, then turned.

And found Dion standing in the doorway, a distinctly uncomfortable look on his face. How much had he watched? He gave me a look like one might give an unfamiliar dog that had just been barking frantically but now seemed calm. Through that whole exchange, I'd been a crazy man, stalking around and talking to himself.

No. I'm not crazy. I have it under control.

Maybe that was my only real madness. Thinking I could handle all of this.

"You found your mother?" I asked.

"In the backyard," Dion said, thumbing over his shoulder.

"Let's go talk to her," I said, brushing past him.

15

I found Ivy and J.C. outside, sitting on the steps. She was rubbing his back as he sat with hands hanging before him, gun in one of them, staring at a beetle crossing the ground. Ivy gave me a glance and shook her head. Not a good time to talk to him.

I headed across the well-tended lawn with Audrey and Tobias in tow. Mrs. Maheras had finished pruning and was now inspecting her tomato plants, pulling off bugs, pulling weeds.

She didn't look up as I approached. "Stephen Leeds," she said. Her voice bore a distinct Greek accent. "You're famous, I hear."

"Only among people who like gossip," I said, kneeling down. "The tomatoes look nice. Growing well."

"I started them inside," she said, lifting one of the plump, green fruits. "Tomatoes do better after the late frosts are past, but I can't help wanting to get an early start."

I waited for Ivy to give me a prompt on what to say, but she was still on the steps. *Idiot,* I thought at myself. "So . . . you like to garden a lot?"

Mrs. Maheras looked up and met my eyes. "I appreciate people who make decisions and act on them, Mister Leeds. Not people who try to make small talk about things in which they obviously have no interest."

"Several pieces of me are very interested in gardening," I said. "I just didn't bring them along."

She regarded me, waiting.

I sighed. "Mrs. Maheras, what do you know of your son's research?"

"Almost nothing," she said. "Ghastly business."

I frowned.

"She thinks it took him away from the church," Dion said behind me, kicking at a clump of dirt. "All of that science and questioning. Heaven help us if a man spends his time *thinking.*"

"Dion," she said, "don't speak stupidity."

He folded his arms and met her gaze, defiant.

"You work for the people who employed my son," Mrs. Maheras said, looking at me.

"I just want to find his body," I said. "Before anything dangerous happens. What can you tell me of your priest?"

"Father Frangos?" she asked. "Why ever would you want to know about him?"

"He was the last person to see the body," I said. "He visited the coroner on the night before your son's corpse vanished."

"Don't be silly," Mrs. Maheras said. "He did nothing of the sort—he was here. I requested a house blessing, and he visited."

To the side, Tobias and Audrey shared a glance. So we had a witness that Father Frangos had *not* gone in to see the body. Proof an impostor was involved. But what good did that knowledge do us?

"Did Panos give you anything, before he passed away?" I asked her.

"No."

"It might have been something trivial," I said. "Are you sure? There's nothing you can think of?"

She turned back to her plants. "No."

"Did he spend time with anyone in particular during the last few months?"

"Just the men from that ghastly laboratory."

I knelt beside her. "Mrs. Maheras," I said softly. "Lives are at stake because of your son's research. Many lives. If you are hiding something, you could well cause a national disaster. You don't need to give it to me. The police—or, better, the FBI—would work just fine. Just don't gamble with this. Please."

She glanced at me, lips pursed. Then, her expression hardened. "I have nothing for you."

I sighed and rose. "Thank you." I walked away from her, back toward the steps, where J.C. had perked up a little at Ivy's prodding.

"Well?" he asked me.

"Stonewalled," I said. "If he did give the key to her, she wouldn't tell me."

"Coming here was a mistake," J.C. said. "A distraction from what we need to do."

I glanced at the mother, who had continued to regard me, trowel in her hand.

"Admit it, Skinny," J.C. continued. "If we don't do something soon, the world is going to get cancer." He hesitated. "Smet, it sounds stupid when I say it like that."

". . . 'Smet'?" I asked.

"Future curse."

"Why does it sound so much like—"

"Future curses *always* sound like our curses," J.C. said, rolling his eyes. "But they're not, so it's okay to say them when prudes are around." He thumbed at Ivy, still sitting beside him.

"Wait," Ivy said. "I thought you were from another dimension, not from the future."

"Nonsense. I've always been from the future."

"Since when?"

"Since two days from now," J.C. said. "Look, Skinny, do I need to repeat myself? You know what our next move is."

I sighed, then nodded. "Yes. It's time to break into Exeltec."

Part Three

16

"**Are you** *sure* about this?" Ivy said, rushing along beside me as I strode out of the front of the house.

"It's our best lead, Ivy," J.C. said. "We don't have time to investigate new threads. Exeltec has the body. We need to find out where it is and steal it back from them."

I nodded. "Panos's key could be almost anywhere, but if we destroy the corpse, then the key doesn't matter." I raised my phone, noticing that I'd missed a call from Yol. I nodded for J.C. to watch the perimeter as I texted Wilson for a pick-up, then dialed Yol back.

Yol picked up the line.

"Hey," I said. "I—"

"I don't have much time," Yol interrupted, voice muffled. "This is bad, Legion. *Seriously* bad."

I grew cold. "What happened?"

"Panos," Yol said, talking quickly, his accent growing thicker in his haste. "He let something out. Damn it. It's—" He cut off.

"Yol?" I said, growing tense as Ivy and Tobias crowded in, trying to hear what was being said. "Yol!"

I heard voices on the other end of the line, followed by rasping. "I'm being arrested," Yol said a moment later. "No more information in or out. They're going to take my phone."

"What did Panos let out, Yol?" I asked.

"We don't know. The feds tripped a hidden file on his computer. It erased the damn thing and popped up a screen that taunted us, saying he'd already released his infection. They're freaking out. I don't know anything else."

"And the things I asked you to do?"

"Did some. Set others in motion. Don't know if I'll be able to finish."

"Yol, my life could depend on whether or not—"

"*All* of our lives are in danger," Yol snapped. "Didn't you hear me? This is a disaster. Hell! They're here. Find that body. Find out *what that man did*!"

The phone rustled again, and the line went dead. I had the distinct impression that Yol hadn't hung up—someone had taken the phone from him. The feds now likely knew I was involved.

I lowered the phone and looked at my aspects as Wilson pulled up. Behind us, Dion trailed out of the house, hands in his pockets. He looked troubled.

"We need to get moving," J.C. said, rushing back from watching the perimeter. "Zen could show up here at any moment."

"If she does," I said, "Mrs. Maheras is in danger. I'm surprised Zen hasn't been here already—if not her, then another Exeltec flunky." I frowned. "I feel like we're a step behind. I do *not* like that sensation."

I ignored the car waiting for us, and I barely noticed Dion as he walked up. Instead, I closed my eyes. "Tobias," I whispered.

"Have you noticed the beauty of the landscaping here?" Tobias said. "Those are tuberous begonia, challenging flowers to raise, particularly in this region. They require lots of light, but it can't be direct, and are very sensitive to frost. Ah, I remember a story about them . . ."

He talked on. The other aspects fell silent as we thought, collectively. I would not proceed, feeling I'd missed something. Something that one of us should have spotted. What was it?

"Zen," J.C. interrupted suddenly. "Her ambush."

"People are far less secure," I whispered, opening my eyes, "than their security measures." I reached up to my shoulder, where Zen had grabbed me in the alleyway to pull me away from the building, then I moved up to touch under my shirt collar.

My fingers brushed metal.

"Oh, *holy hell*!" J.C. said.

Zen had bugged me. *That* was what the attack in the alleyway had been about. It hadn't been nearly as reckless as she'd made it seem. My mind raced as J.C. explained to the other aspects what had happened. What had I said out loud? What did Zen know?

She'd heard that I intended to break into Exeltec. But what about the instructions I'd sent Yol? Did she know about those?

Sweating, I traced back through my memory. No. I'd only written that information down in the email. But she did know what I'd said to Mrs. Maheras. She knew that I was at a dead end.

"I'm an idiot," J.C. said. "We thought to have you scrub down after the restaurant, but not after actual *physical contact* with the assassin?"

"She hid her intentions well," Audrey replied. "Masked it as a frantic attempt to get the flash drive."

"At least now we probably don't have to worry about her coming to hurt Mrs. Maheras."

Probably. I stared at my phone. How had we missed this?

"Calm, Stephen," Tobias said, resting a hand on my shoulder. "Everyone makes mistakes, even you. We can use this one—the assassin is listening to us, but she doesn't know you've figured that out. We can manipulate her."

I nodded, taking a deep breath. Zen knew about the plan to infiltrate Exeltec, which meant I couldn't go through with that. I needed something new, something better.

That meant relying on the things I'd set in motion with Yol. Making Exeltec's owners frantic, then playing upon that. Why did missions always go this way, lately? I looked up at my aspects, then made the decision, punching a number on my phone.

Someone picked up. "Oh, honey," a sultry voice said on the other end of the line, "I was *hoping* you'd call me today."

"Bianca," I said.

Tobias groaned. "Not *her*."

I ignored him. "I need information," I said to the woman on the line.

"Sure thing, sugar," she said. How *did* she purr like that? I was half-convinced she used some kind of sound effect machine. "What about? Your . . . date the other night? I can tell you the names of the people who set you up."

"It's not about that," I said. "There's something going on with a company called I3 and their rival, Exeltec. I think they might have released a deadly virus into the wild. Do you know anything about it?"

"Mmm . . . I can look," Bianca said. "Might take some time."

"Anything you can get me on Exeltec would be heartily appreciated," I said.

"Sure," she said. "And honey, next time you need a date, why not give me a call? I'm *so offended* that I wasn't even considered!"

"Like you'd show," I said. Three years, and I'd never seen Bianca face-to-face.

"I'd at least contemplate it," she said. "Now, you've got to give me *something* for the newspapers. About your date?"

"Get me information on Exeltec," I said, "and we'll trade." I hung up, looking over my shoulder as Dion stepped up to me on the sidewalk, looking confused.

"What are you hoping to find out?" the kid asked.

"Nothing," I replied, fully aware that Zen was listening to all this. "Bianca is a *terrible* informant. I've never gotten a drop of useful information out of her, and after I call her, most of what I say ends up on the internet within minutes."

"But—"

I dialed another informant and initiated a similar, but more circumspect, line of inquiry. Then a third. Within a few minutes I'd ensured that very, very soon everyone who cared about Exeltec would be reading about how they'd been involved in a major public safety breach. With 13 being investigated and me being involved, the kernel of truth to the rumors I'd started would set off a media frenzy.

"You're pushing them up against the wall, Steve," Ivy said as Wilson finally pulled up. "Zen's employers were desperate before; they'll be *rabid* once this hits."

"Hoping to make them ignore you and focus on damage control with the media?" J.C. asked. "Not smart.

Whipping the tiger won't distract it; the thing will just get angrier."

I couldn't explain, not with Zen listening. Instead, I got out my note pad and scribbled a few instructions to Wilson, assuming the aspects would see and catch on.

Surprisingly, Audrey seemed to get it first. She grinned. "Oooh . . ."

"Dangerous," Ivy said, folding her arms. "*Very* dangerous."

Wilson rolled down the passenger window. "Master Leeds?"

I finished writing and leaned in through the window, handing him the message. "Some instructions," I said. "I need you to stay here, Wilson, and watch Mrs. Maheras. I'm worried the assassin might try to get to her. In fact, you should probably get her to the nearest police station."

"But who will drive you?"

"I can drive," I said.

Wilson looked skeptical.

"Funny," Audrey remarked, "how a man can trust you to save the world, but not to feed or drive yourself."

I smiled reassuringly at Wilson as he looked down at the instructions in his hand, then back at me with a worried expression.

"Please," I said to him.

Wilson sighed and nodded, climbing out of the car.

"You coming?" I said to Dion as I opened the side door of the SUV for my aspects and let them pile in,

"You said that people could be in danger," Dion said.

"They are," I replied, closing the door behind Audrey. "What your brother let out could cost the lives of millions."

"He said it wasn't dangerous," Dion said stubbornly.

Damn. The kid was holding out on me. Did *he* have the key? Unfortunately, I didn't want him to talk and let Zen hear. Well, either way, I needed him with me. I might need an extra pair of nonimaginary hands, now that I'd sent Wilson away.

I settled into the driver's seat, and Dion climbed into the front passenger seat. "Panos didn't do anything wrong."

"And what *did* he do?" I asked, resigned. If I didn't prod, it would look suspicious to Zen.

"Something," Dion said.

"How pleasantly descriptive."

"He wouldn't tell me. I don't think he even actually finished it. But it wasn't dangerous."

"I . . ." I trailed off, looking back as J.C.'s mobile phone went off. The ring tone was "America the Beautiful." I shook my head, starting the car and pulling away—leaving an overwhelmed-looking Wilson on the curb—as J.C. answered his phone.

"Yo, Achmed," he said. "Yeah, I've got him here. Video? I can do that. Hey, you gonna fix that Chinese stuff for us again?"

"It was *Indian* food," Kalyani said, now on speaker. "Why would you assume it's Chinese?"

"Had rice, didn't it?" J.C. said, kneeling beside the armrest between driver's seat and passenger, then holding the phone out for me.

"Coconut rice, and curry, and . . . Never mind. Mister Steve?"

"Yeah?" I said, glancing at the phone. Kalyani waved happily, wearing a simple T-shirt and jeans. Her bindi was black today and shaped like a little arrow between her eyebrows, rather than being the traditional red dot. I'd have to ask her about the significance.

"We've been talking," Kalyani said. "And Arnaud wants to tell you something." She turned the phone to the punctilious little Frenchman. He leaned forward, blinking at the screen. I kept my time divided between him and the road.

"Monsieur," Arnaud said, "I have spoken with Clive and Mi Won. The three of us, you see, had some upper-level chemistry and biology courses as part of our schooling. We cannot dig too deeply, because . . . Well, you know."

"I do." Ignacio. His death had ripped away most of my knowledge of chemistry.

"Regardless," Arnaud said, "we have been pouring over the information given to us. Mi Won is insistent, and we have come to agree with her. It is our admittedly amateur opinion that I3 and the man named Yol are lying to you."

"About what specifically?"

"About giving up on a viral delivery method into the body," Arnaud said. "Monsieur, Panos had too many resources—was progressing too well—on his supposedly 'secret' project to have been cut off. They were investigating that line, no matter what they told you. In addition, we are not convinced that this cancer threat is as viable as it first seemed. Oh, that is *theoretically* where this research could lead, but from what we've gathered from the notes, I3 had not reached such a point yet."

"So they didn't want to tell me what the real crisis was," I said. "The rogue bacteria or virus that Panos spliced, whatever it is."

"That is for you to consider," Arnaud said. "We are scientists. All we are saying is that there are layers here beyond what we are being told."

"Thank you," I said. "I suspected, but this confirmation is helpful. Is that everything?"

"One more item," Kalyani said, taking back the phone and turning it around toward her smiling face. "I wanted to introduce to you my husband, Rahul." An Indian man with a round, mustached face stepped into view beside her, then waved at me.

I felt a chill.

"I told you that he is a good photographer," Kalyani said, "but you do not need to use him that way. He is a *very* clever man. He can do all sorts of things! He knows computers well."

"I can see him," I said. "Why can I see him?"

"He's joined us!" Kalyani said, excited. "Isn't it wonderful!"

"Very pleased to meet you, Mister Stephen," Rahul said with a melodic Indian accent. "I will be very helpful, I can promise you."

"I . . ." I swallowed. "How . . . did you . . ."

"This is bad," Ivy said from the back seat. "Have you ever manifested an aspect unintentionally?"

"Not since the early days," I whispered. "And never without researching a new topic first."

"Man," Audrey said. "Kalyani gets a husband and I can't even have a gerbil? Totally unfair."

I pulled over immediately, not caring about the car that honked beside me as I swerved. As we lurched to a stop I yanked the phone from J.C.'s hand and stared at the new aspect. This was the first time any family member of one of my delusions had appeared to me. It seemed a very dangerous precedent. Another sign that I was losing control.

I hung up, making their smiling faces wink out, then tossed the phone over my shoulder to J.C. Sweating, I pulled the car forward, earning a honk from another car. I took the first off-ramp I saw, veering down into the city.

"You okay?" Dion asked.

"Fine," I snapped.

I needed a place to go, a place to think. A place that would look natural, but where I could stall and wait for my plan to proceed without Zen getting suspicious.

I pulled into a Denny's. "Just need some food," I lied. This would work, right? Even a man trying to save the world had to eat.

Dion glanced at me. "You sure you're—"

"Yes. I just need an omelet."

≡≡
≡≡

17

I **held the** restaurant door for my aspects, then
walked in after them. The place smelled of coffee,
and was occupied by the late-morning breakfast
crowd, which was perfect. Zen was less likely to try
something with so many witnesses. It took some work
to get the waitress to give us a table for six; I had to
lie and say we were expecting more people. Eventually,
we settled down, Dion opposite me and two aspects on
either side.

I held up a menu, fingers sticking to syrup on one
side, but didn't read. Instead, I tried to calm my breathing. Sandra hadn't prepared me for this. The family members of aspects appearing suddenly, without research
being done?

"You're crazy," a voice whispered across from me.
"Like . . . *actually* crazy."

I lowered my menu which—I only now realized—I'd
been holding upside down. The kid hadn't touched his.

"No I'm not," I said. "I'll give you, I might be a touch insane. But I'm *not* crazy."

"They're the same thing."

"From your perspective, perhaps," I said. "I see it differently—but even if we admit that the word applies to me, it applies to you too. The longer I've lived, the more I've realized everyone is neurotic in their own individual way. *I* have control of my psychoses. How about you?"

Beside me, Ivy sniffed at my use of the word "control."

Dion chewed on this, leaning back in his chair. "What do they say my brother did?"

"He claims to have released something. A virus or bacteria of some sort."

"He wouldn't have done that," Dion said immediately. "He wanted to help people. It was the others that were dangerous. They wanted to make weapons."

"He told you this?"

"Well, no," Dion admitted. "But, I mean, why else would they try to force him to give up his projects? Why would they watch him so closely? You should be investigating *them*, not my brother. Their secrets are the dangerous ones."

"Typical pseudo-intellectual teen liberal prattle," J.C. said from my right, looking over his menu. "I'll have the steak and eggs. Rare and runny."

I nodded absently as the others spoke up. At the very least, the server wouldn't have reason to complain about us taking up so many seats—seeing as how I'd be ordering five meals. Part of me wished I could have them give the meals to others after I was done imagining my aspects cleaning their plates.

I turned my attention to the menu, and found I wasn't that hungry. I ordered an omelet anyway, talking to the waitress as the kid dug in his pocket, obviously determined not to let me pay for him. He came out with a few wadded-up bills and ordered a breakfast burrito.

I kept waiting for a beep from my phone, telling me that Wilson had followed my instructions. Nothing came, and I felt myself growing increasingly anxious; I wiped the sweat from my temples with my napkin. My aspects tried to relax me, Tobias chatting about the origin of the pancake as a food, Ivy engaging him and acting very interested.

"What's that?" I asked, nodding at Dion, who was staring at a little slip of paper he'd found among the wadded-up bills.

He blushed immediately, moving to tuck it away.

I snatched his hand, moving with reflexes I didn't know I had. Beside me, J.C. nodded appreciatively.

"It's nothing," Dion snapped, opening his hand. "Fine. Take it. Idiot."

I suddenly felt foolish. Panos's data key wouldn't be a slip of paper; it would have to be on a flash drive or some other electronic storage medium. I pulled my hand back, reading the piece of paper. *1 Esd 4:41*, it read.

"Mom slips them into my pockets when she's folding laundry," Dion explained. "Reminders to give up my heathen ways."

I showed it to the others, frowning. "I don't recognize that scripture."

"First Esdras," Ivy said. "From the Orthodox Bible—it's a book of Apocrypha that most other sects don't use. I don't know that particular verse offhand."

I looked it up on my phone. "Great is truth," I read, "and strongest of all."

Dion shrugged. "I suppose I can agree with that. Even if Mom won't accept what the truth really is . . ."

I tapped my finger on the table. I felt as if I was close to something. An answer? Or maybe just the right questions to be asking? "Your brother had a data key," I said, "which would unlock the information stored in his body. Would he have given it to your mother, do you think?"

Ivy watched Dion carefully to see if he reacted to mention of the key. He didn't have any reaction I could see, and Ivy shook her head. If he was surprised we knew about the key, he was hiding it very well.

"A data key?" Dion asked. "Like what?"

"A thumb drive or something similar."

"I doubt he'd give anything like that to Mom," Dion said as our food arrived. "She hates technology and everything to do with it, particularly if she thinks it came from I3. If he'd handed her something like that, she'd have just destroyed it."

"She gave me quite the cold reception."

"Well, what did you expect? You're employed by the company that turned her son away from God." Dion shook his head. "Mom's a good person—solid, salt-of-the-earth, Old World stock. But she doesn't trust technology. To her, work is something you do with your hands. Not this idle staring at computer screens." He looked away. "I think Panos did what he did to prove something to her, you know?"

"Turning people into mass storage devices?" I asked.

Dion blushed. "That's just the setup, the work he had to do in *order* to do the work he wanted."

"Which was?"

"I . . ."

"Yeah," Ivy said. "He knows something here. Man, this kid is not good at lying. Take a dominant position, Steve. Push him."

"Might as well tell me," I said. "Someone needs to know, Dion. You don't know that you can trust me, but you have to tell someone. What *was* your brother trying to do?"

"Disease," Dion said, looking at his burrito. "He wanted to cure it."

"Which one?"

"All of it."

"Lofty goal."

"Yeah, Panos admitted as much to me. The actual curing wasn't his job; he saw the delivery method as his part."

"Delivery method?" I asked, frowning. "Of the disease."

"No. Of the cure."

"Ahhh . . ." Tobias said, nodding as he sipped his coffee.

"Think about it," Dion said, gesturing to the sides, animated. "Infectious disease is pretty awesome. Imagine if we could design a fast-spreading virus which, in turn, *immunized* people from another disease? You catch the common cold, and suddenly you can never get smallpox, AIDS, polio . . . Why spend billions immunizing, trying to reach people? Nature itself could do all the work for us, if we cracked the method."

"That sounds . . . incredible," I said.

"Incredibly *terrifying*," J.C. said, pointing at the kid with his knife. "Sounds a little like using a smarkwat to fight a viqxuixs."

"A what?" Ivy asked, sighing.

"Classified," J.C. said. "Smet, this steak is good." He dug back into the food.

"Yeah, well," Dion said. "I was going to help him, you know? Go to school, eventually start a new biotech company with him. I guess that dream is dead too." He stabbed at his food. "But you know, each day he'd come home and Mom would ask, 'Did you do any good today?' And he'd smile. He knew he was doing something important, even if she couldn't see it."

"I suspect," I said, "that your mother was prouder of him than she let on."

"Yeah, probably. She's not as bad as she seems sometimes. When we were younger, she worked long hours in menial jobs, supporting us after Dad died. I shouldn't complain. It's just . . . you know, she thinks she knows *everything*."

"Unlike your average teenager," Audrey said, smiling toward Dion.

I nodded, toying with my food, watching Dion. "Did he give you the key, Dion?" I asked him directly.

The kid shook his head.

"He doesn't have it," Ivy said. "He's too bad a liar to hide this from us, in my professional estimation."

"What you should be doing," Dion said, digging back into his burrito, "is looking for some crazy device or something."

"Device?"

"Sure," Dion said. "He'd have built something to hide it, you know? All that maker stuff, you know? He was always gluing LED lights to things and making his own name badges and things. I'll bet he hid it like that. You pick up a potato, and it knocks over a penny, and a hundred geese fly into the air, and the key drops on your head. Something like that."

I looked at my aspects. They seemed skeptical, but maybe there was something to this. Not a device like Dion described, but a process. What if Panos had set up some sort of fail-safe that would reveal the truth if he died—but it hadn't been tripped for some reason.

I forced myself to eat a bit of omelet, just to be able to tell Wilson I'd done so when he inevitably asked. Unfortunately, my phone still hadn't beeped by the time we finished. I stalled as best I could, but eventually felt it would look suspicious to Zen if we stayed any longer.

I led the way back out to the SUV, and held open the side door for my aspects before rounding to the driver's seat. I'd just settled in, planning my next move, when I felt the cold metal of a gun barrel press against the back of my neck.

18

Dion climbed into the passenger seat, oblivious. He looked at me, then froze, going all white. I glanced at the rearview mirror and caught a glimpse of Zen squatting behind my seat, gun pressed against my head.

Damn. So she hadn't been as willing to wait as I'd hoped. My phone hung in my pocket like a dead weight. What was taking Wilson so long?

"Join me in the back, if you would please, Mister Leeds," Zen said softly. "Young Maheras, remain in place. I assume that I needn't warn you how willing I am to resort to violence?"

Sweating, I noticed J.C. in the rearview mirror, his face red. He'd been sitting in the seat that Zen now squatted before, but hadn't seen her until now. Twice she'd gotten the drop on us, and J.C. hadn't been able to do a thing. Her skill at this was far better than my own.

J.C. took out his gun, for all the good it would do, and nodded for me to obey Zen. Getting into the back would put me into a better position to engage her.

She moved to the far back seat—scrunching Ivy and Audrey to the sides—as I moved, her gun on me at all times.

"Your weapon," she said.

I removed it, just as I had in the alley, and placed it before me on the floor. Why was I even carrying the blasted thing?

"Phone next."

I passed it over.

"Good job on finding the bug," she noted to me. "We will discuss the matter further, Mister Leeds, as we go for a stroll together. Young Maheras, you are not involved in this. Move to the driver's seat of the car. Once we are out, you are to leave. I don't care what you do—go to the police, if you wish—but stay away. I don't like killing people I haven't been hired to hit. It's bad business to . . . give away too many freebies."

Dion was all too quick to move, scrambling into the driver's seat, where I'd left the keys.

"This is good," J.C. said softly. "She's letting the boy go and is moving us out into the open." He scrunched up his face. "I can't figure out why she'd do either one, but I think it indicates that her superiors have demanded she not actually kill anyone."

I nodded, sweat trickling down the back of my neck. Zen waved with her gun and I opened the side door, letting my aspects file out, J.C first, then Ivy, then Tobias. Audrey rested a hand on my arm encouragingly and I nodded, then moved to climb out before her.

Zen snapped forward, grabbing me by the shoulder and throwing me back. She snatched the door and slammed it closed.

"Maheras," she said, turning the gun on him. "Drive. *Now*."

"But—"

"Go or you're a dead man!"

The kid floored it, running over a parking lot divider. I lay stunned against the side of the car, blinking, tracking what had happened. Zen . . .

My aspects!

I cried out, turning and pressing my face against the window. Ivy and Tobias stood out in the parking lot, looking baffled. Zen instructed Dion to pull out of the parking lot onto the street, and then told him to continue at a normal speed—no trying to get picked up by cops, please.

I barely listened. She'd lured my aspects out, then isolated me from them. Only Audrey was left, and that was by a fluke. Another moment, and she'd have been gone too. I turned, stunned, to look at Zen, who had settled into the seat by the now-closed door, her gun held on me.

"I do my research," she said. "As a side note, the amount that has been written about you in psychological journals was *quite* useful, Mister Leeds."

Audrey sank down onto the floor between us, wrapping her hands around her knees, whimpering. She was all I had, for now, and—

Wait.

J.C. I hadn't seen J.C. out the window. I turned, searching, and there he was! Charging along the sidewalk at a full run, gun in one hand, look of determination on his face. He kept pace with us, barely.

Bless you, I thought toward him. He'd reacted when the other two were caught flat-footed. He dodged around some people on the sidewalk and leaped a bench in an almost superhuman move.

Audrey perked up, looking out the window. "Wow," she whispered. "How is he *doing* that?"

The car was moving at around forty miles an hour. Suddenly, I couldn't pretend any longer. J.C. ran out of breath, lurched to a stop on the sidewalk, his face flushed. He collapsed, exhausted from a run he shouldn't have been able to manage.

The illusion. I *had* to keep the illusion. Audrey looked at me, then seemed to shrink upon herself, realizing what she'd done. It wasn't her fault, though. I'd have eventually noticed how fast we were going.

"You," Zen said to me, "are a very dangerous man."

"I'm not the one holding the gun," I said, turning to face her. How was I going to do this without Ivy and Tobias to help me interact? Without J.C. to pull me out of a deadly situation?

"Yes, but I can only kill the occasional individual," Zen said. "You bring down companies, destroy hundreds of lives. My employers are . . . concerned about what you've done."

"And they think having you grab me is going to help?" I asked. "I won't find Panos's key for you at gunpoint, Zen."

"They're not worried about the body anymore," she said, and sounded faintly troubled. "You've toppled their fortunes and sent the government after them. They don't want to be associated with this hunt any longer. They just want . . . loose threads to be pulled out and disposed of."

Great. My plan was working.

Too well.

I tried to come up with something more to say, but Zen turned from me, giving Dion a series of driving instructions. I tried to get her talking again, but she refused, and I wasn't about to try anything physical. Not without J.C. to give advice.

Maybe . . . maybe the other aspects would find their way to wherever we were going. Given time, they probably would.

I wasn't sure how long that would take.

Audrey spent the ride seated in the middle of the floor between our two seats, arms wrapped around her legs. I wanted to talk to her, but didn't dare say anything with Zen watching. The assassin thought she'd isolated me without any aspects. If I let her know that one was still here, I would lose a big advantage.

Unfortunately, our drive took us to an area on the outskirts of the city. There were some new housing developments out here, as the city's creeping expansion slowly consumed the countryside, but there were also big patches of fields and trees waiting for condos and gas stations. Zen had us pull into one of these large wooded spots, and we drove on a dirt road up to a solitary house of the "my fathers farmed this land for generations" variety.

This was far enough from neighbors that shouts would not be heard and gunshots would be attributed to the removal of vermin. Not good. Zen marched Dion and me to a cellar door set in the ground and ordered us down the stairs. Inside, sacks slumped against the wall, spilling potatoes so old they'd probably witnessed the Civil War. A bare lightbulb glared where it hung from the center of the ceiling.

"I'm going to go report," Zen told us, taking Dion's phone from him. "Get comfortable. My expectation is that you're going to be living down here for a few weeks while things blow over for my employers."

She walked up the steps and locked the cellar door.

Dion let out a deep breath and put his back to the cinder block wall, then slumped down to a sitting position. "Weeks?" he asked. "Trapped in here with you?"

I paused a moment before speaking. "Yeah. That's going to suck, eh?"

Dion looked up at me, and I cursed myself for hesitating before giving my reply. The kid looked frazzled—he'd probably never been forced to drive at gunpoint before. First time is always the worst.

"You don't think we're going to be down here for weeks, do you?" Dion guessed.

"I . . . No."

"But she said—"

"They're trained to talk that way," I said, fishing out Zen's bug from under my collar, then smashing it just in case. I walked around the chamber, looking for exits.

"Always tell your captives they have more time than they do; it makes them relax, sets them to planning, instead of trying to break out immediately. The last thing you want to do is make them desperate, since desperate people are unpredictable."

The kid groaned softly. I probably shouldn't have explained that. I was feeling the lack of Ivy's presence. Even when she didn't guide me directly, having her around made me better at interacting with people.

"Don't worry," I said, kneeling down to inspect a drain in the floor, "we probably won't be in real danger unless Zen decides to take us individually into the woods 'for questioning.' That will mean she's been told to execute us."

I prodded at the grate. Too small to crawl through, unfortunately, and it looked like it just ended in a small pit of rocks anyway. I moved on, expecting—despite myself—to hear commentary by my aspects analyzing our situation, telling me what to investigate, theorizing on how to get out.

Instead, all I heard was retching.

I spun on Dion, shocked to find him emptying his stomach onto the floor of the cellar. So much for the breakfast burrito he'd so stubbornly paid for. I waited until he was done, then walked over, taking an old towel off of a dusty table and draping it over the sick-up to smother the smell. I knelt down, resting my hand on the young man's shoulder.

He looked awful. Red eyes, pale skin, sweat on his brow.

How to interact? What did one say? "I'm sorry." It sounded lame, but it was all I could think of.

"She's going to kill us," the youth whispered.

"She might try," I said. "But then again, she might not. Killing us is a big step, one her employers probably won't be willing to make."

Of course, I *had* made them very desperate. And desperate people were . . . well, unpredictable.

I stood up, leaving the kid to his misery, and walked to Audrey. "I need you to get us out of this," I whispered to her.

"Me?" Audrey said.

"You're all I have."

"Before this, I'd only been on a *single* mission!" she said. "I don't know about guns, or fighting, or escaping."

"You're an expert on cryptography."

"Expert? You read *one* book on cryptography. Besides, how is cryptography going to help? Here, let me interpret the scratches on the walls. They say we're *bloody doomed*!"

Frustrated, I left her trembling with worry and forced myself to continue my inspection of the room. No windows. Some sections of bare earth where the cinder-block wall had fallen in. I was able to dig at one, but heard the floor groaning above as I did. Not a good idea.

I tried the exit next, climbing the steps and shoving my shoulder at the doors to see how strong they were. They were tight, unfortunately, and there was no lock to pick—just a padlock on the outside that I couldn't reach. I might be able to find something to use as a ram and break us out, but that would certainly alert Zen. I could hear her through the floor above, talking. Sounded like a terse conversation over a cell phone, but I couldn't make out any specifics.

I went over the room again. Had I missed anything? I was sure I had, but what? Without my aspects, I didn't know what I knew. Being alone haunted me. As I passed Dion, I found the expressions on his face alien things, no more intelligible as emotions than lumps in mud. Did that expression mean happiness? Sorrow?

Stop, I told myself, sweating. *You're not that bad.* I was without Ivy, but that didn't suddenly make me unable to relate to members of my own species. Did it?

Dion was upset. That was obvious. He stared down at a few small slips of paper in his hands. More scriptures he'd found in his pockets from his mother.

"She just left the verse numbers," he said, glancing at me, "so I don't even know what the scriptures say. As if they'd be a help anyway. Bah!" He closed his fist, then threw the papers, wadded up. They burst apart from each other and fluttered down like confetti.

I stood there, feeling almost as sick as Dion looked. I needed to say something, connect with him somehow.

I didn't know *why* I felt that, but I was suddenly desperate for it.

"Are you so frightened of death, Dion?" I asked. Probably the wrong words, but speaking was better than remaining silent.

"Why wouldn't I be?" Dion said. "Death is the end. Nothing. All gone." He looked at me, as if in challenge. When I didn't respond immediately, he continued. "Not going to tell me everything will be all right? Mom always talks about how good people get rewarded, but Panos was as good a man as there was. He spent his life trying to cure disease! And look at him. Dead of a stupid *accident*."

"Why," I said, "do you assume death is the end?"

"Because it *is*. Look, I don't want to listen to any religious—"

"I'm not going to preach at you," I said. "I'm an atheist too."

The kid looked at me. "You are?"

"Sure," I said. "Almost fifteen percent—though, admittedly, several of my pieces would argue that they are agnostic instead."

"Fifteen percent? That doesn't count."

"Oh? So you get to decide how my faith, or lack thereof, works? What 'counts' and what doesn't?"

"No, but even if it did work that way—if someone could be *fifteen percent* atheist—the majority of you still believes."

"Just like a minority of you probably still believes in God," I said.

He looked at me, then blushed. I settled down beside him, opposite the place where he'd had his little accident.

"I can see why people want to believe," Dion told me. "I'm not just a petulant kid, like you think. I've wondered, I've asked. God doesn't make sense to me. But sometimes, looking at infinity and thinking of myself just . . . not being here anymore, I understand why people would choose to believe."

Ivy would want me to try to convert the boy, but she wasn't here. Instead, I asked a question. "Do you think time is infinite, Dion?"

He shrugged.

"Come on," I prodded. "Give me an answer. You want comfort? I might have a solution for you—or at least my aspect Arnaud might. But first, is time infinite?"

"I don't think we know for certain," Dion replied. "But yeah, I'd guess that it is. Even after our universe ends, something *else* will happen. If not here, then in other dimensions. Other places. Other big bangs. Matter, space, it'll continue on without end."

"So you're immortal."

"My atoms, maybe," he said. "But that's not *me*. Don't give me any metaphysical bull—"

"No metaphysics," I said, "just a theory. If time is infinite, then anything that *can* happen *will* happen—and *has* happened. That means you've happened before,

Dion. We all have. Even if there is no God—even sup-
posing that there are no answers, no divinity out there—
we're immortal."

He frowned.

"Think about it," I said. "The universe rolled its
cosmic dice and ended up with you—a semi-random
collection of atoms, synapses, and chemicals. Together,
those create your personality, memories, and very
existence. But if time continues forever, eventually that
random collection will happened again. It may take
hundreds of trillions of years, but it *will* come again. You.
With your memories, your personality. In the context of
infinity, kid, we will keep living, over and over."

"I . . . don't know how comforting that is, honestly.
Even if it is true."

"Really?" I asked. "Because I think it's pretty amazing
to consider. Anything that is *possible* is actually *reality*,
given infinity. So, not only will you return, but your every
iteration of possibility will play out. Sometimes you'll
be rich. Sometimes you'll be poor. In fact, it's plausible
that because of a brain defect, sometime in the future
you'll have the memories you have now, even if in *that*
future time you never lived those memories. So you'll be
you again, completely, and not because of some mystical
nonsense—but because of simple mathematics. Even the
smallest chance multiplied by infinity is, itself, infinite."

I stood back up, then squatted down, looking him
in the eyes and resting my hand on his shoulder. "Every

variation of possibility, Dion. At some point, you—the same you, with the same thought processes—will be born to a wealthy family. Your parents will be killed, and you will decide to fight against injustice. It has happened. It will happen. You asked for comfort, Dion? Well, when the fear of death seizes you—when the dark thoughts come—you stare the darkness right back, and you tell it, 'I will not listen to you, for I am *infinite Batmans.*' "

The kid blinked at me. "That . . . is the weirdest thing anyone has ever told me."

I winked at him, then left him lost in thought and walked back to Audrey. I wasn't sure how much of that I actually believed, but it was what had come out. Honestly, I don't know that the universe could really handle everyone being infinite Batmans.

Perhaps the point of God was to prevent nonsense like that.

I took Audrey by the arm, speaking softly. "Audrey, focus on me."

She looked at me, blinking. She'd been crying.

"We're going to think, right now," I told her. "We're going to scrounge everything we know, and we're going to come up with a way out of this."

"I can't—"

"You *can.* You're part of me. You're part of all of this; you can access my subconscious. You can *fix this.*"

She met my eyes, and some of my confidence seemed to transfer to her. She nodded sharply, and adopted a look of complete concentration. I smiled at her encouragingly.

The door to the building up above opened, then shut.

Come on, Audrey.

Zen's footsteps rounded the building, then she began working on the lock down into the cellar.

Come on . . .

Audrey snapped her head up and looked at me. "I know where the body is."

"The body?" I said. "Audrey, we're supposed to be—"

"Zen's company doesn't have it," Audrey said. "I3 doesn't have it. The kid doesn't know anything. I *know where it is.*"

The door down into the cellar opened. Light flooded in, revealing Zen silhouetted above. "Mister Leeds," she said. "I need you to come with me so I can question you alone. It will only take a short time."

I grew very cold.

20

"**O**h hell," Audrey said, backing away from me. "You need to do something! Don't let her kill you."

I turned to face Zen—a woman dressed in chic clothing, like she was the CFO of a Manhattan publishing company, not a paid assassin. She walked down the steps, feigning nonchalance. That attitude, mixed with the tension of the call above, told me all I needed to know.

She was going to eliminate me.

"They're really willing to do this?" I asked her. "It will leave questions. Problems."

"I don't know what you're talking about." She got out her gun.

"Do we have to play this game, Zen?" I replied, frantically searching for a way to stall. "We both know what you're up to. You'll really follow through with orders that are so incompetent? It leaves you in danger. People *will* wonder where I've gone."

"An equal number will be glad to have you out of their hair, I assume," Zen said. She took out a suppressor, affixing it to her gun, all pretense gone now.

Audrey whimpered. To his credit, Dion stood up, unwilling to face death sitting down.

"You pushed them too hard, Mister Crazy," Zen said. "They have it in their heads that you're trying specifically to destroy them, and so they have responded as any bully does when shoved. They hit as hard as they can and hope it will solve the situation." She raised the gun. "As for me, I can take care of myself. But thank you for your concern."

I stared down the barrel of that gun, sweating, panicking. No hope, no plan, no aspects . . .

But she didn't know that.

"They're around you," I whispered.

Zen hesitated.

"Some people theorize," I said, "that the ones I see are ghosts. If you've read about me, then you'll know. I do things I shouldn't be able to. Know things I shouldn't know. Because I have help."

"You're just a genius," she said, but her eye twitched to the side. Yes, she'd read about me. Deeply, if she knew how to drive off without my aspects.

And nobody could dig into my world without coming away a little bit . . . touched.

"They've caught up to us," I said. "They stand on the steps behind you. Can you feel them there, Zen?

Watching you? Hands at your neck? What will you do with them if you remove me? Will you live with my spirits stalking you for the rest of your life?"

She set her jaw, and seemed as if she was trying very, very hard not to look over her shoulder. Was this actually working?

Zen took a deep breath. "They won't be the only spirits that haunt me, Leeds," she whispered. "If there is a hell, I earned my place in it long ago."

"So you say," I replied. "Of course, what you really should be wondering is this: I'm a genius. I know things I shouldn't. So why have I placed us here, right now? Why is it that I *want* you right there?"

"I . . ." She held the gun on me. A cool breeze blew in down around her, rustling the lips of old potato sacks.

My cell phone chirped in her pocket.

Zen practically jumped to the ceiling. She cursed, sweating, and rested her hand on the pocket. She thrust the gun at me and fired. Wild. The support beam beside me popped with exploding bits of wood. Dion dove for cover.

Zen—eyes so wide, I could see the whites all around her pupils—held the gun in a trembling hand, focusing on me.

"Check the phone, Zen," I said.

She didn't move.

No! It couldn't go this way. So close! She had to—

Another phone rang. Hers this time, I assumed, buzzing in her other pocket. Zen wavered. I met her stare. In that moment, one of the two of us was mad, insane, on the edge.

And it wasn't the crazy guy.

Her phone stopped ringing. A text followed. We waited, facing one another in the cold cellar until, at long last, Zen reached down and took out her phone. She stared at it for a few moments. Then she laughed a barking laugh. She backed up, placing a call, and had a whispered conversation.

Letting out what had to be the biggest breath of my life, I walked to Dion and helped him to his feet. He looked up at Zen, who laughed again, this time louder.

"What's going on?" Dion asked.

"We're safe," I said. "Isn't that right, Zen?"

She giggled wildly. Then she hung up and looked right at me. "Whatever you say, sir."

". . . 'Sir'?" Dion asked.

"Exeltec was on unstable footing," I said. "I released rumors that it was involved in a federal investigation, and had Yol push all the right buttons economically."

"To make them desperate?" Dion asked.

"To crash the company," I said, walking back to Zen, passing a flummoxed Audrey. "So I could afford to buy it. Yol was supposed to do that part, but only got halfway done. I had to have Wilson do the rest, calling the various Exeltec investors and buying them out." I proffered my hand to Zen. She gave me my phone.

"So . . ." Dion said.

"So I now own a sixty percent stake in the company," I said, checking the text from Wilson. "And have voted myself president. That makes me Zen's boss."

"Sir," she said. She was doing a good job of regaining her composure, but I could see a wildness in the way her hands still trembled, the way she stood with her expression too stiff.

"Wait," Dion said. "You just defeated an assassin with a *hostile takeover*?"

"I use the cards dealt to me. Probably wasn't particularly hostile, though—I suspect that everyone involved was all too eager to jump ship."

"You realize, of course," Zen said smoothly, "that I was never actually going to shoot you. I was just supposed to make you worried so you'd share information."

"Of course." That would be the official line, to protect her and Exeltec from attempted murder charges. My buyout agreement would include provisions to prevent me from taking action against them.

I pocketed my phone, took my gun back from Zen, and nodded to Audrey. "Let's go collect that body."

☵

21

We found Mrs. Maheras in the garden still. She knelt there, planting, nurturing, tending.

I walked up, and from the way she glanced at me, I suspected she realized that her secret was out. Still, I knelt down beside her, then handed over a carton of half-grown flowers when she motioned toward them.

Sirens sounded in the distance.

"Was that necessary?" she asked, not looking up.

"Sorry," I said. "But yes." I'd sent a text to Yol, knowing the feds would get it first. Behind me, Audrey, Tobias, Ivy, and a downcast J.C. stepped up to us. They cast shadows, to my eyes, in the fading light, and blocked my view of Dion standing just behind. We'd found them all walking along the road, miles from Zen's holding place, trying to reach me.

I was tired. Man, was I tired. Sometimes, in the heat of it all, you can forget. But when the tension ends, it comes crashing down.

"I should have seen it," Ivy said again, arms folded. "I *should* have. Most Orthodox branches are pointedly against cremation. They see it as desecration of the body, which is to await resurrection."

We had been so focused on the information in Panos's cells that we didn't stop to think there might be other reasons entirely that someone would want to take the corpse. Reasons so powerful that it would convince an otherwise law-abiding woman and her priest to pull a heist.

In a way, I was very impressed. "You were a cleaning lady when you were younger," I said. "I should have asked Dion more about your life, your job. He mentioned hard labor, a life spent supporting him and his brother. I didn't ask what you'd done."

She continued planting flowers upon her son's grave, hidden in the garden.

"You imitated the cleaning lady who worked at the morgue," I said. "You paid her off, I assume, and went in her place—after having the priest place tape on the door. It really was him, not an impostor. Together, you went to extremes to protect your son's corpse from cremation."

"What gave me away?" Mrs. Maheras asked as the sirens drew closer.

"You followed the real cleaning lady's patterns exactly," I said. "Too exactly. You cleaned the bathroom, then signed your name on the sheet hanging on the door, to prove it had been done."

"I practiced Lilia's signature exactly!" Mrs. Maheras said, looking at me for the first time.

"Yes," I said, holding up one of the slips of paper with scriptures on them that she put in her son's pockets. "But you wrote the cleaning time on that sheet as well, and you didn't practice imitating Lilia's *numbers*."

"You have a very distinctive zero," Audrey explained, looking supremely smug. Cryptography hadn't cracked this case after all. It had just required some good, old-fashioned handwriting analysis.

Mrs. Maheras sighed, then placed her spade into the dirt and bowed her head, offering a silent prayer. I bowed my head as well, as did Ivy and J.C. Tobias refrained.

"So you'll take him again," Mrs. Maheras whispered, once she had finished. She looked at the ground before her, now planted with flowers and tomatoes.

"Yes," I said, climbing to my feet and dusting off my knees. "But at the very least, you're unlikely to be in too much trouble for what you did. The government doesn't recognize a body as property, so what you did wasn't actually theft."

"A cold comfort," she muttered. "They'll still take him, and they'll burn him."

"True," I said idly. "Of course, who knows what secrets your son had hidden in his body? He'd been splicing secret information into his very DNA, and he might have hidden all kinds of things in there. The right impli-cation at the right time might prod the government into a very, *very* long search."

She looked up at me.

"Scientists disagree on how many cells there are in the human body," I explained. "Somewhere in the tril-lions, easily. Perhaps many more than that. Could take decades upon decades to search them all, something I doubt the government will want to do. However, if they think there *might* be something important, they could likely set the body into storage just in case they need to do a thorough search at some point.

"It wouldn't be a proper burial, as you want—but it also wouldn't be cremation. I believe the church does make provisions for people donating organs to help oth-ers? Perhaps it's best to just consider it in that light."

Mrs. Maheras seemed thoughtful. I left her then, and Dion stepped forward to comfort her. My suggestions did seem to have made a difference, which baffled me. I'd have rather seen a family member cremated than spend forever being frozen. However, as I reached the building and looked back, I found that Mrs. Maheras seemed to have perked up visibly.

"You were right," I told Ivy.

"Have I ever *not* been right?"

"I don't know about that," J.C. said. "But you *do* make some really bad relationship choices sometimes."

We all looked at him, and he blushed immediately.

"I was talking about her *dumping* me," he protested. "Not picking me in the first place!"

I smiled, leading the way into the kitchen. I was just glad to have them back. I walked down the little hallway lined with pictures, toward the front door. I'd want to meet the feds when they arrived.

Then I stopped. "There's a bare patch on the wall. It looks so odd. Every surface, desk, and wall in this place is covered with kitsch. Except here." I pointed at the pictures of the family, then two pictures of saints. Two spots, empty save for little nails. Ivy had said that Mrs. Maheras had probably taken down the picture of Panos's patron saint in preparation for his funeral.

"Ivy," I said, "would you say it's safe to assume that Panos knew if he died, this picture would be removed and placed with his corpse?"

We looked at each other. Then I reached up and pulled on the nail. It resisted in an odd fashion. I yanked harder, and the nail came out—but had a knob and string tied around the back end.

Behind the wall, something clicked.

I looked at the aspects, suddenly worried, until the wall's nearby light switch—plate behind it and all—rotated forward like a hidden cup holder in a car's dashboard. The portion that had been hidden inside the wall had LED lights blinking on the sides.

"Well I'll be damned," J.C. said. "The kid was right."

"Language," Ivy mumbled, looking closely at the contraption.

"What happened to the future curses?" Audrey said. "I kind of liked those."

"I realized something," J.C. said. "I can't be an Interdimensional Time Ranger. Because if I am, that means all of *you* are too. And that's just a little too silly for me to accept."

I reached into the holder that had come out and extracted a thumb drive. Written on it, with a label maker, were a few words.

"1 Kings 19:11–12," I read.

"And He said," Ivy quoted in a quiet voice, "Go forth, and stand upon the mount before the Lord. And behold, the Lord passed by, and a great and strong wind rent the mountains and broke in pieces the rocks before the Lord, but the Lord was not in the wind; and after the wind an earthquake, but the Lord was not in the earthquake. And after the earthquake a fire, but the Lord was not in the fire; and after the fire a still small voice."

I looked at my aspects as a fist pounded on the door. Then I pocketed the thumb drive and pushed the holder back into the wall before going to meet with the feds.

Epilogue

Four days later, I stood alone in the White Room. Tobias had covered over the hole in the ceiling, as he'd promised. The place was refreshingly blank.

Was this what I would be, without my aspects? Blank? I'd certainly felt that way while being held by Zen. I'd barely been able to do anything to save myself. No plans, no escaping. Just some stalling. Ivy had sometimes wondered if I was growing good enough on my own that I eventually wouldn't need her or the others any longer.

From what had happened to me when I'd lost them, I figured that day—if it ever came—was a long, long way off.

The door cracked open. Audrey slipped in, wearing a blue one-piece swimsuit. She trotted up to me and delivered a sheet of paper. "Have to go catch a pool party. But I did finish solving this. Wasn't too hard, once we had the key."

On the thumb drive, we'd found two things. The first was the anticipated key to unlocking the data on Panos's body. The body had been seized by the government, and I'd convinced them to put it on ice for the foreseeable future. After all, there might be very, very important data on it, and someday the key might turn up.

Yol had offered me an exorbitant amount to track down the key. I'd refused, though I had forced him to buy Exeltec from me for another exorbitant sum, so I came away from this in a good enough position.

The CDC failed to find evidence that Panos had released any kind of pathogen, and eventually determined that the note on Panos's computer had been an idle threat, meant to send I3 into a panic. Earlier that morning, Dion had sent me a thank-you note from him and his mother for stopping the government from burning the body. I hadn't yet told them I'd stolen this thumb drive.

It contained the key, and a . . . second file. A small text document, also encrypted. We'd stared at it for a time before realizing that the key had been printed on the outside of the thumb drive itself. Chapter nineteen of First Kings. Any string of letters or numbers, or mixture of the two, can be the passphrase for a private-key cryptogram—though using a known text, like Bible verses, wasn't a particularly secure option.

Audrey went out, but left the door cracked open. I could see Tobias outside, leaning against the wall, arms folded, wearing his characteristic loose business suit, no tie.

I raised the sheet of paper, reading the simple note Panos had left.

I guess I'm dead.

I shouldn't be surprised, but I didn't think they'd ever actually go through with it. My own friends, you know?

He'd gotten that wrong. So far as I, or anyone else could determine, his fall really had been an accident.

Did you know every person is a walking jungle of bacteria? We're each a little biome, all to ourselves. I've made an alteration. It's called Staphylococcus epidermidis. A strain of bacteria we all carry. It's harmless, for the most part.

My changes aren't big. Just an addition. Several megs of data, spliced into the DNA. I3 was watching me, but I learned to do my work, even when supervised. They watched what I posted, though, so I decided to use their tools against them. I put the information into the bacteria of my own skin and shook hands with them all. I'll bet you can find strains of my altered bacteria all across the world by now.

It won't do anything harmful. But if you've found this, you have the key to decoding what I've hidden. You make the call, Dion. I leave it in your hands. Release the key on this thumb drive, and everyone will know what I've studied. They'll have the answers to what I3 is doing, and everyone will be on an even playing field.

I studied the paper for a time, then quietly folded it and slipped it into my back pocket. I walked to the door.

"Are you going to do it?" Tobias asked as I passed him. "Let it out?"

I pulled out the flash drive and held it up. "Didn't Dion talk about about starting a new company with his brother? Curing disease? Doing good each day?"

"Something like that," Tobias said.

I tossed the drive up into the air, then caught it. "We'll set this aside, to be mailed to him on the day he graduates. Maybe that dream of his isn't as dead as he thinks. At the very least, we should honor his brother's wishes." I hesitated. "But we'll want to see if we can get the data ourselves first and check out how dangerous it might be."

As my aspects had guessed, my contacts among the feds said the cancer scare had been a fake on Yol's part, an attempt to make my task urgent. But we had no idea what Panos had really been working on. Somehow, he'd hidden that even from the people at I3.

"Technically," Tobias said, "that information is owned by Yol."

"Technically," I said, pocketing the flash drive again, "it's owned by *me* as well, since I'm part owner of the company. We'll just call this my part."

I passed him, heading to the stairs. "The funny thing is," I said, hand on the bannister, "we spent this entire time searching for a corpse—but the information wasn't just there. It was on every person we met."

"There's no way we could have known," Tobias said.

"Of course there was," I said. "Panos warned us. That day we studied I3—it was proclaimed right there, on one of the slogans he'd printed and hung on his wall."

Tobias looked at me, quizzical.

"Information," I said, wiggling my fingers—and the bacteria that held Panos's data, "for every body."

I smiled, and left Tobias chuckling as I went searching for something to eat.

Acknowledgments

First off, I'd like to thank Moshe Feder who edited this book for me, along with the Inscrutable Peter Ahlstrom, who did some serious bonus editing. Thanks to Isaåc Stewart and Kara Stewart for their assistant-fu on this and many other projects. Howard Tayler also helped me brainstorm at lunch one day, and gets a writer high-five for his help.

My beta readers on this volume were: Mi'chelle Walker, Josh Walker, Kalyani Poluri, Rahul Pantula, Kaylynn ZoBell, Peter & Karen Ahlstrom, Ben & Danielle Olsen, Darci & Eric James Stone, Alan Layton, Emily Sanderson, and Kathleen Dorsey Sanderson.

I love the Jon Foster art on this edition—he's done five covers for me so far, and I think this might be my favorite. At Subterranean, the publisher, I'd like to thank Yanni Kuznia, Bill Schafer, Morgan Schlicker, and Gail Cross.

As always, many thanks to my wonderful family, including my three very excited—and very busy—little boys.

LEA DER SHIP

LESSONS FROM AN ILLITERATE MOM

*Against all odds, a mother
dedicates a lifetime of excellence
to deliver unmatched results.*

DR. MAJED YAGHI

ARCHWAY
PUBLISHING

Archway Publishing books may be ordered through booksellers or by contacting:

Archway Publishing
1663 Liberty Drive
Bloomington, IN 47403
www.archwaypublishing.com
844-669-3957

ISBN: 978-1-6657-1656-7 (sc)
ISBN: 978-1-6657-1650-5 (hc)
ISBN: 978-1-6657-1657-4 (e)

Library of Congress Control Number: 2021925313

Print information available on the last page.

Archway Publishing rev. date: 12/31/2021

CONTENTS

To my mother, Nazira Yaghi, a legendary mother, a business leader, an inspiration, and an angel.

GRATITUDE

To DDSS, who never stopped supporting me in whichever global assignment I accepted, whichever crazy idea I followed, and whichever path I took.

I love you.

MORE GRATITUDE

To my seven siblings, forever entwined in heart, in soul, and in life, for their unconditional love, support, and commitment to excellence for their unrivaled and constant pursuit of academic heights.

I love you.

RECOGNITION

To other leaders with little formal education who continue to inspire this world, including the following:

- William Shakespeare
- George Washington
- Abraham Lincoln
- Thomas Edison
- Mark Twain
- Henry Ford

PREFACE

I started writing this book soon after two significant events—one personal and another professional. My mother had just passed away and I was coping alone, separated from my family, which was back in the United States, and from own siblings, who were scattered around the world. The professional event was uncovering the true toxic nature of a leader at work, someone whose selfish and narcissistic behavior was visibly appalling, not to mention organizationally destructive. The idea and framework for this book came to life as an encapsulation of insights gained in my journey and also to defuse a myth that leadership lessons are only learned from the rich and famous or the seasoned corporate veterans.

Many leadership and personal development books are written every year. From business leaders (current and retired) to athletes and celebrities, there is a plethora of authors sharing valuable advice. Even politicians write autobiographies to chronicle their time in public office. So it is not unusual to learn from such people and be inspired. However, what is unusual is for a mother to inspire great leadership lessons with the same visceral drive as those corporate and established leaders. What is even more exceptionally profound is for an illiterate mother to be the source of such exceptional schooling.

My mother, Nazira Yaghi (RIP), never went to school a day in her life. She wasn't even fortunate enough to get homeschooled. No, her only education was the school of life, one that would have granted her a doctorate with distinction, if one had ever existed. She succeeded in building a thriving enterprise grounded in her relentless passion for winning and her will to overcome all odds. Until her passing on August 7, 2012, at the age of seventy-five, she was the consummate leader displaying the same passion and determination my mom was known for in her youth. Throughout her life, she demonstrated leadership qualities that are typically the marks of Ivy League graduates and corporate executives, except she was neither. My mother was merely an illiterate head of our household of eight children.

How could that be? Are there really parallels between raising a family and leading a company? Could an illiterate yet strong-minded mother possess similar traits to million-dollar CEOs? I'm not trying to belittle the role of the corporate chief executive at all. It certainly is more complex and dynamic with immense pressure every single day. But the truth of the matter is that at its core, leadership is neither about size of the organization nor the complexity of the job. Leadership can show up be in the smallest things we do. The qualities of successfully running a Fortune 500 organization, a startup, a sports team, a nonprofit, or any other organization for that matter are arguably similar if not identical. Managing and leading a household are not very different, albeit at a much smaller and informal scale. Similarly, just like large companies struggle with great or toxic leadership, households face those same challenges, and just as corporations seek great leaders, households also seek great parents. Great mothers are astounding leaders, which may explain why several moms have become successful corporate leaders. In fact, a 2017 *Forbes* story chronicled why mothers make great CEO and noted that both set high expectations and set stretch goals while holding everyone accountable for their work. However, my mother was illiterate. Let me take you back to where it all started.

It was the 1940s in old Palestine, in a small village called Masmiyya. The sleepy west coast town was known for two things: its beautifully vast citrus orchards and its two prominent families: the Yaghis and the Mhannas. At the time, both of those families were landowners with immense power and influence in the area. Besides the orchards, the Yaghis were especially distinguished for educating their children by sending them off to Egypt, the region's knowledge destination at the time, for university studies. A highly unique privilege for farming villagers. Remember this was the 1940s in the Middle East, which was mostly underdeveloped, and Palestine was essentially dominated by farming communities. It was quite unusual for a family to think so progressively and send kids off to another country for higher education. Unfortunately, that privilege was extended to boys only and not girls. To be fair though, the Yaghis' seemingly gender bias did not preclude them from educating their daughters. The village did have both boys and girls schools. However, girls typically finished school and either taught in elementary schools or stayed home with their parents until marriage. That was the culture then. Remember this was the 1940s in the Middle East!

My mother was not as fortunate as some of the village girls; she never went to school. She remained illiterate for a good part of her life. Little Nazira was the second eldest in the family but the oldest of four girls. By default, that position limited her future options as she was not sent to school and instead was assigned home duties. Someone had to help their parents with chores. It was years later when her second sister was born that the family realized the importance of educating girls, and from then on, all girls born in subsequent years got formally educated. Unfortunately for my mother, it was too late; she missed the education bus. Instead, she endured a childhood of hardship, house chores, and fieldwork. Her daily routine was quite straightforward: get up in the wee hours of the morning, help her mother prepare breakfast for the whole family, and clean the house before heading out to the fields. All before the crack of dawn. She told us she enjoyed the work and loved that life. Mind you, she didn't know any better at the time. Despite the hardship, my mom would later in her life refer to those hard childhood years as the foundation that defined her character and shaped the determined mother she had become.

The Yaghis owned citrus orchards that needed daily supervision, and my mom's typical operational responsibilities were to be her dad's right hand and do whatever was needed. Both my mother and my grandfather liked that aspect of their daily routine, the mentor coaching his protégé and passing valuable hands-on business knowledge. She did it all: working the fields, tending to the horses, and fetching water from the well. Occasionally, she would go back home to pick up lunch, make tea, and return to the orchards. That was not an easy feat as it was a good 4K walk back and forth. Those days were long and hard, the kind that most often put her straight to sleep as soon as she returned home in the evening.

That was the daily routine from sunrise to sunset. Six days a week with only Fridays as her off days. Moreover, she stood by her dad's side when he negotiated business deals. Season after season, she witnessed buying and selling of oranges, grapefruit, and the rest of their crops. She was there when prices and payment terms were discussed and when delivery or bartering terms were finalized. That is likely the source of her knowledge, where she gained her early education in commerce, and where she developed her business acumen.

However, things took a different turn in 1948 when Israeli militias moved into Masmiyya village and forced all its residents to desert their land, their properties, and their livelihood. Alas, the town was going to be part of the newly created state of Israel, as determined by the United Nations. The Yaghis and the Mhannas were forced to leave everything behind and head to the unknown. They had to abandon the land they owned and worshiped, the life they lived, and the roots they had planted decades ago. There were few options for them to choose from: flee or fight. Flee to safety but also to the unknown or fight the mighty and well-trained Israeli militias. Fighting was not a viable option, especially given the news of all the neighboring villages who resisted and were terminated; the Yaghis were farmers, not fighters. They ran for their life with nothing but the clothes they wore and whatever they managed to carry on their shoulders. Some headed south to Gaza and Egypt, some north to Lebanon, and the rest east to modern-day West Bank, which at the time was part of Palestine. But for the fleeing Yaghi family, the West Bank might as well have been another country, as most of them had never visited the region.

Over the following ten years, the Yaghi family was humiliated and suffered deeply by living as nomads in refugee camps with no work or security prospects. Their temporary housing entailed tin-roofed shacks. That was a proud and prominent family that now endured both embarrassment and harassment from their new neighbors.

Villagers in the West Bank ridiculed them for being too quick to flee their land and not fight the invading Israelis. They used to mock the Yaghis and chant, "The minute they heard the knocking, they ran away," insinuating they were cowards. Those West Bank villagers didn't understand the Yaghis' predicament, that they were simple citrus farmers, not warriors. Besides, how could they have fought a mighty army with heavy equipment and international backing? The only firearms the Yaghis owned were antiquated guns meant for protection from coyotes and hyenas, not combat.

In any case, they withstood all those jokes and ridicule for the better part of a decade, until they found a permanent home. In 1959, my maternal grandfather, the patriarch of the family, decided to move the Yaghi family to Amman, Jordan. He was told by men who traveled before him that in Jordan there was peace and respect. Jordan has since been the family's proud permanent home country. For my grandfather, he thought Amman was the best option for the family because it was across the Jordan River and close enough to return to the homeland when the political situation improved. At least that was his thinking. Little did he know there would never be a return to Palestine and he would never see those citrus orchards again, not in his time or my mother's.

During the transition period, before they settled in Jordan, my mother was married in the refugee camp to a gentleman six years her senior. However, she was only nineteen years old and knew as much about life as she knew about basic reading and writing: nothing. That was the start of a lifetime of suffering. But what to do? Such is life! "Whatever God gives you is good and a blessing" was her popular reminder of how to approach life.

A year after marriage, she gave birth to her first child, a baby boy. He was the first of eight children born over the years: five boys and three girls, all in the span of fifteen years. Imagine the level of pain of bearing eight children, physically as well as mentally, without the luxury of a maid or even financial comfort. Over the subsequent fifty years, my mother worked tirelessly to ensure each one of her children had great opportunities to succeed. She never grumbled or made any of us feel as if we were underprivileged.

My mom made a promise that none of her children would suffer the way she did. She made that promise to herself and to God, who she prayed to endlessly. It was that determination that grounded all her work. "What God gives you is good and a blessing" was a reminder to her kids to appreciate even the smallest things in life and a reminder of her spirituality and optimistic approach to life.

Speaking of spirituality, her relationship with God was unbelievably strong and unwavering. My mother lived her entire life as a God-fearing and loving devout Muslim. It was always that way, ever since she was a little girl. Her dad and mom prayed daily, and she was the same. It was her most defining relationship and her top priority, the only thing to supersede her children. She prayed every occasion she had, much more than the compulsory five times a day. However, and despite her devotion, my mom was also open-minded and moderate. She never forced her children to follow her steps and pray five times day; rather she encouraged them and educated them on the benefits of prayer. She left it to her children to make their own decisions. Some grew up more devout than others, and she was OK with that.

She herself prayed often and every day. She prayed so much that she would often fall asleep at night in the middle of her evening prayers. Moreover, she was never big on sleep, so she would wake up in the middle of night and pray, sometimes until sunrise, when she would get up and start her daily household management routines. When done with chores, although she had a TV and a radio, she rarely turned on either for entertainment, preferring to spend her free time either resting or praying.

My mom's most favorite prayer was the Quran's first *surat*, "Al Fateha" (the opening chapter), which reads,

> In the name of God, the infinitely Compassionate
>   and Merciful
> Praise be to God, Lord of all the worlds
> The Compassionate, the Merciful. Ruler on the Day
>   of Reckoning
> You alone do we worship, and You alone do we ask
>   for help
> Guide us on the straight path
> the path of those who have received your grace
> not the path of those who have brought down wrath,
>   nor of those who wander astray.

This particular prayer is an expression of gratitude and contentment, acknowledgment of being a small part of a bigger design, goal setting, and a search for guidance. It was her daily reminder of the bigger picture and a reference point, which inspired her to focus on accomplishing the family's goals. She would repeat this prayer while working, when relaxing in the garden, and even during the few rare occasions when she turned the TV on. She would cite it in her heart and diligently every single night before going to sleep.

Her spiritual connection was so strong that when she died in 2012, it was the peaceful death she had hoped for, quietly and following a midmorning prayer. Indeed, she was blessed. Throughout our adult lives, my siblings would often call on our mother to pray for us, especially ahead of a big business decision, a job interview, or an important business trip. I cannot recall a single important decision in my life where she was not consulted. It was part of our due diligence process. All of us felt her prayers were always answered because of her sufferings in life. Her spirituality was the foundation for her strong values and virtues. It was the main driver of her belief, in the ability to accomplish hefty goals.

As a wife, my mother had to take charge of the house affairs because my father was always working either out of the country or a great distance away from where we lived. As a household head, she was as tough as nails, firm in decision-making, and always leveraging her experience and the hands-on knowledge she gained working alongside my grandfather. She was always in planning mode and recalibrating her affairs against those plans. In hindsight, my mother fundamentally managed her family affairs with similar precision a CEO leads their organization. My mother had a bold vision for the family (her enterprise) and was laser focused on that target her entire life. She had rules and regulations we adhered to, and she had roles and responsibilities for each of her children. She established routines to ensure we were all on target with our performance. She inspired all of us every single day to be the best we can be and to believe in our ability to overcome all odds.

So what was her secret? How did this magnificent, uneducated, untrained mother manage her family of eight children toward accomplishing the hefty goal of succeeding in everything they did and become the most accomplished group of boys and girls? What rules did she follow? What leadership qualities did she have that enabled her to lead successfully? What was her motivation for doing all this?

As I observed my mother later in my adult life, and as I thought of all the accomplishments she achieved over her lifetime, it became evident that four qualities defined this woman more than anything else. Four behaviors that exemplified her leadership style are the following:

- passion
- planning
- persistence
- perpetual optimism

Now I know what you might be thinking, *Why not title the book 4 P's of Something?* The reality is I wanted the title to be true to the core idea of the book: leadership lessons from the most unexpected source. An illiterate mom who compensated for her limitations with unparalleled drive and commitment.

Sometimes we learn the greatest lessons when least expect. Haven't we all been taught a lesson or two in selflessness from a youngster who shares their lunch with a classmate or an elderly gentleman who gives up his train seat to a young lady? I got my formal higher education from universities in the United States and United Kingdom, but my proudest education I acquired at home, from my mother.

My mother taught me the greatest, most fact-based, and most effective lessons in leadership. Learning that shaped the individual and corporate executive I have become. Yet my mother, my ultimate teacher, was illiterate!

INTRODUCTION

My mom never got any formal education, so she never read any leadership or business management books. She never watched business shows on TV, nor did she ever ask us to teach her basic business concepts. Her personal style of leadership was self-created. It evolved over the years and certainly became more refined later on as she had more children and got more practice.

The fundamental belief in my mom's head was that her family was her proud investment and she would do her utmost to ensure this investment paid off, for the children and not her. This was her top priority, and she did the impossible to see her plans through to her destination. Her investment decisions, every major expenditure, and every acquisition or significant purchase—all of it was grounded in this central belief.

She was working toward one central objective her entire life: *inspire her children to become the most successful group of individuals in the whole extended Yaghi family.* This was her way of ensuring history never repeated itself. Her way of providing the children a much better life than the one she herself had had. This was not an easy task, given the roots of this successful family and the abundances of high achievers.

Even in beautiful Jordan, the Yaghis persevered and found success, with many family members building enterprises in construction, real estate, trading, and other ventures. The Yaghis also had households with children who became successful educators at all levels. However, my mother wanted to outperform all of them. She wanted her children to be become the best of the best, the most successful group; it was indeed an aberration. Success to my mother was not measured by materialistic standards, as many sought, but by education (who attained the highest levels) and being the best in respective fields (self-leadership). Her performance metric for this was percentage of household's children with post graduate degrees. The objective my mother set for herself was 100%, a high and unprecedented standard for a family of refugees. That was my mother's precise thought process, and that was what shaped her vision for the entire household (i.e., her family of eight children becoming the most successful at their respective fields). A proclamation that she proudly achieved against all odds and a powerful demonstration to the world how being poor, under resourced, and underprivileged is not a barrier to success. Given the right leadership qualities, those same barriers can be turned into powerful assets.

Over the years, watching my mom operate her family's business was akin to the management approach I was experiencing at my Fortune 100 employers. I couldn't help but notice the parallels within my two worlds: the family run by an incredibly determined illiterate mother and the world-class organizations run by well-educated corporate leaders. In fact, I would even argue one of my former employers, a large multinational company, failed miserably in areas where my mom succeeded, and they could have benefitted from some of her business acumen. That company faced a major transshipment issue in one of its biggest markets. An official distributor of its confectionaries line knowingly sold and shipped product outside its designated, and contractual, territory. That's a clear violation of distribution terms. Due to the laissez-faire leadership of the parent company, the issue was never addressed in a timely manner and later created instability in the market, in addition to disturbing market prices.

I parallel this situation to how my mom handled a similar situation in the mid-1970s, when my eldest brother was in high school. A distant uncle, a businessman who also owned the largest construction supplies company in the area, secretly propositioned my brother with an afterschool part-time job at one of his stores. "A way to earn some much-needed money," he told my brother. Unfortunately, when my mother learned of this offer, she unequivocally rejected it and warned my brother about being distracted from his schoolwork. Her follow-up action was decisive and timely. She was masterful at problem-solving. She interpreted the afterschool job offer was a cheap shot at humiliating her family, an insinuation that due to our poor financial position, the uncle's gesture was an unwarranted charitable contribution. If accepted, she would have shown weakness and vulnerability. Rather, my mother addressed the situation immediately and went for a meeting with the uncle. No need to call ahead or make an appointment; she just showed up at his office and asked for a private meeting. She articulated her case for turning down the offer and suggested to him leaving all her kids alone. Her argument was threefold.

1. Do not interfere and leave her son alone as his focus should be on schoolwork and studying, not some meaningless job. She emphasized the importance of school and education to her teenage son. So working after school was a distraction and his grades would have suffered.

2. If the job offer was intended as financial help for the family, then she was in no need for charity. She clarified that her family was self-sufficient and had everything they needed. She restated to my uncle and told him, "We in fact have more than we need." In truth though, we barely had enough to keep my brothers and sisters satisfied, but she had to project strength and confidence.

3. All her other children were off-limits and in the same boat as their eldest, focused on schoolwork and nothing else. She wanted my uncle (her own cousin) to not approach any of the other children.

She articulated this to my uncle and stormed out of his office refusing any of the customary Middle Eastern social gratuities like tea or coffee, as another sign of determination. Shocked and disbelieving were the least descriptions of his reaction. He was an important business figure in the community and strangers sought him out for help. That was the end of it. Never again were any of her children approached by that man with such part-time work offers. Her timely and firm response was the key to her effective problem-solving mindset.

Her formula for successfully managing a family of eight children and leading them to maximize their personal potential was approached with the same focus and determination. Four main leadership qualities defined my mother that I watched her exemplify day in and day out. To her, it was her way of life, her own manifesto for growth, if you will. At the same time, as I reflect on my professional career with the likes of global giants Coca-Cola, Gillette, and Kimberly-Clark, I can't help but notice the parallels between the two worlds. The leadership behavior I experienced and developed with those corporate giants is not vastly different from the leadership behavior my mom exhibited. Those leadership qualities are what defined this illiterate woman, and I call them the four P's of leadership.

Those four lessons apply to managing big and small corporations, for-profit and nonprofit organizations, and in my case, my mother applied them to manage her family. In the following chapters, we will dive deeper into each leadership quality and learn how an illiterate mother mastered all of them with unmatched precision.

We'll also parallel my personal experience with those from my corporate experience. As a reminder, unknown to her, this woman was applying a high-level business mindset to managing her family's affairs, without the benefits of a formal education or the complicated algorithms.

Those four principles my mother led with can work for you as well. The results tell the whole story. My mother's destination of building the most successful family was finally realized when in 2007, exactly fifty years after the birth of her first child, her youngest offspring got a teaching position at Kennesaw State University. It was as if her last cycle of investment just paid out in full. When it was all said and done, my mother was proud of all her accomplishments. Her eight boys and girls represented a true testament to high academic achievement with a selection of degrees—four doctorates and four master's degrees to be exact. Each one of her children has leveraged academics to pursue successful careers, and they now include

- a college dean at a major university
- a chief information officer at a leading company
- a head of global customers across a large part of the world
- a head of retail banking at a major regional bank
- a university professor
- a registered nurse and educator
- a high school teacher
- an elementary school teacher

Certainly, this is quite an accomplishment by one visionary mother, one brilliant leader, who never allowed her illiteracy to handicap her ability to lead and dream big. The accomplishments of those eight individuals are not only her proud personal achievements but also the culmination of a perfectly executed business plan. Like a baseball pitcher throwing a perfect game: no hits, no walks, and no errors. My mother's plan came together as she had envisioned, and she succeeded in achieving her lifelong dream of developing the most successful family, from top to bottom.

That is a substantiation of the power of those four leadership qualities. That passion, planning, persistence, and high sense of perpetual optimism combined led to excellence. The same leadership qualities companies seek in their leaders, my mother mastered without attending business school or any school for that matter.

Now let's look into how this illiterate mother applied those four P's of leadership and draw parallels from the business world.

1

PASSION

The ancient Greeks' word for passion was *pasckho,* meaning "to suffer." Suffering for the sake of what you love and care about. Suffering for your dreams and what you aspire to achieve. There's no passion without suffering and no suffering without passion. This particular dimension of passion is possibly more relevant today given the advent and convenience of technology, which has simplified a lot of our daily routines but may have also complicated the essence of suffering.

Take political campaigning as an example. Traditionally a challenging process to the mind and body, today it is made easier with technology and especially social media. You can reach millions of followers with the push of a button. In the past, it was the norm for political candidates to tour the country on a bus or train, speaking to potential voters and promoting their political agenda. The physical suffering of time and energy has been reduced by the use of new digital tools. Meanwhile, mental suffering is still there, and passionate candidates stress over their route to victory until the mission is accomplished.

Whether passion is applied in the personal or business sense, suffering is at the heart of it. The epitome of passion is the suffering in the name of something or someone you profoundly care for or love. Passion is enduring more agony, more pain, and more hurt than others, making the person more driven, and that more than likely leads to success. Marathon runners agonize over twenty-five miles and overcome various unforeseen elements like weather, road conditions, cramps, and exhaustion in pursuit of their passion. Similarly, race car drivers suffer, sometimes for up to 250 miles. They endure fatigue, heat exhaustion, and the prospects of crashing at high speed, all in the name of passion for their favorite sport.

The late, great Nelson Mandela had a well-articulated perspective on passion when he said, "Everyone can rise above their circumstances and achieve success if they are passionate about and dedicated to what they do." History will forever recognize Mr. Mandela as a passionate leader who spent a large part of life suffering while fighting for civil liberty.

In business, passion is an important quality in any leader. It's what powers them to inspire their people, to lead by example, and achieve exceptional results. It is the core of what differentiates them. It is likely the one quality many leaders activate to fuel their great sense of purpose. Some people will even argue that in business, PQ (passion quotient) is more important than IQ (intelligence quotient), and my practical experience leads me to agree. I would take a passionate employee with the right set of work ethics and track record any day over an employee who brings high grades or an elite college degree but lacks the motivation to go over and above the call of duty. You can't teach passion.

There are many passionate leaders in today's corporate world, and certainly people like Bill Gates, Sir Richard Branson, Warren

Buffet, Elon Musk, and Jeff Bezos are on top of any list. Passion is one quality that separates those leaders from any crowd and allows them to inspire people in ways others couldn't. They have inspired investors to make billion-dollar decisions, attracted and assembled support for philanthropic causes, and led their respective organizations to new heights. They possess other qualities, of course, but passion stands out because you see it every time they speak and in everything they do. Warren Buffet donated more than $2 billion to the Bill & Melinda Gates Foundation because of his passion for the foundation's work on improving health and reducing poverty in Africa. In fact, he made his plans public when he announced intentions to donate his entire wealth to various charitable organizations. That is passion for philanthropy, for giving back to the community, and for leaving a positive mark on the world. Another example is Ted Turner, who in the 1990s gifted the United Nations $1 billion, which at the time was the largest charitable gift ever to that organization. It reflected his passion for the work of the United Nations. That donation helped create the UN Foundation, and he was personally involved in raising millions more from other billionaires. That is passion!

In 2010 Coca-Cola chairman Muhtar Kent hosted the esteemed Ursula Burns, Xerox CEO, at the company's world headquarters in Atlanta, Georgia. It was part of a leadership series the company organized, and I was fortunate to have been in attendance at this event. She is dynamic and wise, and she engaged all of us with ease. I still carry, to this day, the pocket notepad with my key learnings from that visit. During the Q&A portion of the event, Ursula was asked the tough question "What is the role of a CEO?" She outlined three things every chief executive officer should focus on in order to lead a successful organization.

1. Recruit the right leadership team. It ensures organizational stability and strengthens the executive bench. When CEOs

recruit high-integrity direct reports, each of them will naturally hire high-integrity people like themselves for the next leadership level and so forth. That trickle effect will have a hugely broad and positive effect on the organization. While the premise of such a top-down approach may seem obvious, the reality is far from it, and many corporations struggle to find senior leaders who implement this approach. In fact, as part of my doctoral research, I interviewed a number of senior executives, including C-level leaders, who called out favoritism and cronyism at their workplace. It was this type of toxic behavior that led to their eventual voluntarily departure.

2. Set a vision for the company. Naturally, every chief executive should have a vision for their organization, a destination everyone could drive toward. The challenge is to have a clear vision and to articulate it in such a way that every employee buys into it. But not many CEOs communicate their vision to the masses in a succinct and relatable manner. Ursula Burns said this was key to her success because a vision "allows everyone to know your destination, which way to row, so to speak." Without a clear vision, the whole organization will lose sight of the essential purpose of its existence.

3. Inspire the people. Ursula Burns explained to us how as CEO she always traveled to all her company office locations in order to talk with and inspire associates. I recall during this talk that Muhtar Kent chimed in, "The ivory tower is the wrong place from which to watch the street." Clarifying that CEOs need to be in the field, where value is created, to get a great perspective and feel the pulse of their organization. Inspiring people for a CEO takes on a wide spectrum, especially given the range of stakeholders they have to manage. Internal stakeholders include employees, leadership

team, and board of directors, while external stakeholders is an even wider group and could include investors, customers, vendor partners, financial analysts, government officials, and many others. Chief executives have to influence and inspire all those internal and external constituents in the pursuit of attaining organizational success.

Therefore, passion is the fuel that powers leaders, such as Ursula Burns and Muhtar Kent, to excel in their respective businesses. If you speak to any former Xerox or Coca-Cola associate, passion is more than likely to be mentioned as one of those leaders' greatest qualities.

Passion is also what powered my mom toward her own greatness, despite her lack of formal education. Her passion was her family, the five boys and three girls that she bore—the one and only thing (besides her spirituality) she cared about for her entire lifetime. Her passion was for seeing those children maximize their potential and succeed. Her personal commitment to such a vision was profound. She sacrificed so much of her life and suffered for decades in order to provide to her family and drive toward accomplishing her main objective, making her family the most successful group of high-caliber individuals. I witnessed her suffering firsthand as a child and later as an adult and successful corporate executive. A few of her life sufferings are the following:

1. Dependence on others. Lacking basic education and the ability to read and write made my mom depend on others, which hindered her leadership work—something she immensely despised. Imagine the hurt and mental pain she endured every time she needed to sign a document or go somewhere, for example. It was a reminder of her misfortune, but also she accepted the suffering and used it as motivation to improve. Much later in her life, she would overcome that

shortcoming with the help of her kids, and she learned very basic reading and writing.

2. Poverty. Since she lived poor for the better part of two decades, my mom was stripped of the ability to provide her children with many of life's basic necessities. Meanwhile, her siblings had traveled overseas to get higher degrees. Two of her brothers came to the United States and one went to Spain. One became a pediatrician, another a university professor, and the third one a businessman. Meanwhile, her three sisters went on to become teachers. All her siblings enjoyed prospering professional careers except for her. My mom was the Lone Ranger, the one to never sit in a classroom, the one who paid a hefty price for her unfortunate circumstances.

3. Small house. After living as a refugee for close to a decade, and following her marriage, my mom spent the better part of twenty years crammed in a small two-bedroom apartment with one bathroom. It meant the rooms were multifunctional. One room was used as a bedroom and storage, and the other was used as a family room where we studied and played. "At least we don't have to pay anyone rent," she used to say. Later in life, my mom would save enough money to gradually expand that two-bedroom apartment into a four-story residential tower. A major accomplishment in of itself for this dynamic mother.

4. Large family. With eight mouths to feed, everything was a struggle: the daily house chores, the cooking, the clothing, etc. With most of the children two years apart, my mom was always caring for a baby in the house. I remember when she would make fried battered vegetables, a favorite childhood dish, we would sit down waiting for the food. As soon as she took a patch out of the fryer, the food would be gone in seconds, as each of the eight children grabbed a piece. By

the time she was done cooking, there would often be little to nothing for herself.

Despite the hardship, my mom's passion for success never relented. It inspired her to overcome obstacles in more than one way. Here're a few examples:

1. Her passion gave her perspective and guided her through tough years of a difficult marriage but kept her focused on the children, her pride and joy and her top priority in life. Whenever she was mentally drained of the constant marital problems, she reminded herself of the big picture, sacrificing her own happiness for her children's future.

2. Her passion helped her identify and differentiate between her allies and nemeses. While she competed with what essentially were her cousins and other Yaghi households, my mother viewed most of them as competition and a risk to her long-term family plan. Interestingly, but not surprisingly now that I think about it, her allies were relatives who shared similar values and beliefs. They were few, but those allies were also her support group and they understood what she was doing through and the sacrifices she was making. One of the group members was a big brother who helped her eldest son with his studies and inspired them to excel scholastically and be the first in the family to attend a university—the best university in the country.

3. Most importantly, my mother's passion empowered her to see a greater purpose in life. Mainly, to persevere, beat all those odds, and to prove to the naysayers—and they were many—that despite her limited abilities, she was a winner. Winning was all she did. My mother's passion grounded her

outlook and empowered her to singularly laser focus on one goal: a successful and high-achieving family.

Channeling Passion

Is there such a thing as "too much passion?"

You heard the saying "Too much of anything is not good"? Indeed, too much passion is not good, but *only* if uncontrolled. If you don't control it and let is get out of hands, it is likely to return and cause damage. One aspect that distinguishes many successful leaders is their ability to channel their passion. Ted Turner is able to focus and channel his passion toward the planet. Nelson Mandela toward racial and social justice, Sir Richard Branson toward space exploration, and Michael Jordan toward basketball perfection. All of those individuals mastered the art of compartmentalizing passion in order to stay focused and deliver better results.

Uncontrolled and unchanneled passion makes us more vulnerable and more susceptible to mistakes. Emotions take over common sense and rational decisions become more questionable. Sports fans in particular tend to be notorious for uncontrolled passions. With so much passion to their team, some will engage in physical altercations with fans of opposing teams. Some will go as far as avoiding wearing any clothing with the team colors of their archrivals. Some people will go as far as severing family ties if those ties clashed with the individual's personal preferences. In college, I had a classmate who vehemently opposed dating and marrying someone from division rivals. The worst example of uncontrolled passion from recent memory could be that University of Alabama football die-hard fan pouring herbicide and poisoning two oak trees more than a hundred years old at the campus of their in-state archival, Auburn University. Those trees are part of Auburn University's history and legend. It's a campus landmark where students celebrated their team's wins and milestones, so there is a strong historical connection to both the school and its athletics. Violating the trees and campus was unfathomable, but it was fueled by one man's uncontrolled passion his football team.

Of course, the most famous example of uncontrolled passion is Romeo in Shakespeare's fictional masterpiece. Romeo's passion for Juliet clouded his thinking and judgment, which led him to killing himself while thinking his lover had died, when in fact she was only pretending and was actually waiting for him to come and rescue her. It could be said that Romeo had too much passion and was unable to control it.

Foundation of Passion

There is no empirical evidence to validate the origins of passion. It is unclear whether passionate people are genetically wired that way or develop such a unique personal attribute during the journey of life, possibly after experiencing life-changing events. Events that could have left a profound impact on the individual, good or bad. When one develops a successful track record at a job or professions, passion is expected to be part of the mix.

Passion could also develop overtime, through hardship, strong will, or just plain experience. Tennis superstar Serena Williams trains so hard throughout the year because of her quest to become the best player of all time. She remains passionate about her sport even after winning twenty-three majors, more than any other player in the modern era. Personally, I love soccer as a sport, but I developed a passion for coaching youth sports after getting involved with my daughter's soccer team. I later gained a coaching certificate and have coached her team for years.

I believe my mother developed her passion for success through hardship and adversity. She developed it as a young girl working the fields and doing house chores while her brothers and sisters went to get educated. She also developed it with the birth of her children, as the more children she birthed, the tougher life became and the more passion she developed for her family. The hardship of raising a large family with a monthly budget smaller than that of a normal couple is what infused my mom with passion for winning and success.

Genetics could also be a key factor in passion. Some people are definitely born with it and show their passion at an early stage, such as the toddler who plays the piano like a maestro or the nine-year-old computer genius who codes in multiple languages. Music figureheads, such as Mozart and Michael Jackson, were known as prodigies for their accomplishments at such an early age. Politics, sports, business, and music are just a few fields where genetics could be the source of passion. An insatiable love for politics runs deep. Genetics is apparent in families across a range of fields. Here're a few:

1. Politics: The Kennedys are one of America's premier political dynasties; the family has produced generations of savvy politicians. For the Kennedys, tragedy has accompanied their political fame, as a number of family members were assassinated. Another iconic American political family is the Bush family, led by former US president George H. W. with his two sons, George W. and Jeb. George W. is a former two-term president of the US as well as former governor of the state of Texas. Jeb Bush is a former state governor of Florida. Currently, one of Jeb's sons is also in politics as a Texas state official. Meanwhile, the Gandhis are the preeminent political dynasty in India with more than five generations carrying the Gandhi name.

2. Business: There are many families in this field. The Ford family, including Henry and his grandson Bill, and the Murdochs, with Robert and sons Lachlan and James, are two. Finally, the Waltons are another example with patriarch Sam starting the Wal-Mart empire and now his offspring Alice, Christy, and Jim are following his footsteps.

3. Sports: Genetics is at the heart of passion for several sports families, including tennis superstars Venus and her sister Serena; the Mannings with father, Archie, and sons Peyton and Eli, all playing football; the Earnhardts racing dynamic duo; and many more. Besides their bloodlines, those families have one other common feature. They all participated in the same sport. Now that's passion.

Can you see similarities among all those families? Across the many spectrums, passion for a specific cause was genetically passed on across generations.

Drivers of Passion

Suffering

Passionate people commonly suffer physical and mental pain in pursuit of their destination. Think of what most of the aforementioned dynasties endured on their pathway to success. The politicians with the long and hard hours of campaigning and fundraising, not to mention the agony of occasional defeats and personal tragedies. What about business dynasties whose founders built legacies for the ages? Future generations remain challenged by good standards their predecessors established. Certainly they suffered greatly in order to maintain those legacies and continue growing business. Then of course there are the sport heroes we all relate to who experience great physical suffering with long daily practice sessions, hard gym workouts, and then of course the actual games they have to play against similarly fierce competition. Their suffering is in the name of their passion for their sports and the fulfillment of lifetime goals.

It appears the Greeks had it right: it is difficult for passion to exist without pain and suffering. Certainly the popular adage "No pain, no gain" is spot-on, although passionate individuals control their passion. My oldest daughter, much like her grandmother, suffered in a different way in the spirit of pursuing her passion, tennis. Since the tender age of five, she endured years of physical and mental pain before becoming a promising junior USTA player. She suffered through hard personal training sessions, grueling weekly practice schedule, and endless out-of-town tournaments, some held during harsh Minnesota winters. Through it all, her passion for tennis drove her to persevere and excel at the sport she loved. When her friends were doing other things that seemed fun at the time, my daughter was polishing her game. She had to suffer mentally in order to become tougher physically.

Focus

The second driver of passion is focus, and highly passionate leaders are great at focusing and channeling their passion. They focus on a singular area where they station their energy and time to make a difference. Bill Gates, long retired from the business of Microsoft, and his ex-wife focused most of their energy on supporting the work of their foundation, Bill & Melinda Gates Foundation. Bill replaced his passion for Microsoft and computers with one for disease eradication in Africa. Whether it is polio, AIDS, or malaria, Mr. Gates is using his foundation, his connections, and his financial position to influence and inspire the production of drugs to fight those diseases. He is personally engaged and focused on that goal. Bill and his ex-wife certainly have the capacity and capability to engage in a wide range of other philanthropic opportunities, but their passion is focused and channeled on disease control.

My mother was focused on one goal: to see her eight children excel in their respective fields. She never lost sight of that destination, and she ensured all of us understood the relevance of achieving that mission. She contextualized how the mission benefited each of us individually. She constantly reminded me of how much I loved business and always reiterated her confidence that one day my dream would come true. Of course, she lived to see it materialize.

Personal Commitment

Another driver of passion is a deep personal commitment. Passionate people are often deeply involved in their business affairs and enjoy a great feel for the pulse of their organization. They understand that without personally being engaged and committed, business results will not be optimum and their path to success may be hindered.

Take the great film director Peter Jackson as an example. The cinematic works of this genius are well-document and recognized, but the maker of such Hollywood blockbusters as The Lord of the Rings trilogy and *King Kong* gets personally invested in every single one of his films. He summed it up when noting the reason for his success was his ability to make movies that he personally would like to watch. He makes movies for himself, not for the studio that hired him, the producers, or even the public. Using his personal preference as benchmark, he believes his stakeholders and general public will follow a similar choice and like the movies he likes. Mr. Jackson's personal commitment to producing great films is profound.

My mother was deeply committed to her mission and helping her children achieve their personal goals. She fully comprehended that collectively it was greater than the sum of the parts. She taught each of us to mentor our younger siblings and assigned us roles and responsibilities. When my oldest sibling sought to come to the United States and complete his higher education, my mother told him not to worry about the money and she would go on to secure the needed funds for him to attend the University of Kansas. Later, she would repeat the same process with my older brother and sister, as well as my own journey. Her personal commitment was clearly focused on one goal.

Sacrifice

The fourth and final driver of success is sacrifice. Passionate people make voluntary sacrifices during their journey toward mission accomplishment. Child prodigies often reflect on their younger years and discuss missing out on common activities that every child experiences. Tiger Woods sacrificed his childhood and some might argue part of his adulthood in the name of golf. His pursuit of being the best golfer in the world superseded everything else he did. When recovering from severe back injuries, Tiger sacrificed playing time and competing for the record books in order to rest and return stronger. In 2019, he won his fifth Masters Tournament, after being away from the game for two years. Other sacrifices are well-documented, including his practice habits. Tiger spent years in the habit of going to the driving range and hitting over 1,000 golf balls after every round of major tournaments. When other golfers were resting or having fun, Tiger Woods was sacrificing all of that in order to perfect his game.

When I coached youth soccer, those kids taught me lessons about passion. I had about ten girls on each of my teams, and although their ages ranged between six and ten, some of those girls demonstrated amazing passion for the sport, even at that tender age. So I developed the ability to recognize those types of passionate young girls almost from the first practice session. It would be clear from day one the girls who played only to please their parents and those girls who had the drive to play their beloved sport. Indeed, passionate players consistently arrived on time to practice and stayed late afterward to work on certain skills. Those girls stood out and hustled both on and off the field. They were the same ones who hated being subbed because they wanted to play all ninety minutes. Once identified, my focus shifted to building their skill set, and I recognized their passionate commitment to play. Much like good soccer coaches, great business leaders must recognize those passionate individuals in their organizations and work to harness that passion, such that it permeates throughout the entire organization and nurtures an effective culture.

My mother was more passionate about her family than any other mother I ever knew. It powered her every action and fueled her energy. Passion helped her withstand some of the hardest suffering a mother could ever dream of facing. Her family was the one subject she talked about most often, proudly reciting the most recent or appropriate personal achievements of her eight children. Moreover, my mother's passion fueled her focus and she literarily ignored anything else. She did not care whether she stayed up all night in order for a son or daughter to study or complete an assignment. She also did not care if she went hungry all day. As long as her children finished their schoolwork and had food to eat, everything else was immaterial to my mother. She focused on them and the vision she set out to achieve (i.e., creating the most accomplished group of children among the Yaghi family).

Her commitment to her family was personal. Determined to accomplish the mission regardless of many obstacles, her personal commitment to see the mission came to fruition regardless of the economic hardship she faced. And finally, it was her passion for her family that inspired her to spend a lifetime of sacrifice for the greater cause. She sacrificed her happiness, her relations with her own siblings, and even her well-being for the benefit of seeing her children succeed and achieve their individual goals. My mother's passion was her family.

Closing Thought

Passion is an incredible quality of leaders and might be the greatest attribute to drive success. However, it is plausible for passion to be a bad leadership quality at the same time. The difference between the two is the leader's own ability to control and channel that passion toward a meaningful goal that benefits the broader ecosystem. If the passion scale tilts one way or the other, it is likely to have negative effect on the individual and their organization, because too much uncontrolled passion is not wise. Great leaders have a talent for balancing that scale.

2

PLANNING

The definition of planning is to think ahead and prepare for what may lay ahead, vis-a-vis your desired goals. It is about anticipating the path forward and being well-positioned to manage the ups and downs. Planning is having a blueprint for accomplishing organizational goals and objectives.

At the heart of it, planning is a very streamlined and highly scientific approach that follows a tight critical path and incorporates specific milestones and check-ins that serve great purpose. Even senior-level meetings and reviews follow a precise schedule to ensure alignment and gain final approval on the business plan document.

A business plan is the main outcome of the planning process. An effective plan outlines how results will be delivered and what resources are needed to accomplish such a plan. In business and especially at successful organizations, planning is a complex, highly orchestrated iterative process led by a dedicated strategy team. Good planning processes culminate with a presentation to senior leadership or the executive committee for review and approval.

Sometimes, plans are rejected for any number of reasons, including wrong assumptions, excessively conservative or aggressive growth estimates, etc. In such situations, plans are typically revised and resubmitted to top leadership for final approval. Once approved, the next phase is implementation and putting critical elements into action within the agreed parameters.

Like clockwork, planning should be an ongoing process, essentially an iterative articulation of the critical work needed to achieve sustainable growth. The majority of well-established and efficiently managed organizations do some type of formal business planning, but not everyone does it with consistency and precision. I have worked with companies where strategic planning never stops, evolving with periodic tweaks and updates. Annual business planning for some starts as early as April of the calendar year and goes through an elaborate series of strategy sessions, consumer research, industry guest speakers, and rigorous financial analysis.

Some companies kick off their business planning cycle later in the year, due primarily to the nature of their industry. The restaurant industry is one that tends to start late because it is a heavily franchised industry and operators prefer to wait until the back half of year for a more accurate read on the actual business performance. Honestly, there is no right or wrong approach because it all depends on factors like industry norms, organization size, and type. What is worth reiterating is the imperative need to have a planning process in place and for your methodology to be cross-functional and well thought out.

Planning for my mom was an ongoing process too, always moving things around while looking ahead for any opportunities or potential headwind. Of course, not as organized and intricate as a professional business, but it was strikingly well thought out. Planning her house affairs was more seasonal moves and adjustments, especially since cash flow was scarce. For my mother, the planning cycle centered around the school year because there were eight children going to different levels of school. For context, when the eldest son was attending university, her youngest was just starting elementary school. They had different needs, and resource allocation was key for my mother.

Months before the school year started, my mom would have already figured out all the supplies and material her children would need. Uniforms, stationery, school supplies, and of course fees. However, it was more than what to buy and where to source the material. It was rather how to generate enough money to be in a position to purchase all those goods when the time was right. If she calculated $500 was needed at the start of the following school year, she planned backward and outlined where that money was going to come from. With cash flow driving all her decisions, it was the most important consideration for my mother. She did not have the luxury of a savings account to pull from, and her emergency fund was largely nonliquid assets. Later in life, she would use some of her savings to buy gold as a safety nest. If there was going to be a shortfall, other expenditures would be cut. Before the school year started in the fall, my mother would spend her springs and summers filling her food supply pipelines and stocking her pantry. She would buy seasonal food in bulk to dry and pickle for the winter. Of course, she did the same with winter food and extended seasonal bounty well into other seasons.

However, to contextualize my mother's planning approach in a more relative business context, her methodology resembled these five main steps:

- situational assessment
- opportunity assessment
- goals and objective setting
- systems alignment

- final sign-off

Planning Process Step 1: Situational Assessment

The Situational Assessment, often referred to as SWOT (Strengths, Weaknesses, Opportunities, and Threats) is foundational and absolutely the most important piece of any viable planning process. It is an evaluation of the operating environment, both internally and externally. The equivalent of an annual medical checkup that must be thorough, it is an honest review of past performances and an outlook on future spaces where the organization may want to play. It is where you identify your growth corridors and your competitive landscape.

The standard SWOT breaks into four key buckets; each is equally critical to the planning process, and each plays a role in developing a great assessment of the current situation. You start off looking internally at the forces that drive your business and brands, then shift your outlook externally at the forces that influence your business and brand. Failing to perform an accurate situational assessment puts your entire business plan at risk and in serious jeopardy.

Strengths

The first step in the SWOT is to complete an internal evaluation, a deep dive, of what makes you and your organization strong. This is the core of who you are and what you do best. It's your identity that others recognize and give you credit for. Strengths differentiate your brand from others, making you unique and the stuff that you've become known for over the years. Your strengths are your competitive edge against others and what drives people to seek you out.

Coca-Cola, for example, has been operating around the world for over 130 years, and some of the company's strengths may include the following:

- iconic Spenserian script
- contour-shaped glass bottle
- operating in over two hundred countries worldwide
- the brand's secret recipe

That is what distinguishes Coca-Cola as the leading soft drink company in the world and most valued brand in the consumer packaged-goods industry. Similarly, this is one of those things that makes it undeniably difficult for other beverage companies to replicate. Meanwhile, Pepsi, primary competitor for more than seventy years, has their own set of strengths that differentiates them from others. One of their biggest strengths is a diverse snack and food portfolio with leading brands like Frito Lay and Quaker. Having this range of food and drink products helps the company deliver greater value to their customers and stakeholders.

As the first step in the situational assessment, you should look deep inside and identify those differentiators that empower your brand identity and make you stronger than the competition. Strengths could be different things to different organizations and could be both tangible and intangible assets you possess. People, technology, or even advertising slogans are potential strengths.

Weaknesses

Once strengths have been identified, the other part of your internal assessment is understanding your weaknesses. You cannot consider what makes you stronger without understanding what makes you weaker and slows you down. Think hard and candidly about yourself/your organization and identify those forces that hamper your ability to grow and the things you wish you excelled at. That is not any easy task because we're all humans, and most do not want to admit their shortcomings, especially entrepreneurs who spend time and money building their brands. That being the case, it is always a good idea to seek input on your weaknesses from others who are outside your organization. Ask customers, suppliers, partners, and investors about your flaws. It's 360-degree assessment of your brand and organization.

When conducting this step of SWOT analysis and thinking of your system weaknesses, keep in mind that much like strengths, weaknesses are a checkup of your internal business. This has nothing to do with the other players in your field or the marketplace. It is not the competition that make you weak. It might be your own deficiencies that do, so it's all on you, whether you want to admit it or not. External factors are responsible for your lack of international routes if you are an airline or logistics company, for example. Weaknesses must not be viewed negatively because this is your chance to address such shortcomings, especially if you are honest with your assessment.

Opportunities

Business and life in general are constantly evolving, and so are consumer needs, albeit the latter at a much faster pace. The competitive landscape also evolves, and as an organizational leader, you have to relentlessly be aware of what's happening in the marketplace. Such change brings vast opportunities for your company and brands. As such, in the situational assessment process, opportunities represent the white spaces your organization could exploit for growth. Where you aspire to take your brand, those things you would like to possibly acquire and the areas you could expand into.

Opportunities are fertile grounds for growth, provided the organizational resources exist to capture the incremental business. However, it is noteworthy to understand some of those opportunities are available to your competitors as well, so be judicious in identifying viability for you. What works for a competitor may not yield similar results for you, and the opposite is true of course. Opportunities have to align with your strengths, and there needs to be a strategic fit with the overall organizational destination.

Coca-Cola built its long, successful track record in the consumables industry on the foundation of its ubiquitous flagship brand and namesake. However, when changing consumer drinking habits became too defined, the company recognized that noncarbonated drinks was a key category for future growth. Subsequently, the company went on to build a portfolio of brands away from its core carbonated drinks and across a range of emerging categories, including water, juice, energy, and even dairy. While some of those brands were acquired, most were developed organically from within the company's own innovation center of excellence. In all cases, the new brands complemented the more established sparkling portfolio. For the most part, the new noncarbonated brands are either sold or delivered through the same supply chain system, hence the accretive value and operational efficiencies.

Threats

A business cannot operate effectively without a deep understanding of the macro forces that influence its operation. As such, the fourth and final step in the situational assessment (SWOT) process is an outline of those forces, the external factors that could threaten your ability to deliver the business plan. Those macro forces are naturally overarching and out of your control. They do affect the entire marketplace—you and competitors alike. However, you still have to account for them and recognize their potential threat. They are too important to ignore, and your business plan has to be adjusted accordingly.

For a company like Coca-Cola, which operates in over two hundred countries, a major threat is always foreign currency fluctuations. The company would need to account for that in their annual business planning cycle and track how changes in major currencies could impact revenues. Similarly, chain restaurant brands are heavily monitored by health agencies and as such, companies like McDonald's and Yum! recognize government health regulations as potential threats to be addressed. Some macro forces with potential threat to the restaurant industry include new caloric guidelines, excise taxes, scientific and regulatory standards, customs hikes, and even banning of some material. So if you operate in this industry, your annual business plan must account for such threats and clearly outline potential impact. Responding to caloric regulations, for example, a restaurant chain develops low- and no-calorie menu options, thus responding to shifts in eating habits and preempting negative revenue fall.

Much like the first two steps of the SWOT analysis are internally driven, those last two steps, opportunities and threats, are externally driven. There is little influence anyone can have on external factors, but a deep recognition and understanding of such those forces is imperative for the success of your business planning processes. Together, the four components of your situational assessment complement each other and provide a clear view of business. The typical output of this stage of planning is a one-page SWOT document.

My illiterate mother, despite her nonexistent professional experience, was very effective at doing self-assessments. Unknown to her what a SWOT is, she in essence applied similar tactics in her annual planning for the family. Her analysis for one of the years could have looked something like the chart below, focusing on the things that mattered the most. In subsequent years, she would go on to capture several of the opportunities outlined below, despite her many personal challenges. That's how masterful a planner she was.

Strengths	Weaknesses
- Leadership: With her at the helm, she was the enterprise's biggest asset. - Committed children: Each member of the team was on board with the long-range plan. - Real estate: We owned the land our tiny house was built on.	- Limited funding: Living on a tight budget for close to twenty years, she learned to survive. - Limited space: A two-bedroom house with eight children is tight by all standards. - No education: She could not read or write.
Opportunities	**Threats**
- Higher education: Each of the children could get a higher degree. - Real estate: Expanding on the house was expensive but a viable revenue growth option. - Revenue growth management: Leveraging resources to drive top line results.	- Food inflation: Price of basic goods was increasing year over year. - Geopolitics: Enduring the dynamic politics of the Middle East region.

Planning Process Step 2: Opportunity Assessment

The second step in the planning process is to further substantiate the growth levers identified in the SWOT as the highest leverage drivers. Opportunity assessment incorporates an evaluation and prioritization of those growth levers vis-a-vis the organization's current and long-term positions. Your evaluation must be honest and realistic. Overreach, and you could take the organization on a dangerous and challenging path, while underreaching may cost you dearly as you miss out on real prospects of growing your position in the marketplace.

Opportunity assessment must also consider the overall financial position of the organization and whether the adequate level of investment is available for making such overtures. If not, you may need incremental funding or a postponement of the initiative. The opportunity assessment process could be broken into two parts: opportunities and strengths.

Part 1: Matching the Opportunities with Your Strengths

Once you have identified the growth corridors for the upcoming operating period, each corridor must be studied in relation to your team or organizational strengths. It will ensure there is strong fit and alignment between what you excel at today and what you could be doing next year or years to come.

So if you are a dairy company and "entering the ice cream category" was identified as an opportunity in your SWOT, now you check to see if you have the needed frozen storage capabilities or logistical infrastructure. Without it, it will be impossible to supply products to clients, and in this particular case, the opportunity does not match the organizational strengths/realities. At this juncture, one of two decisions have to be made: set up storage facilities and supply chain logistics or remove "entering the ice cream category" from your opportunities consideration.

Similarly, if you are a chain restaurant company, maybe "home delivery" was identified as a strategic opportunity for growth during the SWOT analysis phase. In this case, this step of the planning process involves understanding if you need to have a few systems in place, things like the following:

- call center to receive and process delivery orders
- fleet of cars or motorbikes to deliver orders

- dedicated team of drivers
- geographical mapping software

If those resources above do not exist in your business today, it will be extremely difficult to enter such a new segment and be successful. Systems and resources have to be in place before you venture into a new business category. However, in some rare occasions, it is possible for someone to start a new growth corridor with limited resources. I personally have seen a restaurant operator launch home delivery services with only limited and at best primitive capabilities, hoping to "start slow" and learn as business progressed. Unfortunately, the move backfired and their venture failed miserably.

Output from this specific step in the opportunity assessment process is a list of the highest leverage and realistic opportunities that match the organizational culture, strengths, and needs. Of course, you would also expand on why each high-leverage opportunity is important to the organization.

A great illustration of applying this balanced approach is my good friend Greg Parker's use of technology in his chain of convenience stores. Greg is one of the most successful businessmen in Savannah, Georgia, and is widely considered an industry innovator. Among his business ventures, Greg owns and operates Parker's, the leading convenience retail chains in southeast Georgia, with a vision to be recognized as the preeminent small box retailer throughout the southern East Coast. Always a vocal thought leader, in the late 2000s, Greg identified technology-based consumer loyalty as a key growth opportunity for his business. At the time, it was white space that no one in his industry and in his operating area had penetrated. Given he was already running an advanced point of sale (POS) network, Greg understood the importance of technology and long positioned it as a distinctive competitive advantage. Leveraging that advantage, he developed and introduced a loyalty program that honored consumers with reward points for both fuel and in-store purchases. The new system was complex and required a lot of integration, but it allowed him to retain his strong consumer base and more importantly attracted new users, while at the same time, the new technology did not interfere or complicate his organizational structure. Today, Parker's is a thriving business enterprise of more than sixty Parker's Market and Parker's Fresh stores across the US Southeast.

My mom also managed this opportunity assessment phase very effectively. In her case, she understood that living in a two-bedroom house was not sustainable, especially with the increasing size of her household. She realized that building a second story on our house was a viable opportunity, given that she owned the land and the cost to build at the time (1970s) was reasonable. Over the span of a decade, she would go on to fulfill that opportunity and gradually expand our house by building not one but three additional stories, giving my mom more living space for all seven siblings as well as prospects of an incremental income stream.

Even with renting the newly built apartments, my mother's strategy was precise and articulate; she insisted on long-term leases only. She used to explain to us how the frequent turnover of tenants was not good business because it increased the upkeep and maintenance charge. Additionally, she advertised the new rental space through word of mouth, before the contractors were even done with their work, guaranteeing the units would generate revenue from day one.

Another opportunity my mother identified and leveraged to perfection was her investment strategy in gold. She recognized early on that a key imperative to delivering her vision was financial resources, which was absent for much of her life. Therefore, she identified gold as a long-term investment instrument with low risk and high potential returns. In order to strengthen her financial position, she started using whatever little savings she had from trading high-quality Syrian goats to buy gold coins. She didn't sell any of those coins unless there was a strategic need, like my eldest brother going off to the University of Kansas for graduate school or my second-eldest brother leaving Jordan to come of the US and attend college. My mother sold enough of her gold reserves to pay their first-semester tuition and expenses. She did not fund subsequent years of college because each of us had to work and generate our own income. To her, selling gold to pay for college expenses was a justifiable move as it aligned with her plan and overarching goals. Gold would become her top investment option and her top source of cash flow for years to follow.

Part 2: Defining Relevant Consumer/Market Insights

Once the highest-leverage opportunities are matched with the company's strengths, you now need research and insight to gain a deeper and better understanding of the consumer and market landscape for those very same growth opportunities. This is critical to the planning process because much of the opportunities at this stage are white space: unchartered territories with little knowledge on the inner working of each. But white space also means new consumers and new dynamics. Some generic market and consumer research is often readily available in the public domain, but you may have to conduct your own primary research specific to your category and brands. There are two reasons for conducting new research at this point: to validate fit between the opportunity and your organization or brands and to better understand the opportunity from your consumers' viewpoint.

The Coca-Cola Company is great at methodically and carefully conducting opportunity assessment. When launching a new beverage-dispensing platform known as Coca-Cola Freestyle in 2009, the company revealed to the public they had actually spent over six years developing and perfecting that new technology.

Clearly Coca-Cola Freestyle plays into what the company does better than anyone else, marketing nonalcoholic, ready-to-drink soft drinks. So that is where the fit between the growth opportunity and existing business was identified. Additional consumer research was done to understand how consumers felt about soft drink options and what they aspired to have in the future. The research provided valuable consumer insights to the company and validated the overall proposition for Coca-Cola Freestyle. Then, in complete confidence, several teams worked to apply the newly acquired insights to develop a dispensing platform that fulfilled consumer needs for variety and customization and reinforced the company's position as the most innovative and market-leading company in the beverage industry. They completely fulfilled the opportunity through a tight consumer viewpoint. Today, Coca-Cola Freestyle offers consumers more than 130 soft drinks and thousands of potential drink combinations.

My mother applied similar scientific opportunity assessment methodologies as Parker's and Coca-Cola, but of course without benefiting from any formal education or the luxury of having access to high-level consumer research. Let me illustrate with an in-depth example. In the early 1970s, my mother completed her opportunity assessment and identified "raising high-quality Syrian goats" as a growth and high-leverage opportunity. No, she wasn't a farmer, but she was a determined entrepreneur and a shrewd businessperson who was in pursuit of an audacious vision. Her thought process for identifying this strategic opportunity was fourfold.

1. Low entry cost: To my mother, setting up the business of raising breeding goats was affordable and easy. She only needed to start with one head and gradually build up her trip inventory. She limited her cash flow exposure and figured hat adding more goats as cash flow became more abundant allowed her to slowly ease into this new business venture,

learn the ins and outs of the trade, and later build it up into a competitive advantage.

2. Low maintenance cost: To my mother, feeding and maintaining those goats was reasonable. During the day, the trip of goats would be out grazing in the nearby pastures, and that was no cost to her. At home, the goats would feed on leftover vegetables. Cooking for eight kids necessitated purchasing a lot of produce, which also generated a lot of waste that became goat feed on a daily basis. My mom hated to throw away anything. For grazing, she did not hire anyone to help. She just had to convince one of her older sons to guide the animals out to the neighboring pastures and watch over them while they grazed. In the meanwhile, her instruction to the son was to do his school homework or read a book while watching over the goats.

3. High demand: To my mother, Jordan in the early 1970s was still a country of traditional Middle Eastern customs and habits. Rural life was the norm at the time, and in Jordan, Bedouin lifestyle was prevalent. One of those social norms was welcoming guests with a feast lunch or dinner—a feast that always consisted of a stuffed lamb or goat served over a sea of white rice. Therefore, demand for goat meat was high. Within this category (Syrian goats), the majority of the country's supply was imported and as such commanded a price premium. This particular breed had the highest quality, especially young goats aged six to twelve months, with tender and tasty meat. My mom recognized this opportunity and built a thriving goat-breeding business.

4. High margin: To my mother, the country's heavy demand for Syrian goats translated into a profitable opportunity. Her goats, grass-fed thoroughbreds, were rare quality and in high demand, which commanded above-average prices

and yielded high profits to her. At the time, it was her second-highest margin investment after gold.

Planning Process Step 3: Goals and Objective Setting

Every organization has goals and a set of objectives that support and justify their investment decision. Before getting into how to properly set goals and objectives, let us define those two terms and consider the differences between them, as they are sometimes used interchangeably. Goals are overarching destinations the organization plans to reach in the short or long term, while objectives are specific actions planned for a predetermined period of time.

Goals and objectives should be differentiated in the planning process. One is broad, extending multiple years, and the other is specific to a year or shorter window. One is loose with some flexibility, while the other is tight with little margin for error. Finally, goals articulate where the organization is heading, while objectives outline how that destination will be reached. Altogether, both goals and objectives should be aligned with the overall mission of the organization.

Let me illustrate with an example from motor racing. A typical Formula One or NASCAR team starts every racing season with a specific set of goals and objectives. One team's goals and objectives may look like this:

Goals	Objectives
Be the most accomplished racing team.	Win at least five races during the season.
Have the best crew team.	Run in top five for at least 75% of the season.
Be the most popular team.	Finish the season with zero penalties.

Looking at those goals above, it is unquestionable where this racing team wants to be. Each of those goals is broad and progressive and will energize the entire organization to be the best they can be. Collectively, those goals would set the overarching mindset of the management team. Moreover, they support the essence of what every car racing team aspires for: winning and being the best. Those goals are strategically aligned with the core values of a winning motor racing organization. You can see how those goals are broad and it may take a team many years to accomplish.

Goal setting must be in full concert with the organization's overall mission and core values. For example, Coca-Cola states a desire "to be our customers' best business partner," which is a goal that aligns with the company's overall mission of "[being] an active member of the communities where Coke operates."

Similarly, if your business mission is "to lead with heart and soul," then one fitting goal could be "to be in the top 10 percent quartile of "Best Places to Work" ranking. It is a great destination and one that is well-positioned against the overall mission. It is also broad enough to allow for effective objective setting.

How those various goals will be achieved is the main reason objective setting is an important step of the annual planning process. Objectives eliminate any confusion about what the team is trying to accomplish during the operating period and what the team must deliver in order to justify the resources being deployed. When setting objectives, remember results materialize over time in a series of events and milestones. You must also recognize that business conditions change and be prepared to pivot or alter your execution. Any business plan without tightly specified objectives is worthless and a recipe for failure.

That said, you have to set your objectives and communicate them to the entire organization in a timely manner. That's one reason I preferred to complete my planning early because it allowed my teams to be involved and understand what the game plan was. Additionally, that allows each team to build their own plans in sync with the team's.

Objective Setting

Let's focus now on how objectives are set. Objectives serve as a reference point to guide you and keep you on course toward achieving your goals. It's a point of closure or learning upon which you can toast your accomplishment or reflect on what you could have learned along the way.

A marathon has an end point. It is that point when the last runner has crossed the finish line, when a winner is proclaimed and runners celebrate their different personal accomplishments. The objectives for each one of those runners could vary to a large degree. Some may have a target time to hit, some a specific position on the pecking order. However, they all have one other objective: to finish the race. In soccer, lacrosse, hockey, basketball, and many other net sports, getting the ball or puck into that net is the objective of every play. Therefore, objectives are an end point to a particular journey.

The proficiency in objective setting varies from one individual to another and takes much trial and error to perfect this skill, so indeed it is both a science and art. The best objectives that have been proven to deliver best results are those that are SMART, meaning specific, measurable, achievable, relevant, and time bound. Those characteristics are what separate effective objectives from ineffective ones and good business planning practice from bad practice. In a way, SMART objectives are reflective of how serious an individual or organization is about the work ahead. At work and home, to achieve meaningful results is to set specific objectives.

Specific

SMART objectives are specific. They are pinpointed and clear. They leave no doubt in anyone's mind about what is being pursued. For example, one who sets a personal objective of "I want to lose fifteen pounds before the wedding" is undoubtedly specific and clear on what they aim to accomplish. With hard work and follow-up, such an objective can and should be achieved. On the other hand, "I want to eat more healthy food" is not specific and therefore not considered a SMART objective. It is unlikely to deliver the targeted results because it's difficult to dimensionalize what is meant by "healthy food" and in what context. What might be healthy to one person is possibly junk to another! One might consider switching to organic food as part of their drive toward healthy living while another might be content with home cooking; either approach could be construed "healthy." Hence, such a broad objective could be destined for failure and is highly likely to be dismissed.

Another example of a nonspecific objective is "Becoming the best manager," which is very subjective and would be difficult to measure and track. That very same manager might be considered "horrible" by some of his own team members; it is all a matter of perspective. This resembles the popular debates on sports talk shows where many heated arguments bubble up from the question of who the GOAT (greatest of all time) is. Without outlining the criteria for answering such a question, it is impossible to have a fruitful debate. Which sport and what era are we talking about? Is it overall winning percentage or number of rings and trophies? Those are a few measurements that would make the debate more effective and potentially reach a consensus on the answer. Therefore, for an athlete or a coach to have "become the greatest of all time" as a personal objective, it would be very broad and ineffective. SMART objectives are specific.

Measurable

SMART objectives are also measurable. They include specific criteria and action that definitively outline how the performance will be measured. At any point in time, you should be able to look back at your delivered results and ascertain your exact position against said objectives. You should be able to determine whether you are on track, ahead, or behind and most importantly what the degree of separation is.

That person aiming to shed fifteen pounds before the wedding could jump on a scale at any point in time and evaluate their performance. Because it was a specific and measurable objective, they would be well-positioned to track their progression on a periodical basis and make adjustments. Conversely, that other person who targeted being the best manager cannot be as definitive because their objective was not measurable. The objective lacked the metrics to assist in achieving such an objective.

It reminds me of a debate I was involved in years ago with a coworker as we discussed whether a certain leader of leaders at our place of employment was a horrible boss. We discussed the habits and qualities the leader exhibited around the office space, but neither of us saw those qualities through an identical prism. For instance, my colleague saw the leader's habit of arriving late to interoffice meetings as acceptable behavior and a sign of power, while I viewed it negatively as a sign of disrespect. The behavior being evaluated was perceived differently because it lacked the metrics to establish a benchmark for measuring performance. Smart people always set measurable objectives because they understand the importance of having a yardstick to gauge performance at all times. Smart people also use measurable objectives as tools to navigate their organization and steward their accomplishments with senior leadership. SMART objectives are measurable.

Achievable

SMART objectives are also achievable and in essence are believable because they are specific and measurable; SMART objectives have a higher probability of achievement. They can be accomplished within the appropriate parameters. Using the earlier example, losing fifteen pounds before the wedding is certainly a realistic and achievable objective, but "losing fifty pounds" may not be. Losing weight in general is a difficult task, so we must be realistic when setting our objectives. Moreover, realistic objectives help us maintain a winning, can-do mindset until the destination is reached.

Similarly, winning a NASCAR or Formula One championship could be an achievable objective for a motor racing team that has a winning track record but not for a new racing team or one that does not have that winning history. A more realistic objective for such a team could be "finishing in the top ten" whereby accomplishing such an achievable objective would set the stage for bigger and more audacious objectives. Setting SMART objectives mandates a good assessment of your capabilities, history, and track record. Achievable objectives must be in sync with your skill set, not just your desires. SMART objectives are achievable.

Relevant

SMART objectives are also relevant. Your objectives should have some degree of connectivity to what you do and who you are as an individual or company. Objectives must tie back to the essence and core of what your organization operates and stands for, including your stated values. Moreover, the objectives you set should be linked to your overall goals and must support organizational strategic priorities. A relevant objective is one that perfectly aligns with the work individuals and organizations do on a daily basis.

"Win best inflight dining experience award" may not be a relevant objective for a low-cost airline that offers limited food on board their planes. Such an objective could be more relevant to premium airlines, such as Emirates or Qantas. A more relevant objective for a budget airline could be something like "Increase operating profits by 10 percent" or "Launch transatlantic services for under $100." Both goals align more fittingly with the nature of budget airlines and their business model. More importantly, such objectives would be expected to deliver more measurable results. SMART objectives are relevant.

Time Bound

SMART objectives are time bound. They specify a time frame for objectives to be accomplished and provide a critical path for the individual to build their planned action. Without a time reference, it would be difficult to make a meaningful contribution to the organization's overall goals. The individuals and organization would not have the focus and sense of urgency to work toward completing the necessary work to achieve the objectives. Also, having a time frame for objectives affords you a chance to break them down into mini objectives or milestones, such that it facilitates achievement and measurement.

Wanting to "lose fifteen pounds" in and of itself is good and a specific objective, but without a time frame, it would not be a SMART objective. Are you planning to deliver on such an objective in six weeks or six months, and how will you measure your progress if you don't have a time reference? On the other hand, "I want to lose fifteen pounds by end of this school year" delivers the time limit when you have to stop your activity and step on the scale to measure how many pounds were actually lost. In between, the objectives could be broken into smaller ones like "lose x pounds in March" or "lose x pounds during the summer months." So time-bound objectives provide proof point and validation that the necessary work was completed and the needed value was delivered. Now you deserve to celebrate your accomplishments and share the learning with others. SMART objectives are time bound.

Despite her illiteracy, my mom was exceptional at setting SMART objectives. She was never formally trained on the subject; it was only her high business IQ and the robust firsthand experience she gained in her younger years, working alongside her dad and watching him do business. It was no surprise that she would later share that knowledge with her children, training them all at an early age of the importance of having SMART objectives. Every single year, my mother would sit us down and ask each one to decide on specific objectives to achieve during the upcoming school year. As noted earlier, my mother used the school year as her planning calendar. So as soon as school finished in early summer, she would have this objective-setting conversation with each of us. Doing it this way helped her understand what the family needed collectively, and each of her eight children could plan ahead. We did this religiously every year, and SMART objectives were mandated from each of us. However, she encouraged us to set mostly education-related objectives, like "read three books during summer vacation" and even "save half of my daily allowance." So our objectives ran the gamut, everything from my middle sister wanting to "learn how to knit a sweater during summer break" to my eldest brother wanting to "publish his first short story before the end of his senior high school year." My mom even taught us to set objectives for the two-month school break. Each had to pick one thing, like my second-oldest brother whose objective for one summer was "learning to play chess," which incidentally he managed to achieve and it was a family friend who taught him the game. Remarkably, that friend was blind.

Yes, my mother was illiterate, but she somehow understood and fully executed goal and objective setting, just like professional organizations do. Some of my mother's actual objectives, which had a familiar corporate tone, were

- sell the entire lot of goats before season end (revenue generation)
- feed the family meat at least once per week (inspiring the core)
- grow the household's entire needs of herbs at home (cost management)
- pickle four twenty-gallon containers of cucumbers every year (supply chain)

Planning Process Step 4: Systems Alignment

Once opportunities have been identified and SMART objectives established, the fourth step in the planning process is to align all stakeholders with your annual business plan. System alignment ensures the business plan you just developed fits and is in concert with the rest of the organization. It is about soliciting and securing the needed support from key decision-makers in your organization as well as others who are central to the success of your plan.

Building a solid business plan requires synchronization with other functions that feed into or link to what you have set out to accomplish. Moreover, it is difficult to execute the plan without proper resource allocation, which requires approval from senior leadership. Therefore, system alignment is the process of ensuring that all internal constituencies are in agreement with the proposed business plan. Internal constituencies include different functions that touch the plan, such as marketing, sales, finance, supply chain, legal, IT, and human resource. Those internal constituents could also be shareholders and business partners, like suppliers and advertising agencies. Imagine you build a plan to expand into a new category without first discussing and vetting the proposition with suppliers of raw material or production machinery. Every function and key supplier should play a role in the development of a viable business plan and be involved in the process from start to finish.

My mother did not report to a board of directors, of course, but she considered her educated children the brain trust of her enterprise. She sat us down most summers to share plans and sought our perspective, especially later in life as the children matured into educated young women and men. Additionally, she religiously consulted her children ahead of big decisions that impacted the family. In all candor, she relied mostly on the opinion of my eldest brother, now a professor of Asian studies, who enjoyed a balanced and even-keeled thought process. However, whenever she shared her plans with the broader family, she gave everyone an opportunity to share a point of view. Like the time when she planned to start that young Syrian goats business, she sat us down and introduced the idea, what it entailed, and why it was a good idea. I remember one of my brothers questioning the merits of investing in expensive imported goats when locally produced goats were cheaper. My mother calmly and in great detail explained the high margin and multiple benefits of Syrian goats, making sure that all the other children listened and learned.

When she had the plan discussed and agreed to, she reiterated the responsibilities of each individual in the new venture. For the three oldest boys, she assigned each a critical role. The eldest was charged with marketing and helping my mother negotiate buying and selling deals. He had a mature and confident personality. My mother put my second-oldest brother in charge of finance because she knew he excelled in math and was more of an introvert, at least growing up. Lastly, for me, as the third-oldest boy, my mother assigned me supply chain responsibilities, which meant sourcing food for the goats. Their food had to be at no cost because we could not afford to pay for goat feed. My job was to roam the produce market on a daily basis, usually first thing in the morning, and collect whatever leftover I could muster, a skill that played to my haggling and problem-solving abilities. With those three critical jobs safely secured, my mother ensured her operations were well positioned to succeed.

Corporations alike must align all intercompany functions to gain agreement on their overall business plans. Various departments and functions, and to some degree key third-party business partners, have to agree with what is being asked of them. Can you imagine a paper goods company planning a new line of feminine care products without engaging their production team? Well, it actually did happen to a popular brand. The brand marketing team in one of their international operations developed a new product line with very unique features that would have been first to market in that part of the world. On paper everything looked good: feminine hygiene pads with wings, and in focus groups consumers loved the idea. Unfortunately their production lines lacked the capability of producing those specific types of pads. The additional tooling cost and lead time to upgrade existing production lines necessitated capital investment, itself a lengthy process that required senior management approval. Without aligning their cross-functional teammates in production and finance, the brand team missed a huge step in the planning process and delayed a key product launch by almost one year.

Successful business plans incorporate feedback from key stakeholders to make certain plans are fully integrated. It facilitates buy-ins and accountability from other departments, with each having a vested interest in materializing those plans. Also, if your organization is global, then various operating units around the world have to be aligned and involved in the annual planning process, lest you aim for dysfunctionality.

Planning Process Step 5: Final Sign-Off

By now in the planning process, valuable time have been exhausted to develop solid plans that address market needs and deliver the desired growth. Next up, and the final step, is to secure approval from senior leadership. It is what your planning effort builds down to, the ability to convince senior leadership that your plans align with the organization's overall mission and values. It is also a reflection of your outlook on the forthcoming fiscal period and commitment to helping deliver on the company's overall goals. In essence, the final sign-off is a request for approval to spend corporate funds and resources as outlined in your proposed business plans.

In the final step, you present or essentially pitch your business plans to senior leaders and articulate the thinking behind those particular growth levers and proposed investments. This breaks into three separate and sequential rounds of approval, each with a realistic probability of returning to the planning boards. It begins by pitching department heads, then business unit head, and finally the C suite. Of course, depending on organizational structures, there may be more or fewer layers to pass through.

1. Department Head Approval

The first person to review your business plan is likely to be your direct boss or department head, depending on your seniority level. Their focus will be to understand the specifics of your plan and fit with both your objectives as well as department's objectives, which in turn are assumed to synch up with those of the overall company. Your boss's or department head's aim here is to evaluate the aggressiveness of your plans and check for any potential room to stretch some deliverables.

Likely to be the most grueling approval layer, you can expect to be drilled here with questions on your assumptions and growth projections, and you may even get asked to benchmark your plan to prior years. Remember objectives have to be realistic and if the prior year you delivered 9 percent growth, as an example, do not expect your department head to approve a business plan that calls for a lower growth rate, without significant justification. Chances are your plan will be rejected on the first round and you will be asked to go back and edit parts or all of it before returning for a repitch. Your boss or department head is also thinking ahead about their own boss and their reaction to your planned action. They have to be able to sell this upstream as well.

2. Business Unit Head Approval

Once the department head approved the plan and whatever revisions you may have made, they will accept your business plan and prepare you for the next round of approvals. They will consolidate individual plans of all their team members and roll them up into one business plan for the entire operating or business unit. At this point, department heads are the ones responsible for pitching the consolidated plans on behalf of their departments; they are in the line of fire with their superiors, business, or operating unit heads.

A consolidated business plan reflects what all the departments and functions within the business or operating unit aim to achieve during the upcoming fiscal period. It is an amalgamation of all the synergies and capabilities across the unit and is an articulation of how those consolidated plans fit with the overarching goals and objectives of the organizational. There is little margin for error here, and your plans must be nearly perfect. A rejection would involve multiple departments and functions having to rework their individual plans to address whatever notations or adjustments asked by the business or operating unit heads. However, if the pitch is successful, and depending on organizational constructs, plan presentations continue to the next level.

3. CEO/COO Approval

In a typical corporate structure, each business or operating unit president will present their plans to the CEO or COO, depending on hierarchy and culture. In some companies, there might be an executive committee that reviews those business plans and grants final approval. That is the final approval step before your business plans are approved and ready for implementation.

Once the plan is approved, it signifies the end of the annual planning process and also triggers finance to allocate the requested funding and resources. But in reality, business planning is ongoing and plans are constantly adjusted and calibrated against market and business needs. Plans often require periodical updates and adjustments for numerous reasons. Firstly, changes in market dynamics play a vital role, especially if a major force (e.g., macroeconomics and geopolitics) adversely affects the business and puts your plan in jeopardy. In such a situation, recalibration is needed. Secondly, year to date performance will ignite a need to adjust plans. Whether your business is facing head- or tailwinds during the fiscal period, adjustments will make your plans more accurate reflection of the marketplace.

My mother's planning skills were exceptional for an illiterate. Early in her married life, she benefited greatly from the coaching and guidance of her father, who recognized the hard circumstances and misfortunes his daughter faced. For instance, my maternal grandfather introduced her to his supplier of foodstuff, a wholesaler with a good reputation. He encouraged my mom to take advantage of the big savings that wholesale purchasing offered. As the child who spent the most time accompanying her on their purchasing trips, I had firsthand knowledge of this as on the way home, she would regularly tell me (coaching mechanism) how much she saved on this or that deal. Those "listen and learn" talks helped shape my growth as an individual and a father.

My mom quickly recognized the value of an important business connection, particularly financially. She estimated that wholesalers saved her more than 20 percent on every shopping trip. She struck a professional friendship with the wholesaler and later in time would leverage it to gain extended credit facilities, something unknown to Jordanians at the time and especially in the wholesale trade where cash was king. She would go on to spend decades sourcing all her household needs from that wholesaler. Gaining credit facilities was another significant financial benefit for my mom, and she recognized the value of it.

It was changes in market dynamics like that that led my mother to recalibrate her plans accordingly. With the enhanced credit terms, she adjusted her business plan and set an objective of maintaining those credit facilities so she used the excess cash flow to fulfill other critical needs like school supplies and clothing for her children. Essentially, she was mastering the art of using OPM, "other people's money," as we say in business. I remember she sat us down on numerous occasions and taught us lessons on the importance of securing such credit facilities and how she did it. It was customary for my mother to conclude those frequent family talks with one of her favorite pieces of advice: "Save your money for a rainy day."

My mother's very first major investment was buying the small, one-third acre of land in Amman, Jordan, where our family's house was built. She recognized renting was an expensive and untenable long-term proposition. She realized that instead of renting, her limited cash flow (she actually sold all the gold from her wedding to complete the land purchase) was better invested in a piece of land where she could accumulate equity. Additionally, she thought land would enable her to potentially increase the size of building and offer some units for rental. She would actually go on to accomplish her plan, and that one land purchase deal turned into an impressive four-story residential building.

My mother was acutely aware of the importance of shelter and security to her overarching vision of bringing up the most accomplished family. Before she purchased that property, she consulted with her dad, who supported the land investment idea. My grandfather's advice was to find a lot closer to where he lived so they could stay close. My mother proceeded and put the gold turned cash as down payment on a lot adjacent to her parents. While Palestinian refugees around her in the early 1960s lived in UN-funded camps and shacks, my mother was proudly enjoying life in a two-bedroom apartment, safe and distanced from trouble and UNHR handouts. She was now a proud landowner.

Closing Thought

Effective planning is both art and science. It requires precision, dedication, and a methodical approach. The process must be followed closely to deliver the desired results and can be perfected with a high level of commitment and excellence. The process requires ongoing maintenance where you frequently tweak and adjust plans based on performance, so plans reflect the realities of the marketplace. Planning starts with a deep internal and external assessment, followed by setting the right smart objectives, and concluding with approval from top leadership and affirmation that your plans align with the company's.

3

PERSISTENCE

Persistence, the third leadership lesson my illiterate mother taught me, is defined by the Merriam Webster Dictionary as "the quality that allows someone to continue doing something or trying to do something even though it is difficult or opposed by other people." As such, it is possessing that drive and determination to achieve your goals despite any challenges. Your will to persevere propels you to overcome any setbacks.

Persistence was a quality of Michael Jordan, arguably the greatest basketball player in the history of that sport, with accomplishments that are yet to be matched. He once said, "I've missed more than 9,000 shots over my career. I've lost almost three hundred games; twenty-six times I was trusted with taking the game winning shot and missed. I've failed over and over again in my life, and that is why I succeed." For Michael it was the realization that missing over 9,000 baskets was imperative to his success as a prolific scorer. He was content with missing a large number of shots because he understood that many more of his shots did succeed. In fact, according to one source, basketballreference.com, Michael Jordan succeeded in hitting exactly 12,192 of his basketball shots during his professional career.

That is the quintessence of persistence, and business leaders must show high aptitude levels of such quality. It is the omnipotent that fuels winners to pursue their goals and objectives with unmatched focus and commitment. It is the will and drive to be what you want to be. It is the singular focus on a goal or an objective and channeling all your energy toward achieving that one goal.

Persistence is also possessing both the fit and fitness to do a particular job, because as we know, not every Ivy League graduate is a thoroughbred and not every seven-foot-tall person is fit to play professional basketball. While a seven-footer may be fit (height) to dunk a basketball, they may lack the fitness (agility) to run and hustle for forty-eight minutes, the duration of a professional game. Manute Bol was a seven-foot, seven-inch (2.3-meter) basketball player from Sudan who had a long playing career in the NBA but was not productive and enjoyed little playing time. He clearly had the exceptional height (fit) to play, but what he lacked were body strength and durability (fitness) to withstand the physical demands—the pushing and shoving of basketball. No matter how long and hard his various teams tried to bulk him up, it never worked for Manute. He bounced around the league, playing for six teams, but at the end, it seems his body just couldn't withstand the daily grind. He did not have the fitness to succeed, and there are many like him today in the NBA.

Successful leaders exhibit persistence in everything they do. It's a way of life for them and they can't do it any other way. They possess the unique ability to zero in on the essentials to accomplish exceptional results. Take, for example, Abraham Lincoln, the sixteenth president of the United States, who learned about failure the hard way. On his way to becoming one of the most iconic leaders in history, he endured years of failure. Lincoln failed twice as a businessman, once was refused admission to law school, and suffered a nervous breakdown. On the politics front, Mr. Lincoln lost elections eight times, but despite all that failure, he persisted on his dream of becoming president. He would go on to become one of the most renowned presidents in American history with a long list of monumental accomplishments. It takes strong character, will, and persistence to withstand multiple letdowns.

When I coached girls youth sports, one of my most repeated nuggets of advice was "Winners never quit and quitters never win." I recall once my daughter, who was nine years old, asked me to explain what that meant. When she heard my simplified explanation, she commented, "Oh, so it's like when I want a new toy. I just have to keep begging you until you agree?" Indeed, that is a child-size articulation of persistence. It's the unique ability to do things over and over, failing multiple times until you get it right and succeed in achieving your objectives.

Persistence could be the difference between winning and losing. You could have other qualities like passion and exceptional planning, but if you don't have the stamina, fitness, and persistence to complement those other qualities and withstand the obstacles, then you are more likely to fail. Lack of persistence is one of the main reasons a majority of great plans fail. In fact, *Harvard Business Review* conducted a study on organizational execution and concluded that 95 percent of all plans fail because of bad execution, a by-product of persistence deficiency. Persistent people execute well and show great attention to detail because they are laser focused and determined. They keep trying and reapplying their learning until they get it right and eventually become a self-fulfilling prophecy of an improbable ability to achieve the most arduous goals.

Persistence is also doing the same thing over and over again without fear of the consequences or the opinion of others. Michael Jordan must have had doubters among his own teammates who may questioned those missed shots he took. That nonetheless never stopped him from continuing to do what he's best equipped for: shoot the ball with every opportunity. He possessed the confidence and willpower to make the key shots when it mattered most. To a certain degree, repetition builds muscle memory when your body and mind sync up and become well-trained on the subject matter that it executes certain tasks automatically without a trigger.

My illiterate mother was a very persistent individual, probably the most of her own siblings, despite her educational limitations. She pursued every one of her main objectives with unmatched determination. To demonstrate this quality in her, let me share the story of our first house expansion initiative. After she sold her wedding jewelry to buy a lot next to my grandparents and went on to build a two-bedroom house, my mom had her mind set on expanding our house as soon as financially feasible. Not because it was becoming increasingly tight to fit a family of eight children, although it was incredibly tight, but in her opinion for the potential of generating incremental revenues through leasing the new build. Even with a very tight budget, sacrificing her comfort and that of her children in return for financial security was a no-brainer to my mother. As she shared with us her plans, she explained her thought process and said that investing in house expansion for rental was a viable idea. She gave us three reasons.

1. There was high demand for rental properties, largely the result of Palestinian refugees fleeing the West Bank after the 1967 Arab-Israel War.

2. It will pay off in the long run. The expansion would provide a lifetime of revenues, so the ROI on that investment is a no-brainer.

3. Cost of building supplies was reasonable. Whether she sourced the material from her cousin's shop or elsewhere, it was still affordable.

However, with a small, one-third-acre lot, city ordinances didn't allow for horizontal expansion because a three-meter (nine-foot) clearance from all four sides of the building was a requirement. As such, the only option for expansion was vertical. So my mother developed a plan to build a second story above our home. Lacking the funds needed to build an entire floor, she attempted to borrow money from her parents, but that avenue failed. So she turned to her life partner and asked my dad to put up the required funds, but he adamantly refused.

My dad did not share her drive or entrepreneurial spirit. His denial to share the costs was rooted in his disgruntlement for not having his name on the deed; instead, it was entirely in the name of my mother. Months later, he offered to support her and provide the much-needed funds, but with one condition: his name replaced hers entirely on the title deed, a proposition that was vehemently rejected. My dad was essentially asking to control the one thing my mother gave up her entire life savings for, her gold, to secure. In a strange and twisted thought process to my dad, funding the expansion of a property he considered not his own was a wasted investment, despite its sentimental and economic value and despite the woman asking for his support being his wife. And although they would go on to be married for fifty-five years, for my dad, my mother was both a wife and a nemesis. She was everything that he wasn't or maybe did not want to be. Maybe deep inside he was a chauvinist and disliked watching a powerful woman lead with her heart and mind. My mother was determined, loyal, and successful. However, despite their many differences and roller-coaster life, my parents agreed on one thing, the importance of higher education. My dad was fully on board with my mom's goal of building the most accomplished family and was fully supportive of every decision ever made on that subject.

Determined to see through her plan of expanding the house and building a second floor, my mom delayed the start of that project until all the funds were secured. That was a new objective she set out to complete. She started saving small amounts of cash every month, including whatever she could spare off house expenses. A couple of years later, she sold whatever gold she had accumulated and, along with her two-year cash savings, had enough money to start the house expansion. With her limited cash flow, she even negotiated a payment plan with the contractor, who was a neighbor of ours. She paid him in installments and her persistence finally paid off as nine months later we celebrated a brand-new extension to our house. Honestly for me and my siblings, it would have been better if we had moved up to the target apartment and enjoyed more room, but my mother was the undisputed leader of this organization and understood the economic value of a new revenue stream. The cost-benefit analysis she never did would have proved her correct.

The newly built second floor consisted of three full bedrooms, a kitchen, a nice sunroom, and one bathroom. Had my mother wavered after every setback, had she not possessed the strong will, and had she not kept her eyes on the big picture, she would not have succeeded in completing this important milestone. Later that same year, our newly built floor was rented out to a family of newlyweds and another of my mother's STAR objectives was successfully accomplished. Over the next thirty years, that same rented second floor became a vital revenue stream and provided much needed financial relief to our family. It only materialized because of my mother's persistence.

Some leaders give up too soon on their goals and move on to new ones. Even leading organizations with vast capabilities, many have pivoted away from sound goals to pursue "new shiny objects." A case in point is a major company I worked for when they launched a product extension for a popular consumer product line, only to retire it from all markets within less than two years. In all candor, little marketing or above-the-line advertising was spent over the two years, and the only promotional support was product sampling and in-store activation. What was even more disheartening was the lack of postmortem analysis or consumer insights to better understand causals for the presumed subpar performance.

How do you expect to succeed if you don't take time to understand why you failed in the first place? Moreover, maybe you should not invest millions to commercialize a new product without doing the necessary due diligence or at least a trial period. It is a mystery why tolerance for failure is unrecognized or runs thin at some organizations. Clearly every product has a distinctive life cycle, and growth is derived from persistent management of that cycle. The goal is to extend the shelf life of new products such that they turn into solid and permanent contributors to the value chain.

In that particular experience, the product itself had all the basic ingredients to prosper, both intrinsic, as validated through consumer research, and extrinsic, given its health benefits and the modest but positive share gains the line extension established during a two-year span. It is plausible that the brand manager or head of marketing lacked the desire to take risks in supporting the initiative. It is also possible that senior management demanded aggressive or even unrealistic returns from that investment, which shortened the sights. In both cases, lack of persistence contributed to the product failure, taking away a potential growth driver and in the process sending a negative message to those who worked tirelessly to bring it to market.

Three Ways to Solidify Persistence

Persistence can be learned, nurtured, and eventually mastered. Like many leadership qualities, genuine commitment and hard work are mandated in order to maximize results. Indeed, as already discussed, persistence develops over time with repetition and drive. That said, it can be strengthened with the right mind and skill set. In my combined professional corporate and personal experience watching my mother operate masterfully, there are three ways to do that: having a strong stomach for failure, a strong will to win, and a strong focus on the target. You get the picture. You have to be multidimensional in strength, but let's delve into each of those elements.

Strong Stomach for Failure

Thomas Edison was said to have failed more than 1,000 times before he discovered the light bulb. That is a rarity for innovators, who have a habit of quickly pivoting to new places and new ideas. However, what is enlightening is his perspective on failure, where he viewed it as "learning 1,000 different ways of how not to make a light bulb." So we succeed because of failure, and while we set out to win and not fail, what matters is the connection of the two mindsets.

Even in today's highly entrepreneurial culture, young aspiring business minds are admired for being bold, taking more risk, and not fearing failing. It is what some have coined "failing fast culture" as an embodiment of a new innovative culture where iterative thinking, meaning to learn from mistakes, continues until success is attained.

Edison certainly had the stomach to swallow his pride and risk failure so many times in similar ways to Michael Jordan, who did not mind swallowing his pride and looking silly missing those 9,000 basketball shots. In both cases, those two geniuses were confident of their eventual success. Persistence drives an individual to believe in their abilities and skill set, providing "an extra gear" of sort to jump-start multiple attempts to accomplish a task.

In a similar vein, my mother encouraged us to take calculated risks and not fear failing in order to strengthen our chances of succeeding and becoming the winningest group of highly educated people that has ever been assembled in her family. When my oldest sister graduated from high school, my maternal grandmother hard-pressed my mom to marry off my sister, as was the social norm in Jordan during the 1970s. My grandmother's Middle Eastern thought process was still old-fashioned. But my mother vehemently rejected that notion and instead encouraged my sister to focus on applying to colleges. My sister did go on to complete a master's degree and is now a successful educator. Had my mom, and sister for that matter, not persisted, who knows what would have happened to her future?

Strong leadership promotes trial and error and interactive thinking, as long as people are smart enough to learn from mistakes and apply such learning to future trials. My mother often said, "If you don't try, you don't know," alluding to the importance of trial as part of the learning process. A child never learns to walk, ride a bike, play any musical instrument, or play a sport without first failing.

Strong Will to Win

While some people have a strong stomach for failure, others have a strong will to win. They are locked in and focused on winning whatever activity they engage in. People with that ability go into every endeavor expecting to prevail, and it shapes both their mindset and behavior. Similarly, those people will dislike losing and vocalize their frustration with not winning through words and body language.

Earvin "Magic" Johnson Jr. was my idol growing up, and to me, he was the best basketball player in the world. He always exhibited a strong will to win, and I even saw it on TV, much like everyone else watching Los Angeles Lakers games. His energy during the game, when he was on the bench catching his breath, or even when he was inside the huddle when coaches were mapping out plays. His upbeat personality on and off the court, exceptional basketball talent, and winning attitude were all great qualities to be idolized. But in 1991 when he shocked the world with an announcement of contracting the deadly HIV virus, all odds were against him. He battered the resentment of some players on opposing teams and the rejection of fellow players, some of whom publicly voiced strong reservations about playing alongside his blood-infected condition. Magic Johnson also fought the backlash of public opinion, which often is quick to judge people. His strong will to win the fight against a deadly disease propelled him to prevail.

Magic Johnson was determined to beat AIDS and endured over twenty years of strong medications, sometimes taking more than fifteen types, a strict diet plan, and a rigorous workout routine. Today Mr. Johnson is fit and lives a very healthy and successful life. Moreover, his persistence guided him to venture into the business world and to bring to the corporate board room the same level of dedication he demonstrated on the basketball court.

Today, Magic Johnson is a very accomplished business titan with an enterprise incorporating urban-focused movie theaters, fast food franchises, and most recently part ownership of the Los Angeles Dodgers baseball team. He is said to be worth significantly more than during the peak of his professional basketball career. His strong will to win propelled him to overcome devastating setbacks and succeed when society minimized his chances. His strong will carried through the toughest times of his life.

Strong Focus on the Target

Having a strong stomach for failure and will to win are complemented with a laser focus on the planned destination. Keeping that target in sight and aligning all activities against a singular objective are hallmarks of persistent leaders. They masterfully channel all their energy and resources into narrow paths to success.

Becoming the first human to climb Mount Everest was clearly the biggest objective for Sir Edmond Hillary. He failed in his first attempt but he didn't give up. On his second attempt, it is reported that he camped out overnight about 3,000 feet from the mountaintop, almost 90 percent of the climb complete. That night he fought strong winds all night long, but his biggest struggle was inside his head, keeping his mind sharp and alert. He later recounted the experience and mentioned how in making the climb it wasn't struggles of the mountain that he conquered but the internal struggles that he controlled so effectively. That type of determination is what drives persistence and eventually renowned success. Sir Hillary could have quit many times. He could have resorted to the other mountains he's conquered, but he didn't waver. His resolve to go where no other person had gone was his primary target, and he remained zoomed in until he prevailed.

Persistence is a very unique quality testing the human's ability to stay focused on the objective and at the same time energizes us to do what is required over and over again until we triumph. It is the powerful energy that fuels our drive to keep marching on. It is a test of our appetite for failure, a test of our will to win, and a test of our focus on the goal at hand. Persistence is one of the biggest tests in life. If you develop that winning formula, you are destined for success, and in the process, you would have obtained a great quality that will fuel you for life.

My illiterate mother was the most inspiring and persistent leaders I have ever known. In the 1980s, our family faced an extremely challenging period when one of my younger brothers drifted off the path my mother and the rest of us were on. It was a time when the four older siblings (three boys and one girl) were all here in the US attending college, so he was in many ways "the man of the house," if you will. While in high school, he hooked up with a troubled group of friends who were bad news from the very first day they met. While it is common for teenagers and especially high schoolers to revolt against society, my brother's friends were thugs and losers. Before he met them, my brother was an exemplary student, highly intelligent, and an honors student. He was blessed with high IQ, strong physical abilities, and street common sense. My mother relied on him to look after business affairs, and just like the rest of us, he grew up having specific responsibilities in line with my mother's plans. My mom often called on him to go downtown to the Friday market to sell different merchandise that she handmade at home. He was to sell the goods at the highest possible price and use the revenue to purchase household necessities at the lowest possible prices of course.

Through such experience, my brother gained his practical skills, which also complemented his physical strength. However, when he reached high school, it was another world for him, one that he possibly was not ready for. His friends were the complete opposite of him: careless about school and no regard for social order. My mother saw right through them. She noticed the signs early on and monitored my brother's ever-frequent rendezvous with his band of bad news bears. His grades slipped, and behavior changed drastically during that period. He spent less time at home studying and more time outside partying with his friends. He often returned home late at night with blood-red eyes, which was my mother's biggest concern. She didn't know what he did away from home, and my brother never told the truth about his friends.

Despite his newfound confrontational behavior, my mom continued to support him and encouraged my troubled brother to refocus on school as it was the only pass to a life of prosperity. All of us, his siblings, tried different tactics to bring him back to his senses, his old self, but he rejected our intervention attempts, even resorting to violence on a few occasions. In later years, my brother would go on to share with us his evaluation that it was anger that filled my brother's unruly youth demeanor. It appears he was angry at everything: the world he lived in, the miserable life he wanted to get out of, and society at large.

My mother was the only individual who maintained her undivided support of my troubled brother and never lost hope. If she had any doubt, she certainly made sure not to show it. She stayed up many nights until early hours of the morning praying while waiting for her lost son to come home. My mother was lost and for once didn't have the right answers. Her only solace was prayer. She would pray and raise her arms up to the heavens and ask God for help. She would ask for guidance and for mercy on her lost son.

Those terrible circumstances lasted for a couple of years until one day my brother almost did the unthinkable. He returned home dazed and in no mood to listen to my mom's questioning of his whereabouts. She had just finished praying and wanted to understand what was going through his head. She thought she could reason with him and wondered whatever happened to her really smart and strong son. Unfortunately, my brother was not in the mood for such talk and the conversation got louder and more heated. Their argument reached a point when my troubled brother ran to the kitchen and, in the spur of a moment—a terrible moment for that matter—picked up a jug of kerosene and was about to pour it on his crying mother.

Suddenly, the magnitude of his action and the grave crime he was about to commit dawned on him. Call it divine intervention or a higher power, but in a split second, he dropped everything on the floor and fell to his knees crying in my mother's lap. He apologized endlessly, kissing her hands and begging for forgiveness.

Her response was as motherly as ever. She hugged him tightly, kissed him, and reassured him she never lost hope. She calmed him down and told him that deep inside he was still a good boy and the smart son she raised. She also reminded him it was only the unfortunate circumstances of mixing with the wrong friends that led to his predicament. She shared with him how all her prayers for the past couple of years, the entire time he was with that band of troubled friends, were focused on him and his safe return.

When she retold the story years later, my mother explained it was an attempt to teach us lessons from that experience, not to chastise my brother. My mother's strong will to win and her laser focus on the target guided her effort to save my brother. Her persistence guided her to persevere and succeed in saving a troubled son. She was as solid as a rock and never gave up on a cause she believed wholeheartedly in.

My troubled young brother would go on to gain a doctorate in financial science and build a successful career as a senior banking executive.

Closing Thought

Persistence is all about will and an individual's ability to hone that will against achieving meaningful results. The will to accept failure and view it in a positive context as a learning opportunity and a time to recalibrate systems. It is having the hunger and humility to fight the odds and pursue important goals. Persistence is also having the will to focus on key objectives that matter the most and direct all energy against that destination.

History is filled with overachieving names whose accomplishments defy conventional wisdom, and persistence is a clear attributable factor that cuts across many of those cases. The old adage "No guts, no glory" is possibly a good layman articulation of the essence of persistence.

4

PERPETUAL
OPTIMISM

Perpetual optimism is a brilliant and rare leadership quality. It's a state of mind that propels certain individuals to view the world through a different and very unique prism. Such individuals always see things in a more optimistic context, regardless of the difficulties and challenges. Those "optimists" view challenges positively, rather as opportunities, and often expect to be rewarded for their effort with positive outcomes. They often choose to see the glass as half full and try to convince others of their perception. Hence, perpetual optimism is the propeller of positive thinking, which instills in people a self-fulfilling prophecy that things will always get better, and after every down there is definitely an up.

Perpetual optimism is also a "force multiplier," as one of my leadership idols, the late General Colin Powell, put it. It impacts entire organizations and permeates positive thinking everywhere. It multiplies faster and larger than pessimism. General Powell's optimism trickled down to his commanders and from there on throughout military units. That was one of his drivers to succeed as a four-star general. Can you imagine the idea of war being led by someone who is a pessimist, someone who can't motivate their troops to march toward an enemy and sacrifice their lives for the good of their country? That would be a doomed battle and deadly results.

In 2009 I watched General Powell keynote the annual conference of National Association of Convenience Stores in Las Vegas, and perpetual optimism was his topic. He described it as "a belief in yourself, in your purpose, and in success." In the military, great leadership and a great deal of optimism go hand in hand. It is impossible to win any battle, let alone a war without a positive outlook to inspire and lead the charge. Troops in the line of fire are focused on survival and expect confidence from their superiors, reinforcing their ability to defeat the enemy and return home safely. A pessimistic commanding officer would fail at drawing a winning plan or projecting confidence to their troops, causing major mental and physical damage.

Perpetual optimism is an attitude, a belief, and a state of mind. It plays into your psyche and gives you the confidence to overcome serious adversity. It is that shot of energy that boosts your body, invigorates you, and fuels your drive. Leaders with such a quality project their confidence on to their teams, and employees recognize the power of their positive thinking.

My mother epitomized perpetual optimism, especially when you consider her background as a Palestinian refugee, married early, financially challenged, and with eight children to care for. Her positive attitude was her hallmark—one that allies admired and adversaries resented. She was often the lone positive voice, so much that one day my grandmother, her own mom, shouted at her, "Wow! I don't understand where you get all this confidence from.

Your kids are not even in college and you think they are going to go on, earn degrees, and become more successful than their uncles and everyone else in the family?"

My mother's optimism was ingrained in all of us at an early age. Whether it was the chances of getting new clothes for the holidays, having protein for Friday dinner, or the prospects of succeeding in school, she trained us to value what we have and taught us the virtues of seeing the glass the way she saw it: half full. She used to frequently repeat, "As long as we have a roof over our heads, it will protect us from the rain." This means as a family with limited resources, having a house, albeit a small one, is a blessing and we should be thankful because others are not as fortunate. My mother was confident in her ability to succeed in life and beat all the odds. She never doubted it, and I believe her passion, planning, and perseverance were all attributed to her perpetual optimism.

In forty years since her family was forced out of Palestine and they fled to Jordan, she progressed from being a refugee to living in a small, two-bedroom apartment to owning an impressive residential compound in one of the best areas in the city. She evolved from a tiny house surrounded by neighbors on every side, looking down on her, to a house with no neighbors as far as the eye can see. A beautiful, white, Mediterranean, stone house surrounded by a garden of lovely Jordanian fruit trees that fulfilled her dreams. Her favorites were the grape vines because of the shade they provided her where she prayed and the sweet golden grapes she enjoyed eating and serving her guests. She also loved the grape leaves, which she boiled and stuffed with rice and minced meat for a delicious Mediterranean delicacy. As her children grew up and moved away, each on their own professional path, she helped build a house that symbolized her vision, a castle for her entire family, a base for all of them to reunite and rekindle childhood memories. The house she built was a central command where they would occasionally gather in the summer for good times and family reunions. She never gave up on the dream of moving out and into a neighborhood of her own, no neighbors for miles, a quiet area, and lots of fresh air and greenery. Yes, her glass was always full. It was her planning, passion, persistence, and optimism that helped her reach the final destination.

Perpetual optimism is a leadership quality every successful business executive must possess. Coca-Cola Chairman and CEO Muhtar Kent radiated optimism across the more than two hundred countries he led between 2008 and 2017. His optimism stemmed largely from his forty years of experience with the company and a successful track record he built. It is not surprising when his optimism was reflected in Coca-Cola's 2010 manifesto for growth, which included an audacious goal, Vision 2020, essentially doubling company revenues in ten years. The magnitude of that goal only magnified by the realization it took the company 122 years to achieve that revenue level. Mr. Kent, the perpetual optimist, planned to double the revenues in one-tenth of the time. Mr. Kent believed it was an achievable objective despite the apparent hurdles. Everyone on his leadership team believed it wholeheartedly as well and bought into that dream, into that optimism. Muhtar Kent encouraged his leadership team to leverage every opportunity to update the organization on their progress against that goal, which ultimately was achieved as planned.

Perpetual optimists are naturally happy and ooze positive energy. They enjoy a positive perspective on life and are hardly saddened by the negativity surrounding them or scared to be themselves. In fact, it is rare for optimists to see negativity around them. Could this state of mind be acquired? Or are leaders born with it? I believe some are born with it, but it can also be developed over time. It requires two things: self-confidence and a track record.

Self-Confidence

Optimists exude confidence and ooze energy in everything they do. They are always charged up and ready to go, ready for any task. They trust their skill set and experience and rely on that trust to help them achieve great results. To others, optimists may come across as arrogant or self-conceited. I know we all have had those conversations that turn into heated arguments about whether it's arrogance or self-confidence. For an optimist, they do not even care.

When the late basketball great Kobe Bryant broke into the National Basketball Association (NBA) as a youngster, fresh out of high school, the seventeen-year-old was not shy about shooting the ball. He was not afraid of taking the tough shots and in fact called for the ball at the most critical time, when the entire game was on the line. When most players, even experienced ones, look for someone else to take the final shot, Kobe relished the opportunity. His self-confidence was viewed by many of his detractors as borderline cockiness. They wrongly associated his lack of college playing experience as immaturity. He proved them all wrong and went on to play in the NBA for nineteen years. His accomplishments are well-documented, highlighted by winning five national championships and scoring more points than all but two players in the history of the National Basketball Association. Kobe Bryant was not arrogant; he was just very confident of his basketball skills and a perpetual optimism who was not scared to be himself

Track Record

When you succeed at doing something the first time, it gets easier the second time around. Doing it successfully repeatedly builds confidence and the ability to build muscle memory, when the action becomes almost habitual.

Let us do a mindset comparison and use cold calling as an example. The first time is always the hardest time, as they say. You may have been reluctant or had difficulty in following the script and deliver a great cold call. Or maybe you were worried about failing or did not trust your skills of selling over the phone. However, the second time around, after you have done it once correctly and effectively, now you are less worried and not as intimated as you were the first time. You think of how vastly improved the chances of success are when you pick up the phone and make another prospecting call.

Now imagine your psyche after making one hundred calls or even 1,000. Muscles have strengthened and memory kicks in every time a cold call is made. You have become seasoned and competent at this particular skill. There is no doubt of your ability to operate at a high rate and succeed in prospecting. In this context, your track record fuels your energy to be a confident and perpetual optimist.

Apple CEOs show high levels of confidence, at least in public. Dating back to their founder and late chief executive, Steve Jobs, the huge success of Apple innovation, particularly the iPhone, has given them reasons to believe. The iPhone track record in generating huge sales worldwide is proven and leads those in charge of the company to be optimists with every new edition of the mobile communication device. In fact, Apple has become such an iconic innovator that consumers and business analysts anticipate success in whatever product category the company enters. However, what is not easily visible to the public eye is the complexity of Apple innovation processes and the multitude of iterations those products cycle through before making it to retail or online shelves,

While it pales in comparison to Apple or their successful product line, my mother's investment in goats is an illustrative example of how she applied those attributes. It was one of her early major investments, long before she ventured into breeding the highly prized young Syrian goats. Her first plan was to purchase only one prized female goat, pay the expense of mating her with a stud, sell the offspring, and use the revenue to invest in another prized female goat. She started with one female goat, her eternal pride and joy, given how productive the goat was in producing offspring and providing steady supply of milk. The flock grew to a sizable number over a short period of time. With one prized goat, she was able to build a small farm and a steady stream of revenue. In addition to buying and selling those goats, she mastered other incremental sources of income.

As the farm expanded, my mom adjusted her business plan and pivoted to another priority: self-sufficiency. She used some of her goat business revenues to buy small supplies of dairy production tools. She started producing milk, cheese, yogurt, and butter. Of course this was not for commercial purposes but family consumption, preserving her cash for emergencies. She never lost sight of her top priority: the family.

Her confidence showed up even in the pricing structure of goats. Market driven and fact based but strategically sound, she would go out or send my oldest brother to survey the market and gather competitive pricing of various breeds. Based on that information, she set her prices for the tribe and insisted on gaining the upper hand in all sales negotiation. She wasn't a hardliner with respect to negotiation but purposely controlled. Her pricing structure had a high/low range, and she always ensured her starting point was the higher price point. She would negotiate hard with the buyers until a mutually acceptable final price was achieved. I don't ever recall her telling us that she sold one goat for less than the midpoint of her high/low price range.

Her marketing strategy was based entirely on word of mouth (WOM) and referrals. In reality she didn't have to market her goats. Her reputation in the local market and that of her goats was so positive that buyers would frequently seek her for new stock. Her self-confidence coupled with a stellar track record in buying and selling goats helped her become a perpetual optimist. Again, she mastered all this exceptional leadership style without the benefits of a formal education.

Closing Thought

Perpetual optimism is an attitude with trickle-down effect on the entire organization. It is a key leadership attribute that separates great leaders from mediocre ones. It spreads like wildfire if projected broadly and followers see and sense the optimism, leading to sustainable organizational productivity.

Two critical elements of perpetual optimism are self-confidence and track record, both interdependently fueling an attitude and belief in the likelihood of success. Repeating a task in and of itself is not enough alone to propel confidence but doing it successfully over and over again does.

5

KEY LEARNING

This chapter is a summary of the key points covered in this book. A book about four leadership lessons I learned from my illiterate mother and parallels with attributes of business leaders. Lessons I hope are useful to your personal leadership journey.

I chose to benchmark her leadership skills against business figures not because my belief of her greatness, although that is a fact, but because I spent over thirty years working at high-performing global companies and have seen what it takes to be a leader. Indeed, throughout my corporate career, I gained firsthand knowledge of the tools for success in the corporate world. I applied those tools, but in the back of my mind, there was always the thought of parallels to my mother's teachings. It was evident her skill set was not vastly different from that of corporate leaders; at least the substance of what she taught her children was consistent with what organizations strive to achieve. Those four qualities are mandates for leaders, and in fact, companies spend millions annually in training and development to build such competencies.

Yes, I am convinced my illiterate mother was not much different from a proficient CEO leading her organization toward prosperity. My mother applied complex management concepts to successfully lead her enterprise, despite her lack of professional training or education, for that matter. While business leaders are compensated handsomely for leading, my mother's pay was zero. No annual bonus and no benefits, just the privilege of enjoying the fruit of her labor and bragging rights. Those leadership qualities also played a significant role in fostering a supportive organizational culture that permeated the entire family. A culture that has had lasting positive effect both internally and externally, helping her children be the best version of their individual selves.

Those are the same leadership qualities that strengthened my mother, both as an individual and as the head of our household. They defined who she was and shaped her relationships with siblings and neighbors. They helped her navigate through the many turbulent surprises of life and guided her toward reaching her goal. Those leadership qualities that supported her were passion, planning, persistence, and perpetual optimism.

Passion is the first and probably the most vital quality in inspirational leaders. It distinctively differentiates you from the crowd and propels you to inspire others, attract like-minded talented individuals, rally support for good causes, and lead organizations to new heights. Four distinct elements of passion are

- suffering: experiencing hardship or adversity along the way
- targeted: laser focus on forward-thinking goals and objectives
- personal commitment: fully vested in the role and mission ahead
- sacrifice: willing to make the hard trade-off in return for success and glory

Planning is the second leadership quality and provides organizations with a road map to success. It is putting pen to paper and articulating how a leader's vision will come to fruition. Planning outlines the work and responsibilities of every member of the organization. It is the one tool that cannot be missed or the organization will stray, rudderless and without direction. The following five steps are for effective business planning:

- situational assessment: an honest inside/outside view of your business
- opportunity assessment: evaluating the highest leverage growth pillars
- goals and objectives setting: charting where the organization is going
- system alignment: getting all stakeholders on board with your game plan
- final sign-off: securing a green light to put your plan into action

One integral component of the planning process is objective setting, the art of articulating what will be accomplished during the short term—usually a fiscal year. SMART objectives are the most effective format as they are specific, measurable, achievable, realistic, and time bound.

Persistence is the third leadership skill and is a unique quality because it is a test of a leader's willingness and ability to stay focused. It is doing an action repeatedly until you prevail and achieve that set objective. It also tests our appetite for failure and desire to learn from pitfalls so we can persevere on the next go-around. To build persistence, three things are needed:

1. Strong stomach for failure: Believing failure is an option and a learning opportunity but you must have the wisdom to learn from it.
2. Strong will to win: Winning has to be your priority, and you need the will to do the impossible in order to reach that destination.
3. Clear line of sight on the target: Focus on the end goal, and drive all your systems toward that one place you want to go.

Perpetual optimism is the final leadership quality and represents a mindset. It is a "force multiplier," as the late General Colin Powell described it. It trickles down to the entire organization and equips you with a belief in yourself, your purpose, and your prospects of success. Two things are core to optimists:

1. Self-confidence: The assurance that you can do whatever task you intend to do, the ability to never quit, and the trust in your competencies.
2. Track record: This is the proof that you have been there and done that before, your gate pass to support your persistence.

Those four leadership qualities are naturally perfected over time and with much focus on being cognizant of the iterative nature of the learning process. Some qualities may be more conducive to certain types of personalities; the idea is to develop competency for all four. Also, there is a plethora of traits that differentiate great leaders, but those four are what resonated most with me when I think about the parallels between development at home versus at the workplace.

Finally, one caution is to watch out for dark forces—destructive traits—that counter the positive effect of those four leadership qualities. Toxic leadership is increasingly seeping through organizations and will be a costly force that must be addressed.

6

LEADING BY AXIOMS

My illiterate mother led by example. She talked the talk and walked the walk. Again and again, she learned from setbacks and usually recalibrated her approach to ensure alignment with planned goals. For a large part of her life, she was amped up and ready to pursue her passions with ferocious focus, especially relative to developing her offspring and teaching them life lessons.

As a teacher, my mother broke down her wisdom into small nuggets for all of her children to process, then she followed up by living and breathing each of those lessons. Role modeling was imperative to my mother.

"Watch me, and learn how it's done" was her favorite go-to preface. Her life experience and best practices were most often encapsulated in stories she recited, both as wholesome entertainment (purposeful bedtime stories) as well as character-building teaching moments. Moreover, my mother applied those stories to amplify key messages, be it targeted or general. She wanted all her children to be equally qualified.

However, my mother also used proverbs to teach us professional lessons in finance, management, and other subjects. She loved sounding them off immediately following an error, for greater impact and "on the job training," if you will. On any given day, it would have been normal for her to repeat half a dozen of those sayings. There were probably hundreds if not more of those sayings, and in later years as adults, my siblings and I often reminisced about them and the knowledge we gained. We took turns attempting to recall our favorites and the circumstances prompting our mother to recite them. Looking back, she was right about the effectiveness of breaking down learning material into small and simple nuggets.

Proverbs are prevalent in every culture, and it is not uncommon for some to be contextually used in similar manner. Having traveled around the world during my executive career, I certainly have heard a fair number of axioms. However, what is unique in my mother's case is the conscious frequency and breadth of application.

What follows are some of her most repeated sayings for your reference, and hopefully they bring both the hero of this book and the four leadership lessons into further context. Those are the proverbs each of my seven siblings have memorized by heart, and by now, we have passed them on to our children. Please bear in mind what follows is a loose and literal translation from Arabic, so bear with me, especially if one may sound funny in English.

1. "Stretch your quilt enough to cover your feet." "Mid el Hafak ala Aad Rejlaik."

    This means to live modestly within means. Spend money wisely, only on the things most needed, and do not waste it. In the early years of motherhood, when crammed into a small, two-bedroom apartment, that was my mother's message when we nagged about things like tight closet space or lack of meat in our dinners. Personally, I recall complaining frequently about things like my small daily allowance, desire to go watch a soccer game with friends, and buying new clothes. We just did not afford all those luxuries and my mother hoped I understood her wisdom. This was an important lesson in economics.

2. "Save your penny for a dark day." "Khabee Ershak Labyad Layoumak Laswad."

This means don't waste your money on things you don't really need. Instead, save it or invest your money wisely so you have it in time of need. My mother built her successful enterprise following this golden rule, making it one of her most repeated sayings. She was a prolific money saver, given her astounding lifetime accomplishments. On many occasions, I was the recipient of this wisdom. More than my siblings, my mother disliked how I spent my allowance almost entirely on food, especially buying candy. She would look me in the eye and repeat this saying with a lovely motherly smile, echoing the importance of saving money. This was another valuable lesson in economics.

3. "Be smart and support each other." "Koono Shatreen w Sanad la Baad."

This means to care for one another, such that siblings are a strong support network. My mother often shared this wisdom after someone helped a brother or sister with a chore or schoolwork. Her feedback was prompt, especially for good deeds. It was usually accompanied with a small treat as reinforcement of positive behavior. I recall my two older brothers being the most helpful in the family; they were always ready to help. They were often the recipients of that wisdom, and to this day, the bond among us eight siblings is as strong as ever. This was a vital lesson from my mother in human resources and talent development.

4. "Whatever God gives you is a blessing." "Elee Min Allah Khair we Barakeh."

This means to be content and satisfied with what you have. Be happy with the blessings you enjoy because it is God's will. With her strong, faith-based ideal, my mom maximized her resources. There were endless days when meals were candidly not sufficient to satisfy a family of eight, but she was content. Moreover, she followed her plans vehemently and refused to be tempted into unwarranted discretionary spending. She repeated this saying anytime one of her children grumbled about the food or clothes they didn't particularly like. That was a key lesson in operating expense management (OPEX.)

5. "If you seek prosperity, stay up at night." "Man Talab al Ola, Sahar al Layalee."

This means nothing in life comes easy and achieving goals requires hard work. It's similar to the adage "No pain, no gain." If you want to reach the mountaintop, you must stay up late and do your diligence. That wisdom we often heard from my mother as we played around the house instead of studying. Also, when after a long night of schoolwork, one complained about the heavy load of schoolwork. Reflecting on what her children have become, it is clear that advice paid off handsomely and the handwork proved worthwhile. That was a key lesson in personal leadership and development.

6. "Eat your food, and enjoy." "Kol Aklatak we Ithana."

This means to have contentment for what you have. Regardless of how little it may be, just be satisfied with what you've been blessed with because many are not so lucky. This was repeated around the dinner table, especially whenever we complained about the small portions or lack of meat. On the occasion chicken was served, it was usually one chicken for the whole family and my mother got the smallest piece or nothing at all. Even when there was visibly no more food left for her to eat, she used a lame excuse, like fasting or being full, to fend off any comments or guilt feeling. A lesson in managing supply chain.

7. "Your neck will hurt you if you look up too much." "Elee Bitalaa Lafook Kthair, Raabatoh Betoujouh."

This particular proverb had multiple meanings and applications. My mom used it to reinforce the need for humility and as a reminder of reality. She didn't subscribe to the theory of living beyond one's means and was content with what little she had. Modesty was her hallmark, and she was proud of that. The proverb also reinforces the virtues of being grounded, akin to "Tortoise and the Hare" tale. She advocated slow but steady progress, underpinned by her advocacy for SMART objectives. This was a lesson in modesty.

8. "Do your good deed, and walk away." "Emal Ma'aroofak we Imshee."

This means don't linger and overstay your welcome, especially when being a Good Samaritan. My mother wanted us to be focused on the real reason we were in such situations (i.e., helping others). She valued time management and viewed socializing as a time-wasting activity. She repeated this saying once when I returned home late from tutoring one of my cousins. While my mother endorsed my supportive action, she disliked overstaying the visit and viewed it potentially becoming a burden on my aunt or her family. She preferred I did my good deed and walked away. That is a lesson in social responsibility.

9. "Make your social visit a blaze." "El Ziyarah Garah."

Similar to the previous proverb, it highlights benefits of short and sweet social visits. She hated wasting time and resented the thoughts of burdening others. My mother used this saying frequently, but especially after someone complained about a short visit to our grandmother or an aunt. When we were thinking more playing time, she was thinking etiquette. Always a big believer in prioritizing schoolwork over other activities, especially time with relatives, which she viewed as time-consuming and of little value. Another important lesson in time management.

10. "People's chatter hurts and has no benefit." "Kalam el Nas Bidor wa Ma Benfaa."

This means don't listen to people's gossip because it is largely negative and hurtful. Whenever my mom overheard one of us bad-mouthing a classmate or a neighbor, she would recite this proverb, typically coupled with a stern face for emphasis. Other times, she coupled it with a firm order to do something more useful like studying or reading. She considered such chatter distasteful and time-consuming. Living the values was my mother's blueprint, and gossiping was never high on her agenda. Even when her dearest sister would do it, my mother would shut her off. This was a lesson in public relations.

11. "Barakesh brought it on their own." "Ala Nafseha Janat Barakesh."

This was a legendary go-to proverb for my mom, one she repeated her entire life. Barakesh is a mythical figure of my mother's creation about a stubborn camel that left its caravan and went its own way, only to get lost and die in the harsh desert. This saying is meant to emphasize the responsibility for one's action and not blaming others.

A popular saying that my mother repeated whenever she did not like any of our action. Like the time when, as an eleven-year-old, I badly scratched my dad's brand-new Toyota pickup truck. He gave me the key with a request to handwash it. When I finished the task and while he was napping, I mustered the courage to get in the driver's seat and drove it around the neighborhood. It was relatively new. My dad had been teaching me to drive the manual stick shift automobile, so I knew the basic controls, or at least that's what I thought. In any case, during my short and unfortunate joy ride, I scratched the front fender while making a sharp right turn. I exacerbated my predicament by running to the hardware store and buying a can of regular blue paint. Needless to say, my brush paintwork was terrible and I was grounded with no allowance for some time. Lesson here is about accountability.

12. "Everyone sleeps on their comfortable side." "Kol Wahad Binam ala Janb ely Birayhoo."

This means don't fret about what others are doing; people are free to do what they see fit. She prioritized controlling the controllable and refused making excuses. Wise advice whenever she heard us complain about how another sibling was doing things. Like the time when my brothers whined about me playing in the neighborhood while they studied. My mother was an excellent teacher who constantly dished out advice but also allowed each of her children to develop their own personality. A valuable lesson in taking responsibility.

13. "Keep your smart friends, and dump your bad ones." "Sahbak el Shater Khaleeh wel Ahbbal Kibooh."

This means to surround yourself with smart people because you learn more from them and you push each other. Conversely, bad friends only bring trouble. She reminded me personally of this on a number of occasions, especially in elementary school. Once she saw me walking home from school with a much taller friend who had repeated fifth grade. She assumed he was bad and not a smart student, thus a bad influence who would hold me back from studying. She also shared this advice with a younger brother of mine when he hung out with the wrong group of friends and his grades dropped dramatically in his senior high school year. A lesson in networking.

14. "Silence is golden." "Al Sukoot Min Thahab."

It is a common and self-explanatory counsel, unless you are illiterate and didn't learn this in school. My mother shared this sage advice whenever one of us uttered the wrong words. She despised rudeness and the thought of her children being impolite, especially in public and definitely not in the presence of elders. Growing up, I was the loudest mouth among my siblings and my mother often reminded me of this wisdom whenever I talked too much. Even in arguments within the children, she suggested staying quiet over talking back to a sibling. This was a valuable lesson in public relations.

15. "When elders talk, youngsters listen." "Itha Hakoo L'Kbar, Sakatoo L'Zghar."

Similar to the previous saying, this was used by my mother specifically following social engagements, formal or otherwise. In Middle Eastern culture, social norms predicate adults lead formal conversations and youngsters, if permitted to join, sit quietly and obediently. My mother echoed the importance of good social manners and expected her children to be polite and selective with words. Whenever we begged her to take us along for her family visits, she would mandate good behavior as a prerequisite. She viewed listening, especially to elders, as respect, in addition to being valuable learning occasion. That was another lesson in public relations.

16. "Patience is a virtue." "El Saber Tayeb."

Another legendary proverb my mother repeated almost her entire life. It is a straightforward wisdom intended to promote the art of patience. She was unusually patient herself and guided by her faith; she believed God had a plan for her and everyone else for that matter. As such, whenever something unfortunate happened to the children, my mother's customary reaction was to remind herself to be patient and put her trust in God.

She was also powered by her perpetual optimism and truly believed in what she preached. To her, whenever one door shut, ten new doors opened up, not just one. For instance, the time when I was job interviewing after college and was turned down by The Coca-Cola Company. My mother encouraged me to keep my head high and prepare for other interviews. Less than a month later, I was offered my first full-time job with Warner Lambert. Incidentally, to further prove my mom's advice right, ten years later, I was recruited by Coca-Cola and went on to spend twenty-two years at the company and rise to a rank of vice president.

Patience may be a poor person's way of make-believe, but it is truly a valuable experience that not only builds character but also reinforces how tribulation leads to perseverance. My mother would never have achieved her monumental milestones without such beliefs. It was a key lesson in patience.

17. "The truth is a peace of mind." "El Saraha Raha."

This means to profess the need for honesty. My mom warned us against lying and despised it, reminding us of its dangerous ethical outcome, including loss of trust. She associated honesty with peace of mind. This was the wisdom I heard from my mom after the car scratching incident as I wasn't totally honest with my dad about the odd-looking blue paint. He was ready to unleash his anger on me and my mom came to my rescue with advice to tell the truth. At the start, I claimed ignorance and only confessed to driving and damaging the bumper after my mother pressed and promised to convince my dad to take it easy on me. That was a valuable lesson in honesty.

18. "The rope of lying is short." "Habel el Kithib Qaseer."

This means you do not get very far with lies and deception. Sooner or later, the liars are bound to get exposed and the truth surfaces, at which point you have to bear the consequences of your action. Similar to the previous advice, my mother's words of wisdom centered on core values designed to shape the character of her children. As a devout Muslim, she comprehended the downside to lying. She reinforced the importance of honesty with her own action as she always was honest and straightforward with her children. This proverb was a valuable reminder and another important lesson in honesty.

19. "The house of the charitable is blessed." "Bait El Mohsen Amaar."

This means if you are a giver and nice to people, God will reward you. My mother was a Good Samaritan and would give money to street beggars or food to those knocking on our doors. Occasionally, she prepared special meals for the neighborhood garbage collector, despite her modest financials. While she wasn't superstitious at all, she believed in good fortune and reciprocity. My mother encouraged us to help others, especially elders and women. Like the time when we were walking back from the market and she asked me to help an older lady carry her groceries all the way to her house. It became customary, whenever I accompanied her. This was a lesson in social responsibility.

20. "Close doors that blow wind." "Bab Eli Bijeek Minoh Reeh, Sidooh We'Stareeh."

Meant as counsel to manage problems, my mother meant to say that in order to have peace of mind, one must focus on the controllable and ignore what is not. Additionally, if something is bothering you, find the source and get rid of it all together. She repeated this after successfully navigating through bad situations. Much of the context for applying this proverb was socially centric, like when my younger brother stopped hanging out with his troubled gang of friends or when an annoying tenant was finally forced out. This was about crisis management.

21. "The wind blows against the desire of ships." "Tajree eRiyah Bima La Tshtahee e Sofon."

While it may not make much sense in English, this is the closest thing in Arabic to the proverbial Murphy's Law. My mother meant that life is life and we don't always get what we want, and as such, we have to be mindful of that reality and just embrace it as opposed to fighting it. She advised us to plan for the worst and always be prepared. Like the numerous times we complained about pop quizzes at school, returning from the market without making a sale, or even when good fortune suddenly surfaced. This was a lesson in planning.

22. "Kiss a dog on its lips until you get what you want." "Boos el Kalb Min Themo, la Takouth Hajtak Minoh."

This means sometimes we have to work with people we don't like or adversaries, in which case focus is on getting the work done, not the personal differences. This is how she managed her relationship with one troublesome neighbor and solved a major property line issue. They remained neighbors for decades, but their relationship was strayed. This proverb was also repeated when a business partnership with one of my dad's cousins fell out and he owed us money for the loader tractor we invested in. My mom's advice was to stay nice to that cousin until we got our money back. A good approach to negotiation.

23. "The eye is never above the brow." "El Ain ma Telaa al Hajeb."

This was another legendary go-to proverb from my mom and was meant to reinforce the value of respect for your elders and superiors. You must follow their lead and direction because in my mother's thought process, that shows respect. Respect is shown by not talking back, bad-mouthing, arguing, or other nuances against elders. In Middle Eastern culture, seniors enjoy a special social status for their wisdom and maturity. Like when a man plans to ask for a girl's hand in marriage, the effort is often led by a group of family elders who do most of the talking on the groom-to-be's behalf. That level of hierarchal standing is commonly predicated.

My mom commonly echoed the merits of respect, including older siblings regardless of age or gender. Even as an elder herself, my mom respected her older brothers, and likewise they showed tremendous respect for their sister. They sought her counsel of various matters and appreciated her perspective. Furthermore, my mom was a staunch feminist who believed in gender equality and as such expected boys to respect their sisters. She encouraged my three sisters to be independent and seek the highest education levels possible, again believing that education is the window to the enlightenment. That was a critical lesson in appreciation.

24. "The ignorant are their own worst enemy." "El Jahel Adou Nafsoh."

Reinforcing the value of learning, my mom consistently prioritized schoolwork above all. The proverb is meant as encouragement to excel at school and pursue the highest degrees possible. In her mind, she equated education to success and even independence. She believed wholeheartedly that schools and universities build knowledge, which opens up windows of growth and opportunity. My mother said this to me personally many times, seeing I was the one child with a host of extracurricular activity. She also voiced it whenever she was unable to read a letter or document that arrived in the mail. She would hand us the papers instead. That was a vital lesson in planning.

25. "He who digs a hole for his sibling will fall into it." "Min Hafar Hufrah Li Akheeh, Waqaa Fiha."

This means be kind to your loved ones and don't plan to do them any harm; otherwise, it would backfire on you. My mother condemned in-house fighting and stressed brotherly love and sorting issues through intelligent and sensible mechanisms. Today, as grown-ups with families of our own, we remain a close-knit group talking regularly and meeting periodically for family reunions. This proverb was particularly her go-to wisdom whenever news spread of distant relatives falling out after fighting. Another lesson in relationship management.

26. "Blood never turns into water." "El Dam Omroh ma Biseer Mayeh."

Yet another legendary quote from my late mother and meant to emphasize the high importance of siblings being supports and not rivals. Also, it means the bond between siblings is eternal and should be strengthened. She realized through experience that brothers and sisters will always care for one another, much more than strangers.

Regardless of what transpires in life, my mom affirmed the need for family to stick together, indeed through thick and thin. She put a hefty price on interfamily fighting and frowned at the idea of hate within her household. She was the happiest when observing her children coming to each other's rescue. Like the time when my younger brother drifted off while in high school, but we all stood by his side and reminded him of his stellar and studious past. We supported him all the way, until he got out of his predicament.

As a family-oriented mother, she cherished nurturing closer ties among us and we did. Strangely enough, today as adults, relationships among all eight children are stronger than any time in the past, including our childhood. That is entirely attributed to my mother's advice and coaching, as well as our desire to live the values she taught us and teach such values to our own sons and daughters. This was another lesson in networking.

27. "Experience over wisdom." "Esaal Mjjarib Wala Tisaal Hakeem."

This means sometimes real-life experience and best practices are a great road map to follow. While she promoted higher education her entire life and was an advocate of science, my mother valued experience and considered life her best school. She attributed much of her success to her ability to learn from mistakes—hers or others for that matter. Like the time during construction when I fell off a scaffolding, despite her repeated cautioning, or when she sent me to buy vegetables from the street vendor and I came back without haggling for a better price. This was a lesson in leveraging best practices.

28. "Stay away from evil, and sing for it." "Ebid an el Shar O Ganeelo."

This means the farther away from danger you keep, the safer your life will be. My mother used it to reinforce the need to stay out of trouble. Also as a warning against friends she considered bad influences, as in her opinion bad company detracted her children from their missions: excelling at school. I recall once in grade school coming home crying after playing soccer in the yard and telling mom about losing my soccer ball. One of the boys angrily kicked it directly in the street and an incoming car inadvertently ran over it. Her advice to me was to stay away from playing with those boys all together, if I want peace of mind in the future. A lesson in problem-solving.

29. "Your tongue is your horse. Protect it, and it will take care of you. Insult it, and it will harm you." "Lisanak Hisanak, in Sunto Sanak win Hintu Hanak."

This means words matter and what you say has consequences. My mother was a disciplinarian who valued respect and good manners, regardless of age or social status. She warned us against being hasty and rushing to utter words that may backfire and inflict sustainable damage. It also means applying both the golden as well as platinum rule when treating people. My mom condemned gossiping and bad-mouthing others, so she promoted care with words. If you promise something, then you must deliver. Another lesson in public relations.

30. "She was ready to celebrate but found no place for herself." "Ejat el Hazeeneh Tifrah, Maa Liyat Matrah."

This means underprivileged people suffer more in life, and even when ready to celebrate, something bad suddenly occurs. My mother used to quote this in response to unfortunate events because she believed intent was always good. As such, she expected positive results and was content with the outcome. Like in the mid-1970s when Amman, Jordan, faced a significant potable water shortage and supply was only possible through government-funded tankers that toured neighborhoods regularly. We would wait in line, ten-gallon jugs in hands, only to be disappointed when the water ran out before we got a turn. Going home emptyhanded, my mom would encourage us to cheer up and just conserve whatever little water we had until the next scheduled tanker visit. All her plans to shower us, clean the house, and do laundry were put on hold until water was available again. That was a lesson in motivation and human resources.

31. "The cooking pot found its lid." "Tinjarah we Liyat Gataha."

This is meant to sarcastically poke fun at one who found their perfect match. Like saying, "Birds of a feather flock together," it was always meant in jest. My mom blared this out when watching me play soccer with my friends in the streets or my brother writing another novel with his favorite classical Arabic music playing in the background, and when my brother and sister played chess.

The proverb also applied to bad or gossip-hungry people banded together and my mom would ridicule their bond. She preferred intellectual gatherings that benefitted participants and advanced good causes as opposed to what she viewed as time-wasting nonsense. This was a lesson to all of us in networking.

32. "He has the height of a palm tree and the brains of a baby goat." "El Tool el Nakhleh we Ael Sakhleh."

This means do not be fooled by people's appearance or size because looks are often deceiving. My mother understood that a most distinguished-looking person could turn out to be puerile and the opposite of general perceptions. She used to cite it whenever someone did something silly, especially my dad. Like the time he threatened to divorce my mom and go marry a young woman. She chuckled at the idea of an old man with eight children considering a new marriage, instead of directing his energy at his children and their needs. She encouraged us to be regal and balanced in conducting ourselves, such that it reflects positively on our character. A lesson in self-leadership.

33. "My heart is with my kid and her heart is with stones." "Qalbee ala Wladee we Wladee Qalbhom ala Hajar."

This means that she (our mother) was more worried and concerned about our well-being, our future, and our schoolwork than we were. She wished for us to see the big picture and be forward-looking thinkers. She disliked short-term thinking and viewed it as ineffective. She strongly believed her kids should leverage her life sufferings and learn from her experience. She repeated this saying whenever someone pushed back at her direction or doubted her advice. Like the time when my eldest brother contemplated accepting a part-time job doing hard work at my uncle's building supplies store. My mom instructed him to listen to her because she knew it would affect his studies on top of being hard physical work, something he was not built for. A valuable lesson in leadership.

34. "Daylight has eyes." "El Nahar Eloh Oyoon."

This means one should not work late at night on an important task. Instead, one should rest and complete it in the morning. My mother said this whenever one of us was doing schoolwork late at night but was visibly exhausted or found sleeping on a book, as I often did. The quality of work or study at that point is diminished and may pose more risk, especially if it's important work. She often repeated this proverb to my elder brother, a notoriously late-night literature reader and writer. A vital lesson in time management.

35. "The eye can see what the hand can't reach." – "El Ain Baseerah We el Yad Aseerah."

Essentially this means you can't have all that you desire. With eight children to care for, my mother repeated this proverb frequently. During our childhood, this was often quoted as our household lacked many of the basic necessities, let alone ancillary luxuries. She recited those words whenever one of us asked for something new, like clothes or a schoolbag, and she just did not have the spare money. My mom had big dreams of her own, but the shortage of money limited her ability to fulfill those dreams while her kids were young. However, with the help of her grown-up children, she would go on and achieve those dreams later in her life. That was a key lesson in operating effectiveness.

Those thirty-five proverbs were exceptionally effective tools my mother mastered over a period of more than thirty years as she brought us all up. They represented important life teachings and had to be appreciated. She lived and breathed every single one of them and embodied all of them. It was her way of leading by example. She recited those sayings indiscriminately whenever they applied. My mom normally followed her proverbs with "Listen and learn!" as an exclamation mark. She viewed every one of those proverbs as a standalone training module that she could deliver for hours.

Again, this was an illiterate mother who never went to school a day in her life. She compensated for that shortfall with best practices and experience. She often quipped that she too had a doctorate, "a

PhD in life" she would say. Despite her illiteracy, she was the greatest teacher I have ever encountered.

The true significance of those proverbs did not crystalize to me personally until I joined Fortune 100 companies and saw firsthand the need for such great leadership. The need for corporate leaders to do what my illiterate mother did so well her entire life: be beacons of hope and catalysts for change.

FINAL WORDS

Yes, my mother was illiterate. She never went to school a day in her life, and she never got any formal education or training. She was cognizant of that, but none of it mattered a bit to her because she grew up learning the hard way: through trial and error as well as from others' mistakes. None of her shortfalls stopped my mother from pursuing her dream of succeeding in developing a highly accomplished family. Her illiteracy did not prevent her from teaching my seven siblings and me vital life lessons that shaped our character today.

It didn't stop her from teaching me personally valuable lessons in leadership long before I joined Gillette, Kimberly-Clark, and Coca-Cola. Now and after more than thirty years of professional work experience and travel to more than seventy countries, I am awestruck by the incredible parallels between the lessons I learned at home and those from work. Today, as I sit down writing this book, I am convinced more than ever that my mother was not only a great mother, but she was a brilliant business leader.

She displayed some of the same qualities witnessed in successful business leaders. My mother's most distinctive four qualities were passion, planning, persistence, and perpetual optimism. Four competencies that test your drive and will to succeed. Four qualities that my mother embodied, practiced, and preached to her children day in and day out and ensured they witnessed her modeling the right behavior. My mom was convinced that teaching those lessons to her children would build their character and support their quest for success. She was 100 percent spot-on. She lived her life convinced teaching her children those important lessons would also trickle down and benefit future generations. She was right in that sense, because my leadership, both at home and at work, is grounded in those valuable lessons my mother taught. At home, my three daughters are being preached the very same leadership lessons. So in essence, my mother was not only shaping the future of her children by also her future grandchildren.

Not only was my mother a great business mind and an educator, but she was also an angel. I honestly believe my mother was a true angel in disguise, sent by God to spread happiness and hope, to withstand an entire lifetime of hardship and struggle, and to look after her eight children and secure their future. I'm sure a lot of people view their mothers as angels, but my mother accomplished so much with so little, and she was illiterate. I watched her for forty-seven years and she was totally different from my uncles and aunts— her siblings. She was unlike the other mothers of our neighborhood. She was an educator despite having no education. She was religious and prayed endlessly but respected religious freedom. She was selfless and sacrificed her own physical well-being for the good of the whole. She prioritized her children well above everything else, other than her love for God and prayer. She was a holy angel sent from God to deliver a message of hope, humility, harmony, and happiness. She spent her entire life caring for her family and never was heard complaining about anything material. She got up after every downfall and found new avenues. She was a visionary and a leader without ever going to a business school.

My mother had a vision for her household to be the most successful group of children in the entire Yaghi family. She never lost sight of that vision, never wavered, and never gave up. That is until one late morning on August 7, 2012, when her time on this earth came to an end. She finished praying in the front yard of her beloved garden and passed away immediately thereafter. In true mom fashion, quietly and peacefully. Exactly four days after the conclusion of the family's annual reunion when she had by her side all eight of her children and their families, including twenty-two grandchildren. Her vision was finally achieved; each of her children is successful in their respective field and enjoying a truly blessed and happy life. She died exactly the way she had always hoped for: in peace and praying to God.

Mission accomplished.

Made in the USA
Coppell, TX
28 December 2023